WOUNDED MAGUS

JOURNALS OF NATTA MAGUS | BOOK 3

ROB STEINER

QUARKFOLIO BOOKS

Sign up for my newsletter at www.robsteinerauthor.com to get a **FREE** compilation of Natta Magus short stories, along with news and previews of upcoming books.
Never miss a new release, and you can unsubscribe at any time.

For Sarah and Amelia, always.

I

I awoke to darkness and the sounds of lapping water. The smells of moldy wood, old sweat, fish, and the sea all mingled into a miasma every bit as potent as Rome's. After a disorienting moment, I remembered where I was: on a sea galley crossing the Mediterranean to Carthage.

The darkness wasn't absolute. Cana had set a dim spark globe above us before we had gone to sleep. We were in the captain's "cabin," which was about the size of my apartment's closet back home in twenty-first century Detroit. Cana lay on the cot, and there was barely enough room for Paetus and me to lie curled up on the floor next to her. It was my letters of credit from Caesar Augustus himself that had earned Cana, Paetus, and I the best sleeping spot in the galley.

But none of that had awoken me. It was the muffled cries of alarm from above us, followed by thumps of bodies falling to the deck. If there had been rousing bouts of laughter, I would've chalked it up to drunken sailors and gone back to sleep. But it was the ensuing silence that kept me awake.

Our galley was under attack.

Out of all the travel methods in the ancient Roman world, boat travel always seemed the most dangerous to me.

No, Natta Magus, you're from the future, Paetus and Cana had said, for once in agreement on something. *It* is *the best way to get to Egypt. It would take weeks to travel the roads through Anatolia and Palestine. You're too used to your aero-planes and horseless trollies, Natta Magus. Trust us, Natta Magus, this way* is *best.*

The four-day crossing from Sicily to North Africa was a nightmare. We encountered monstrous swells that almost toppled our galley and made me *yack* up the meager porridge they served onboard. The hull leaked in six different spots, which required slaves armed with buckets to monitor them round the clock. And then there was the whole day without a breath of wind to move our sails. It made me wonder what it would be like to die of thirst on a salty sea. And this was only the first half of our journey. Once we reached Carthage, we'd board *another* galley that would hug the North African coast and take us straight to Alexandria.

All part of a normal voyage, the Carthaginian captain explained. Nothing to worry about.

I'm not an "I told you so" kind of guy. When I realized the ship was under attack, I simply nudged Cana on her cot. My apprentice's brown eyes shot open.

"Don't panic, *leerling,*" I whispered, calling her the Dutch word for apprentice. "We're under attack."

She opened her mouth to say something, but Paetus shot up into a sitting position next to me. "Attack? Are you—?"

Both Cana and I shushed him at the same time. The whites of his eyes were almost as bright as the spark globe above us.

A man screamed on the deck, and we all jumped. Heavy feet creaked and bent the floorboards above our heads. We stared at the ceiling in silence. Then came a thump and the sounds of many feet rushing across the deck.

"We should help," Cana said, still watching the ceiling.

"Are you mad?" Paetus hissed. "It's probably pirates. They're monsters. I've heard horrid tales. They'll slice us open from neck to groin and let the gulls feast on our innards!"

Cana rolled her eyes and whispered, "Piracy has been extinct for decades. You read far too many fantastical tales." Her tone was impatient as it always was with Paetus, but her Latin's Gallic accent was far more pronounced. It meant she was scared.

Paetus's wan face turned pink with anger. "Just because Pompey Maximus destroyed them doesn't mean he made them 'extinct'. They could still lurk in every cove and—"

"Paetus," I said. I kept my voice low, calm, and firm like a leader should. "Whoever they are, Cana's right. We either do something now or wait for them to find us."

Paetus groaned.

"I have practiced *slapen,*" Cana said. "I can get at least four."

More likely one, I thought. Cana had a habit of overestimating her strength. But what she lacked in strength—at the moment—she more than made up for in confidence and shear stubbornness to learn. She'd grown more in the last two months that I'd known her than I had in all four years of secondary academy in Detroit. I never believed that magi of her strength could naturally develop so early before the Great Awakening. She'd surpass my strength in the next few years.

If we made it through the next five minutes.

"Only if they're kind enough to bunch up for you," I said to her, "*and* if none of the crew are among them to dissipate the spell. If so, go for it. If not, we need another plan."

A shout came from above in a language that certainly wasn't Latin. It sounded similar to the Carthaginian captain's words when he gave orders to his crew and slaves. The freedmen rowers just outside the cabin's thin curtain murmured nervously in their rowing bays.

"Paetus," I said, "do you understand what they're saying up top?"

Paetus knew about a dozen languages, Carthaginian Punic being among them. He looked sick with fear, but he cocked his head and listened. His shoulders slumped and he looked even sicker, if that was possible.

"They just killed the captain," he whispered. "The pirate leader told his men to search the rest of the boat."

My throat seized up and my bowels cramped. I wasn't surprised by my physical reaction to danger. I'd been in many life-and-death scrapes during my three years in Augustan Rome, versus zero in my twenty-first century life. I've fought vampire-like monsters called strix, a sewer basilisk that almost killed Augustus himself, ghosts, daemons, and, most recently, the magically conjured avatar of the Roman revenge goddess Invidia. You'd think I'd laugh off a few mundane pirates.

But this was how I always felt before a fight, from a brawl with drunken Roman plebs to an arena-destroying battle with a deity. And somehow I'd survived all those. I had a destiny, supposedly, and it wasn't to die here.

"Cana," I said, my voice level, "grab all your spell components. We may not be coming back here. Paetus, take only the scrolls and bags you need. Leave your trunk."

Cana was already cinching her leather components pouch before I'd finished my order.

Paetus gave a shaky sigh and then gathered the scrolls on which he'd been writing before we went to sleep and stuffed them into his shoulder bag. He eyed his trunk, filled with even more scrolls, books, and clay tablets, and sighed again.

I made sure my trusty old Wolverines baseball cap was firmly set on my head, secured my own components vest, and fastened my gladius belt around my waist. I also slung my watertight leather bag, which contained Augustus's letters of credit, over my shoulders. I sealed the scroll tubes with these journals you're reading and the cherubic statue of my dearly departed house spirit Lares. I left behind my other sacks with a change of clothes.

I glanced at the wrists of both Cana and Paetus. They both wore the enchanted leather bracelets that I'd given them. I reached out with my cell magic and could feel my feet wanting to walk toward them. As long as they wore those, I could find them if we got separated.

"Think you can swing a *blussen*?" I asked Cana.

"Yes but how will we see?"

"Use cell magic to filter your eyes to heat. You'll see them, but they won't see you."

She nodded, then gave me a worried look. "What are you going to do? Are you going to use—?"

"No," I said firmly.

"I can stop you if you lose control. I know the words—"

"I said no!"

Things weren't that desperate for me to give up a bit of my soul. Yet.

A girl's scream came from the cabin across the hull from us, and then a young man's angry shouts. There were two Carthaginian girls in that cabin, one eleven and one sixteen, traveling with their brother who wasn't much older than them. The brother was yelling something in Punic. The other girl was screaming now, and the harsh laughter of the pirates finally got me moving.

"Put out the spark globe and cast the *blussen*!" I hissed to Cana.

I turned my Wolverines baseball cap around so that the bill faced backwards and flung the curtain aside.

2

I drew my enchanted gladius and charged down the narrow planks that separated the right side rowing stalls from the left. There were two lanterns in the center of the deck still casting orange shadows about the hull. I tangentially noticed the rowers huddling in their stalls as far from the armed pirates as they could get. I only hoped they wouldn't get in my way when Cana's *blussen* went off.

Three black-haired, bearded pirates were struggling with the Carthaginian kids in the far cabin. Two of the pirates must've heard me coming, for they whirled around as soon as I entered the rowing stalls and brought up nasty curved swords. They were shirtless, with pink and white scars crisscrossing their chests and backs as if they'd been whipped in the recent past. They started easing toward me with sneers. The third pirate continued fighting in the shadows of the far compartment, the two girls screaming at him.

I kept heading toward the two sneering pirates. *Damnation, Cana, where's that* blussen*? I'm going to reach them in three more steps—!*

A warm wave of magic rushed past me from behind as if someone had opened an oven. It was a comforting warmth, one that made my cells sigh with recognition and joy. But I didn't want to feel joy at that moment. I was angry and afraid of what the pirates would do to my friends and the kids in that far cabin. I wanted blood.

All the lanterns blew out, dropping the entire hull into pitch darkness. I took a precious moment for pride in my *leerling's* growing magical skills and then yelled in my bastardized Dutch, *"Bekijken!"*

My cell magic released with an icy tingle across my skin. Rather than the colors of visible light, I saw the heat emanations from everyone around me—the rowers, the pirates, and the people in the far compartment—in glowing reds, oranges, and greens. Even the ship's oars and sundry items glowed, but in muted blues and purples. It was damned eerie; it made everyone look like daemons and the ship like Pluto's nightmare.

Now I could see them, but they couldn't see me.

I pointed my enchanted gladius at the nearest pirate, who was conveniently frozen in shock at the sudden darkness. *"Slapen!"* I yelled.

The sleep spell that I had enchanted into the blade rushed out the tip in a mirage-like wave of cell magic and slammed into the pirate. He crumpled the floor. I aimed at the second pirate, who stared wide-eyed into the darkness like his partner, and shot another sleep spell at him. He fell limply onto some shocked rowers who pushed his body onto the hull at their feet.

The last pirate had realized someone was attacking him and his men. He backed into the cabin with his sword raised to block whatever the darkness was throwing at his partners. I saw three orange and red glows behind him, but couldn't tell who was who since they were huddled together toward the back of the cabin.

I aimed my gladius at the pirate, trying to avoid the three figures behind him, and cried, *"Slapen!"*

The spell fizzled like a puff of steam and then dissipated into the air. I stared at my sword a moment and cursed.

I really had to figure out how to store more than two spells in the damned blade.

I got ready to charge the final pirate with my gladius, but one of the orange figures behind him leaped onto his back. From the cursing and snarling, I figured it was the brother of the two girls. His dagger flashed blue and purple in my filtered vision, and he swung wildly at the pirate. The pirate tried to fend him off with his own wild swings, but he couldn't bring his sword around to do any real damage to the brother. Both men screamed and cursed and snarled and grunted as they fought.

In the close quarters of the cabin, though, the brother's dagger proved more useful than the pirate's short sword. The brother landed several cuts and stabs along the pirate's arms and back, and then one across his neck.

It took all of ten seconds for both to reach exhaustion. The pirate finally crumpled, and the brother immediately fell on him, stabbing him over and over.

I didn't wince at all, even though I knew it was my magic that had enabled the pirate's death. Over my last three years in the ancient world, I'd grown accustomed to dealing out death with my magic. I couldn't decide if that was a good thing.

A harsh, questioning voice in Punic came from the open trap door above us. All of us, including the brother, went still. I didn't understand the words, but I understood the meaning.

The pirate captain wanted to know what the hell was going on down here.

Would he send down more men if he didn't get an answer? My enchanted gladius was empty of *slapen* spells. It sounded like there were over a dozen pirates still up on the deck. If they all rushed down here...

The questioning voice came again, this time more angry.

I tightened my grip on my gladius, praying that I remembered the meager sword training that Vitulus had tried to give me over the last two years. *Tried* being the keyword as the greenest legionary recruit could disarm me in seconds.

A muffled Punic voice came from behind me. For a moment I wanted to turn around and stab at the pirate that had somehow snuck past me. But my filtered eyes saw Paetus with his hand over his mouth, his eyes wide, shouting back up at the captain in Punic with a gruff, leering voice.

Silence reigned on the deck for about a minute. The captain called down again, but this time in a more relaxed tone. He ended his orders with an ominous chuckle.

Paetus visibly relaxed. Whatever he had said, the captain had bought it.

Then the trapdoor slammed closed and the latch snapped shut. We were locked down here. The captain yelled something, and the sounds of footfalls on the deck shifted toward one side and then dissipated altogether

I looked at Paetus through my filtered eyes. He'd dropped his hand from his mouth and stared at the closed trapdoor in horror.

"What's happening, Paetus?" I asked.

"I thought he believed me," Paetus whispered. "I thought—"

"Paetus?"

He turned to my voice, his eyes not quite meeting mine in the darkness. "They're going to burn the ship."

3

I conjured a spark globe with barely a twitch of my cell magic. The ethereal white globe swirled and coalesced into existence, illuminating the hold of the ship.

The rowers and three Carthaginian kids looked terrified, partly because they understood what the pirate captain had just said and partly because of the ball of magical ethereal light floating above my head. Cana and Paetus clutched at their satchels, their eyes following the pounding footsteps above us. The two Carthaginian girls had rushed over to their wounded brother, who had collapsed against the bulkhead next to the body of the pirate he had killed. His face was more gray than brown, and blood soaked the right side of his tunic. The twenty or so rowers mumbled in various languages, but I figured they all wondered the same thing I did: *What in damnation are we going to do?*

I quickly wished I'd asked Helva to teach me her gate spell before she—

Helva. The whole reason why I'd left Rome in the first place. Well one of the reasons. She had sacrificed her life, and possibly her soul, to save Rome. To save me, mostly. But in doing so, she had saved a million people from a gruesome death.

And she was stuck somewhere in the Egyptian underworld, possibly being tortured by Invidia or the various daemons the revenge goddess employed. I had to go to Egypt to help her because I refused to let another friend die for my "destiny."

Hey idiot, I chastised myself. *You have friends who are going to die in the belly of this galley* now *if you don't do something.*

One of the rowers was a bit more on the ball than me. He jumped out of his stall and leaped two steps up the ladder to the trapdoor. He tried opening it, but as I suspected, it was locked from the outside. He banged on it with his fists and pushed against it with his back, but it wouldn't budge.

Several *thunks* came from the deck above, and then the smell of smoke filtered its way through the boards. The pirates worked quickly.

"Another *blussen*?" Cana said.

"Won't work," I said. "We need to see the flames."

"Can't you melt the door or something?" Paetus asked.

I shook my head. "That's not a cell magic thing. Maybe Helva could've done it."

Cana put a hand on my arm. "Maybe it is time for—"

I grunted something in the negative and then hurried over to the rower banging his shoulder against the trapdoor. I motioned him aside with my gladius. He stepped down and got as far away from me as he could, eying both me and the spark globe that followed. I got on the first step, aimed the point of my gladius upward, and thrust it into the boards where I suspected the lock was attached. The sword's sharp point stuck deep into the wood. It took me far too many seconds of pushing and pulling to get it to release.

During that time, the smell of smoke strengthened. I coughed once and then somebody else coughed. Before long everyone in the hold was coughing.

I quickened my hacks. I couldn't thrust too strongly or the sword would stick in the wood, so I had to make stabs that took small shards from the wood next to the latch. My progress was far too slow for my comfort.

I soon noticed flickering light through the cracks in the trapdoor. Damnation, the flames were right on top of it. The fire might weaken the wood enough for me to hack through it quicker, but then I'd only open the door to an inferno that none of us could get past.

"Cana," I said, then coughed several times. I pointed to the flickering and managed to say, "See the flames?"

She nodded. I prayed she could concentrate through her coughing and terror. That was a tall order for any magus from my time, much less an eighteen-year-old former slave who'd only discovered her magical talent two months ago. I couldn't maintain the spark globe, hack at the door, and focus on the *blussen* spell all at the same time. I had no choice but to believe in her. I had to have faith in our teamwork or we'd all die.

There is another option...

It was a quiet, seductive thought that always came when things got rough for me.

No. Things were bad, but not that bad. Not yet.

A wave of warm cell magic rolled past me and weaved itself through the cracks in the trapdoor. The flickering and growing heat above me winked out.

Smoke, however, continued to thicken in the air, dimming the spark globe. I coughed and blinked my gritty eyes, hacked again and coughed. My sword thrusts were growing weaker. With the smoke obscuring the hold's ceiling and my eyes going blurry, I couldn't tell how much more I needed to hack before the door came apart.

But the trapdoor nudged a little. It fueled my muscles and gave me hope that I might just get the damned thing open.

And not have to use soul magic.

I grunted between coughs with each thrust. My grunts turned to screams. That little nudge hadn't turned into the shattered lock that I had thought was moments away. All my muscles were like jelly. My eyes felt loaded with sand. Everyone in the hold stared blearily up at me from the floor, trying to get as low as possible to escape the smoke. My brief hope began to fade.

I cried out with my stubborn Detroit-born-and-raised refusal to give up. And my denial to use a magic that could save my life and those around me...but would cannibalize my soul.

I screamed again, hacked, and the trapdoor flew open.

My overwhelming giddiness at having broken through was scorched away by the heat of the flames on deck. There was a patch of blackened wood around the opening from Cana's *blussen* spell, but that didn't help much against the fire surrounding us. At least the smoke in the hold was rising out of the open door. Everyone below me leaped toward the steps.

"Wait," I yelled, which only made me cough some more. "I need to"—*cough*—"clear the"—*cough*—"flames!"

Luckily Paetus was there to translate. He spoke in hurried Punic to everyone, and they reluctantly backed away from me.

I went up one more step, just enough to bring some of the flames within my sight. I released the spark globe that was still floating in the hold and siphoned more magic from my cells. The cell magic sent the familiar icy tingle over my entire body, helping somewhat with the fiery heat. It was enough to focus my mind despite my coughing and clouded sight.

"*Blussen*," I croaked.

My magic leaped out of me with ecstatic release and into the flames that I could see. The fires went to sleep with a sigh. The sudden reduction in heat allowed me to raise my head a little higher to get a line of sight on more flames. I released another *blussen* spell, and then another to eventually create enough space on the blackened deck for the people below to gather without being roasted alive.

I sheathed my gladius and climbed onto the deck. I threw one *blussen* spell after another at the remaining fires, each of them winking out. Without me telling her, Cana came up behind me and did the same with the flames in front of her. Meanwhile, I heard Paetus below urging the rowers and passengers onto the deck. He didn't have to do much urging, as anyone with a brain wanted out of the smoky hold. Several rowers helped the wounded Carthaginian boy out of the hold, followed by the two shaken girls. Paetus was the last one out. Everyone was coughing, but besides the brother, they all seemed okay.

I grinned through my own coughs. *Teamwork.*

Movement to the left caught my eye. The moon was out and the stars were bright, making it easy to see a trireme rowing toward us at high speed. The bronze plated ram and bow glinted in my galley's dwindling fires, which also made it easy to see a bronze Roman eagle at the top of the bow.

My brain couldn't process the sight, not even when the trireme slammed into the side of our small galley, splitting it in two with a horrific screaming of wood.

4

Like some mythological leviathan, the monstrous trireme's metal wedge-shaped ram sliced through our little galley like an ax through a dry log. The impact flung me to the deck where I slammed my shoulder against the bulkhead railing. I felt a vague crunch that brought more shock than pain at the moment. Other bodies fell on top of me, adding to my confusion and terror.

The trireme's momentum carried us sideways for a few seconds. Then the sounds of screaming and ripping wood ended as if they were switched off. A moment of silence, and then I heard water rushing into the hold of the fatally wounded galley. Commands were shouted from the trireme—in Punic, strangely enough. The warship's rowers reversed course to disengage from the galley that they'd just knifed to death. More ripping wood and rushing water. The galley tilted sharply forward. I tumbled along with other flailing bodies into the warm waters of the southern Mediterranean.

I had a primal, unthinking reflex to reach out and grab for something—*anything*—that would keep my head above water. I tried doing this first with my wounded shoulder arm, but a spear thrust of pain made me scream. My mouth immediately filled with salt water and various other tastes spilling from the galley, which I try not to ponder to this day. I gagged and coughed while flailing with my good arm. I found a flat piece of debris that was—*thank all the gods!*—floating. I grabbed onto the jagged wood and literally held on for my life.

With death postponed a few moments, I gathered my wits and controlled my coughing enough to look around. The galley had not actually split in two, but was only held together by a few timbers on the opposite side from where it was rammed. The large warship had already disengaged its ram and backed away about fifty paces. Small fires still burned at the ends of the galley, illuminating the hellish scene of screaming rowers in the water and the glinting Roman eagle on the trireme's bow.

I frantically scanned the dark waters and debris for Cana and Paetus. I couldn't find them for several seconds. Terror constricted my chest. When I finally saw them, I choked out a relieved sob. Paetus was holding on to a timber with the Carthaginian boy who looked on the verge of passing out (Paetus, too, for that matter). Cana had gathered the two girls onto a jagged piece of wooden debris similar to the one I held. They had seen me before I saw them and were paddling toward me as best they could. I just let them come to me since I couldn't swim to them with my apparently dislocated shoulder.

When we finally connected, I was about to ask if they were hurt, but a cry arose from the rowers in the water. I looked up to see the trireme sail around the halves of the sinking galley. About a dozen archers lined the side of the trireme and were shooting arrows into the helpless rowers. The "lucky" ones died instantly from a well-placed arrow through the eye and simply slipped beneath the waves. But most wailed in anguish from the arrows sticking out of their necks and shoulders.

I numbly found myself thinking that blood loss would soon weaken them and they, too, would soon slip beneath the waves. Either that or sharks would get them.

My stores of empathy seemed to have been used up at that point.

I thought I felt something brush past my legs in the black water. I wasn't sure if it was real or in my mind. But it was enough to clear my numbed mind and try to think up a way to live through the next minute before the trireme reached us.

We had gathered close in a circle about ten feet in diameter. I got an idea, but it was a longshot. All my components were likely soaked within my vest, despite the oiled pouches in which I kept most of them. Besides, it's not like I could surround us all in a talc circle at the moment. At least I still wore my Wolverines ball cap. It would help me concentrate on one of the spells without using components, but I'd need help with the second one.

"Cana," I whispered, trying not to cough. "*Stil.*"

She glanced at me, looked around her, and a flicker of doubt crossed her terrified face. I knew she was thinking the same thing I had just thought. *Without components? Are you mad?* Even her confidence had limits.

But I gave her an encouraging nod that said *I have faith in you.* I had to, or we were dead.

Her face relaxed as she began to concentrate on the *stil* spell, which left me to concentrate on *vervagan*.

My cell magic arose from within me, taking a precious second longer than usual due to my fatigue, fear, and dislocated shoulder. But its warmth and peace eased my pain and focused my mind. With the icy tingle swirling across my skin, I imagined a dome above my fellow survivors and me. The magic always came with the confidence to make it happen, and all negativity fled from my thoughts. Once instinct and experience said that I'd gathered enough cell magic, I siphoned it into the spell by saying, "*Vervagan.*"

The magic burst out of me and encircled my friends in a sphere with a ten-foot radius that obscured us from sight. The only catch was that the archers outside the sphere might notice us out of the corner of their eye. Though if they looked directly at us, they'd only see dark water and floating debris. From *within* the sphere, however, I could see everyone just fine.

The magical release, as always, left me a few moments of contentment and peace, but pain and fear quickly rushed in to remind me of where I was. I glanced at Cana. Her face was a mask of concentration, but I could still hear sounds around us. The trireme was getting closer, its archers still shooting at men in the water. They may not be able to see us, but if they heard us, they might stick around longer. They seemed to want to ensure that everyone on the galley was dead.

A warm wave of cell magic blew past me like a desert breeze. And then the sounds around me grew muffled as if I were hearing them from the next room. Cana's *stil* spell hadn't created absolute silence, but it would have to do.

The trireme floated within twenty paces of us, its oars raised above the water to allow it to coast along slowly so its archers could find their victims. Our galley was almost fully below water now and the fires were all out, so the only light by which the archers could see was the moon and stars. The archers shot at anything that made any sort of splashing sound. Arrows whistled through the air around us, *thunking* into floating wooden debris, disappearing smoothly into the dark sea, and sometimes finding an unfortunate rower whose grunt or cry would only invite more arrows.

I saw Paetus and Cana trying to hold it together. They were doing a far better job than the two Carthaginian girls who were crying and saying something, but their voices were thankfully muffled by the *stil* spell. Their brother looked unconscious, draped over the floating wooden beam, with only Paetus keeping him from slipping beneath the surface.

The trireme eventually moved past us, but circled around the area a few more times. Each time it passed us by was a trial in how much we could control our terror without losing our minds. I mean, my sight had adjusted to the moonlight, so I could the faces of each archer pass over me when the trireme coasted by. I could make out their dark hair, beards, and strange tattoos on some of their cheeks. Some seemed to notice us out of the corner of their eyes. Their heads would dart our way and look directly at us, but they wouldn't see us through the *vervagan* spell.

Sure, I had fought daemons before, but those fights were so fast and furious that I'd never had time to be scared until later. But floating there in the dark water, just waiting for an arrow to enter my throat...that was the most scared I'd ever been.

The trireme eventually sailed away, satisfied that it had left no survivors. Once I was sure they were too far away to see us, I ended the *vervagan* spell and motioned to Cana to end her *stil*. The sounds of our coughs and groans, and water lapping against our life-saving debris, seemed to explode into the night after the long silence. I glanced with worry at the disappearing trireme, but didn't see them turn around.

Paetus was the first to speak. "How did pirates get a Roman trireme?" he sputtered.

"Cana's right," I said. "Piracy has been dead on the Mediterranean for decades. I don't think they were pirates."

"Then who?" Cana asked. She cast an annoyed glance at the youngest girl, who was weeping.

I continued to stare after the Roman trireme as it disappeared into the night. "I think Augustus just tried to kill me."

5

About the only lucky break we caught that night was getting attacked a half-mile from the North African shore. With a breeze blowing from the north, the currents helpfully sent us toward the beach without us having to paddle and spend energy we didn't have.

That and no shark attacks. With all the blood in the water, I was *really* worried about that.

I saw a few lights off to our left, but decided we should stay away from any camps or settlements until we figured out if they were friendly. We made for a dark spot on the beach about a mile north of the lights.

We came ashore an hour later exhausted and shivering. Dawn was breaking upon the tan rocks, cliffs, and mountains of the North African shore. The beach was mostly filled with smooth rocks, but there was a small cove with a strip of sand. We stumbled out of the sea and collapsed on the sand. Worries about fresh water, food, and safety would come later. At that moment, I just wanted to sleep for days on the warming sand. Even the awful pain in my dislocated shoulder wasn't enough to keep me from lying on my back, closing my eyes, and letting the morning sun reheat my body.

I was just happy to have survived the night. And that I hadn't lost my Wolverines baseball cap in the process.

Cana plopped down next to me. "Your shoulder pains you. Do you need healing?"

Healing is pretty intense magic, as far as concentration and energy goes. Even after all the experience I'd had in the last three years with it, I could still barely heal a cut without wanting to nap for a few hours. If Cana did it, her strength being what it was now, she'd need to sleep for the night.

I reluctantly shook my head. "Save your strength. I'll reset it the old fashioned way." *In a few minutes*, I thought. *After I rest.* Though it was more me putting off the pain that I knew would come with the "old fashioned" way.

Paetus dropped down next to me. "We have a problem."

I laughed despite my fatigue. I opened my eyes with some effort and looked at him. "What was your first clue?"

Paetus gave me a sour glare. "The Carthaginian boy. He'll die if he's not healed soon."

My laughter evaporated and I suddenly felt like the biggest ass in Africa. I'd been so concerned with my own fatigue and pain that I forgot about the Carthaginian kids with us.

I glanced at the teen boy lying a dozen paces from us. His eyes were half-open, and his chest rose and fell with shallow breaths. I could see knife slashes that had cut open his tunic along with open wounds around his chest and arms. It seemed they had not stopped bleeding. His older sister sat cross-legged with his head in her lap. The younger one sat next to him, holding his hand. They both looked as shell-shocked as anyone would in their situation.

I sat up, trying to use my good arm to do so, but even that motion brought a blast of fire from my shoulder. I cried out involuntarily. It felt even worse than the time I got shot with an arrow—in the same shoulder, no less—outside Aventicum. I looked down at my shoulder for the first time since I'd injured it and grimaced at how it hung much lower than the other one.

Yep, dislocated. Or so said my non-existent medical knowledge. *Cac* on a sandal.

"I'll heal him," I grunted, "but I can't do a damned thing with my shoulder like this." I looked at Cana and Paetus. "Either of you know how to pop a shoulder back into its socket."

Cana shook her head emphatically, her face seeming to pale at the thought of it. But Paetus said, "I read a medical text describing the procedure once. But I've never seen it done."

"Then you know more than me," I said. "What do I do?"

Paetus licked his lips. "Lie on your back, your arm ninety degrees from your body."

I lay back down and nearly passed out when I raised my arm. Paetus sat down on that side of my body, placed his feet against my side, and then gripped my forearm firmly. He paused, and said, "This may hurt a little."

I bit my lip to keep from swearing at him and then nodded.

He pulled, firmly but slowly. I don't know how long he pulled. Seemed like an hour to me, but Cana and Paetus swore it was only few moments. Regardless, it hurt far more than a little.

I felt a sickening pop, and then the pain suddenly diminished to far more tolerable levels. When it didn't get worse, I grunted a relieved laugh. "Thank the gods. And thank you, Paetus." My shoulder was still sore, and I was sweating despite having dragged myself out of the cool sea, but I seemed okay.

Paetus looked relieved, too, and quite proud. "You're welcome, Natta Magus."

I rolled over and used my good arm to support myself as I stood. I shuffled over to the Carthaginian boy and knelt down next to him. The two girls continued to stare at their brother.

The girl who held his head in her lap didn't look up at me, but said in Latin, "He is so cold."

"What is his name?" I asked.

"Juba."

"And what are your names?"

"I am Elissa. My sister is Alishat."

The girls and their brother had come on board our galley in Sicily, but all three had stayed below deck the whole time, so I had never got a good look at them until now. They were far too young to be going through something like this.

"I'm going to try and heal your brother," I said. "I'm not sure how well it'll work but...well, I'm going to try."

Elissa looked up at me for the first time. "What will you do?"

"What I can," I said.

I put my right hand on Juba's forehead and my left—I winced from the dull ache in my shoulder—on his right arm. I allowed my magic to rise from my body's cells to the surface of my skin. Given my exhaustion and pain, it wasn't as much as I normally had, but I hoped it would be enough to keep the boy from dying. The magic, however, eased my pain, and I fell comfortably into the healing trance. It was like I'd shrunk down to the cellular level within Juba's body. I watched my magic flowing into his wounds, repairing each muscle fiber and skin cell one at a time. I had to limit myself, however, since a full healing would've knocked me unconscious due to the extent of his injuries. But by the time I was done, he was no longer bleeding to death.

I fell out of the healing trance with a gasp and some vertigo. Cana was next to me and put a supporting hand on my back to keep me steady.

Juba's eyes were closed and his breathing was still shallow, but it seemed more regular now. Not the halting, raspy breaths from before the healing.

Elissa and Alishat looked from Juba to me, their eyes glistening with relieved tears.

Elissa stammered, "You are...you are the magus who saved Rome, yes?"

I nodded wearily, too tired to explain that it wasn't all me. A few other rookie magi, including Cana, had a hand in it. And Helva...well, I owed her my life.

"What you did on the boat," she breathed, "in the water...and now...you are truly a gift from the gods, my lord."

I grunted in amusement and then lay back on the sand. "I wouldn't say I'm a gift," I murmured. "And my name's Natta, not 'my lord.'" I closed my eyes. "I need to nap a minute..."

Elissa said no more. She continued to hold Juba's head in her lap while I sensed Alishat curl up on the sand next to him.

My brain tried to jump on the problems of water, food, and how we'd get to Carthage *right now*. But for once my brain wasn't strong enough to overcome the soothing waves and warm sun that lulled me to sleep.

6

I awoke to my own hand slapping my face.

After a moment of disorientation, I looked at my open hand and saw a sand fly smeared across my palm. There were a few more buzzing around my head. I got up as fast as my shoulder and fatigue would allow and used my good arm to wave away the flies.

I glanced down at the sleeping forms of Cana, Paetus, and the Carthaginian siblings, all of whom didn't seem to have the problem I had. Typical. Paetus lay on his back snoring softly, Cana was on her right side curled into a fetal position, and the sisters lay on their sides to the right and left of Juba. The boy's breathing was still shallow, and his skin was far too pale, but at least the wounds on his arms and along his chest were sealed with scabs.

The sun was much higher in the deep blue sky, which told me it was almost noon. Where the sand had been pleasantly warm in the morning, it was now broiling hot, along with the air. There was a dry breeze coming off the sea, but it felt more like a twenty-first century heating vent than anything refreshing. My clothes had mostly dried from my pre-dawn swim, but my face and back were drenched in sweat. My mouth was incredibly dry and tasted like salty cotton. My sleeveless arms were pink with sunburn, and the skin on my face felt burned, too. At least I still had my ball cap, my components vest, and the watertight sack with Augustus's letters of credit and the statue of Lares. I opened the sack and found that the parchment letters had survived intact.

Unfortunately there was no market nearby for me to buy water, food, and shelter.

I looked up and down the beach. To my right were sheer, rocky cliffs that dove straight into the foamy sea. To the left was the continuation of the sandy, pebbly beach, but about a hundred paces behind us were more cliffs. They weren't as sheer as the tan and brown cliffs to the right, but they were pretty steep with loose rocks. We were asking for a sprained ankle or worse if we climbed those.

However, there were large boulders ahead and some alcoves that provided good shade from the sweat-draining sun.

I stooped down between Cana and Paetus and nudged them both away with a hand on each shoulder.

Paetus grunted, his sunburned face turning from peaceful sleep to pained awareness. It took him many moments to simply open his eyes and look up at me. He put one arm over his eyes to shield them from the sun. "This is not going to be a good day," he groaned.

Cana, though, immediately sat up, her eyes alert. Wisps of brown hair fell out of her single, tight braid. Her tunica was dry, and she didn't have Paetus's sunburn on her Gallic face since she'd been facing away from the sun while she slept. Her neck, however, looked red. She looked as haggard and thirsty as I felt, but she had already stood by the time Paetus had opened his eyes.

"We need to get out of the sun," I rasped, my throat dryer than I thought. I pointed to the shaded boulders and alcoves in the cliffs ahead of us. "Help me with Juba."

Elissa and Alishat had awakened when I'd spoken to Cana. Alishat, the youngest, stared at me with confused, bleary eyes, while Elissa checked on her brother. Juba's eyes stayed closed.

Elissa gave me a questioning look, so I said, "Between his wounds and the healing, he'll need all the sleep he can get."

"How long must he sleep?" she asked.

"As long as it takes."

She frowned at me, but I didn't know what else to say. I wasn't a true Healer. I had studied the Finder arcanum in the twenty-first century, before my old mentor threw me back in time. When I arrived in ancient Rome, I only knew enough healing to stop a paper cut from bleeding. Yeah, I'd figured out a lot since then, but I still felt like a first-day intern when I tried any healing spell.

The truth was, I didn't know if Juba would wake up at all. I had stopped him from bleeding out, but he had already lost a lot of blood and he'd been in the sea for hours. And healing takes a lot out of a human body. All I'd done was accelerate his body's natural healing process. In doing that, I might have drained all the energy he'd been using to simply stay alive. His heart was still beating, but what if his brain wasn't getting enough blood? What if he was in a coma and would never open his eyes again?

And what if Augustus sent those pirates after me? What if I'm the reason why—?

"You shouldn't carry anything heavy with that shoulder," Paetus said to me. I blinked, and wanted to thank him for breaking me out of my endless litany of "what ifs."

Instead, I said, "I'm the reason he...I mean, I'm responsible for him now. You take his shoulders, I'll take his feet."

Paetus and Cana exchanged glances, and then Paetus said, "Natta, none of this is your fault. Even if it was an assassination attempt—"

"Fine. *Leerling, you* take his shoulders and Paetus can rub my back and tell me it's all gonna be okay."

I stepped around to Juba's legs and tried not to wince from the pain in my shoulder when I picked them up under the knees. Cana shrugged and picked Juba up by the shoulders, and between the both of us, we shuffled him up the beach toward a shaded alcove. Elissa and Alishat walked on either side of Juba. Cana gave me the occasional glance, but wisely didn't say anything.

Paetus mumbled something about going to inspect the debris that was washing up on shore, and then he walked away. I felt more than a little sorry for snapping at Paetus like that, but at the moment I was in no mood to hear someone tell me this wasn't my fault. I was the one dragging Cana and Paetus with me to Egypt. If Augustus had suddenly decided that I was more trouble to him alive than dead, then this would not be the last attempt on my life. What if on the way to save one friend, I managed to get two *other* friends killed?

Juba was far lighter than I thought he'd be, so we were able to get him to the rocky alcove with relative ease. The alcove was deep enough to provide permanent shade from the moving sun. We could also feel a breeze from the sea in front of us, which would freshen the baking air and hopefully keep the sand flies at bay.

When we set Juba down near the back of the alcove, his eyes fluttered open. Elissa and Alishat both gasped, and I felt a surge of hope.

The girls said something to him in Punic. He moved his eyes from one face to the other, licked his dry lips, and said something back. They spoke like that for a minute or so, with Elissa motioning to me at one point. Juba shifted his eyes to me, and then said in Latin, "Thank you for my life, magus. And my sisters'."

I nodded once. "This may be a stupid question, but how do you feel?"

He stared at me a moment. A smile played at the corner of his mouth, and then he coughed out a chuckle. "Yes, magus. A stupid question. Perhaps my wounds were not plain to see?" He chuckled and coughed again. I was relieved to see his eyes had taken on a playful gleam rather than the lifelessness they'd held when he'd first opened them.

Elissa frowned at Juba and then gave me a wary look. "Forgive my brother's impertinence, *magus dominus*, he means no disrespect. Sometimes he thinks his humor is humorous to all." Elissa looked back down at Juba like a stern matron, but Alishat watched her older brother with a growing smile that matched his.

I felt my own cracked lips spread into a smile. "Don't worry about it. I've been accused of impertinence myself at times." I turned to Juba and said, "So, are you thirsty?"

Juba's chuckle broke into full on laughter, and then he winced as the barely healed wounds in his chest reminded him they were still there. But they weren't enough to stop him from laughing. Alishat laughed along with her brother, tears brimming in her eyes, while Elissa just sighed and shook her head at them both.

I stood and walked out of the alcove, leaving the family reunion. Cana came with me. Once we were a few paces away, she said, "You impress me yet again, *leraar*." She used the Dutch word for 'teacher' when she addressed me, as I had taught her (just because I was in ancient Rome didn't mean I had to abandon *all* propriety). "You heal the body with cell magic, and the spirit with your words."

"That's awfully sweet, *leerling*. Still doesn't get you out of your morning meditations. Finish those yet?"

Her mouth fell open, and she spread her hands out incredulously.

I interrupted her before she could protest. "Just because we were attacked by assassins, spent half the night in the sea, and might die of thirst tomorrow doesn't mean you get out of homework."

She glared at me a moment, inhaled deeply—a trick I taught her to calm her anger—and then let it out slowly. "Yes, *leraar*." She held her head high and walked over to a boulder about twenty paces away that provided some shade and solitude for her meditations.

I wasn't simply being the hard teacher: I had used those same meditations when I was a *leerling* to regain magical strength after some grueling practice sessions. They were monotonous and tedious, but they worked.

Cana would need her strength for tonight when we scouted those camp lights we had spotted from the sea.

I walked toward the shore where Paetus was sifting through some debris. My sandals offered zero protection against the blistering sand, so I had to jog the last dozen paces to the cool surf in a very undignified fashion. Paetus didn't look up at me as he pulled a floating trunk wrapped in oiled leather toward shore. I scanned the debris that had already washed up—small barrels, chests, oiled sacks—and grew hopeful that we'd find something in it that would help us. There was even more out in the water, slowly heading in our direction.

I tried not to let my gaze linger on the human bodies that were also coming ashore.

Despite my tunica and breeches having just dried, I waded over to Paetus and grabbed one of the handles on the large trunk. "Sorry about...earlier," I said as I helped him pull it in.

"No matter," he mumbled.

It sure felt like it mattered, but I didn't push him.

"I heard laughing," he said. "Your healing worked?"

"I think so," I said through heavy breaths. My footing was treacherous and the trunk was heavy. "I had to use more magic than I thought. I'm two blinks away from falling asleep again."

We got the trunk out of the water and dragged it up the pebbly beach. Even that amount of effort forced me to sit down on the wet rocks. Paetus, however, proceeded to use a rock to strike at the trunk's lock, his blows echoing off the surrounding cliffs.

"How in damnation did that thing stay afloat?" I had to concentrate just to keep my head up and my eyes focused.

Paetus didn't say anything, but after a final blow, he broke the lock and threw open the trunk lid. "This was the captain's trunk," he said as he rummaged through the contents. "I saw it in his cabin. It was well sealed and has air bladders, so I'm thinking that... Ah!"

He triumphantly held up two wine skins. Judging by the sloshing I heard and the way they hung in Paetus's hands, the skins were full.

I sighed. "Wine will just dehydrate us more."

Paetus uncorked one of the skins and sniffed it. "Not this wine. It is very diluted with water. A child could drink this without feeling its effects."

I shrugged. "We'll use it as a last resort. Our first priority is to find water and food."

"Can't you use your magic to find those?" Paetus asked as he returned to searching the trunk. "I thought finding things was your specialty."

I laid back down on the beach. I was so tired that not even the pebbles in my back bothered me. "It is. But I need a sample of the thing I'm trying to find. Or an image of that thing in the mind of someone I can touch. I don't have a sample of either water or food from this place."

"Maybe the boy and his sisters have been to a market nearby."

"Perhaps," I said, shutting my eyes. "But right now I couldn't even siphon a spark globe."

"I'm sorry to hear that," Paetus said.

"I'll be fine. I just need more sleep."

"No, I'm sorry to hear that because we could use your magic right now."

I looked up at Paetus, who had stopped searching the trunk and was staring wide-eyed at the cliffs behind us. I sat up with great effort and followed his gaze.

Two riders on horseback stood at the top of the cliff looking down on us from less than a hundred paces. They were both dressed in tan linen tunicas and wore dull blue turbans on their heads that also covered their mouths. Both wore curved short swords at their belts. One of them uncovered his mouth, put his fingers to his lips, and issued a loud whistle.

The sound of hoofs on gravel came from cliffs to my left. Six riders dressed similarly to the guys on top of the cliff sped down a hidden path two hundred paces down the beach. Once they reached the beach, they turned their horses and galloped toward us.

7

There's nothing like a charging cavalry to get you moving.

I jumped up, fighting a wave of vertigo. Terror fueled my limbs. I doubt I could've stood without it. Sure these guys didn't have the armor, shields, and red cloaks of a Roman cavalry, but their horses seemed eager enough to trample us if directed to do so. Each man had a curved sword sheathed at his waist, which I'm sure was just as deadly as a gladius.

"What do we do?" Paetus cried, ready to run.

My first instinct was to run back to the alcove and do what I could to protect Juba and his sisters. But what in damnation *could* I do? I had no magical reserves left worth siphoning and wouldn't for several more hours. I had my enchanted gladius, but it was empty of magic; I'd used all of its sleep spells against the assassins on the galley. And brandishing it at the six riders would likely make them giggle as they struck me down from all sides.

I glanced quickly to where Cana had gone to do her meditations. I didn't see her, but I didn't want to turn my head in her direction either, thus alerting the riders to her presence. *Stay hidden,* leerling. *Don't try to be a hero.*

The only thing that made me a fraction less frightened was the fact that none of the men had drawn their swords.

"We talk to them," I said, watching the riders close in on us. "Get your Punic warmed up."

"Are you insane?" he hissed. "They could be bandits! They'll slice us open from—"

"They'll do that whether we run or fight! We talk first. And by all the gods, don't look up at the alcove. Maybe they won't see Juba and his sisters."

"Juno preserve us..." Paetus murmured.

The riders stopped about ten paces in front of us. They all wore a variation of the same tan tunicas that I'd seen on the spies on the cliffs, along with the dusty blue turbans that also covered their mouths. Weathered, brown North African skin surrounded their brown eyes. Two kept their hands on the hilts of their swords. I held out my hands and tried to look as harmless as possible. I thought about unbuckling my gladius to show that I had no intention of using it on them, but I didn't want them to think I was reaching for it.

That, and if this talk did go south, I'd still have a sword with which to go down fighting.

"Tell them we're glad to see them," I said to Paetus. "Tell them our ship sunk and that we need water and food."

Paetus licked his dry lips and then translated my words. But before he made it through the first sentence, one of the riders said in Latin, "We understood you, Roman."

He gave my Wolverines baseball cap a long hard look and then returned his brown eyes to mine. "You will come with us. We have food and water." He glanced directly at the alcove and the spot Cana had chosen for her meditations, and then back at me. "You will all be safe."

"Your offer is kind," I said slowly, "but forgive me for being cautious. Our ship was attacked last night. We're a little...wary of strangers at the moment. With all due respect, how do I know your offer is sincere?"

The man stared at me, his eyes crinkling around the edges. He pulled the blue turban away from his mouth to reveal a smile with straight white teeth. He had a black beard with small braids in it around the chin. His smile didn't seem friendly, nor did it seem deadly. More like a used trolley salesman trying to close a deal.

"You will not know my offer is sincere, Roman, until you accept it," he said. "There is no water for dozens of miles, and Carthage is more than twenty miles to the north over rocks and cliffs. A very treacherous and difficult journey. Especially for your wounded man. And his sisters. And your woman in the rocks behind you."

Damnation. They had probably been watching us for a while before the two riders on the cliff revealed themselves.

"Or fortune could favor you," he continued, "and a Roman patrol galley will pass these shores. But those only happen two or three times per week. And the Romans seem wary of this region of late." He traded a proud smile with his companions who chuckled beneath their turbans. Now *that* smile was quite deadly.

He turned back to me and gave me an irritated look. "If we had wanted to kill you all, we could have done so while you slept on the beach. Come with us or you and your companions will die on this beach of thirst. It is that simple."

I glanced at Paetus, who still seemed ready to bolt for the nearest cave. I wish I had that energy. I felt so tired that it was all I could to do to remain standing. And I had never been so thirsty in my life; my tongue felt swollen and my lips were bleeding. I knew my fellow survivors felt about the same. In our condition, there was no way we could walk to Carthage over that rocky terrain if it was only a mile away, much less twenty.

And it was true; these guys could've killed us while we slept. Hell, they could kill us *now* if they wanted. They seemed to genuinely want to help us. They hadn't even spared a glance at the wreckage washing ashore or the trunk Paetus had just opened. Maybe they were just kind locals who wanted to do the right thing.

Right. If three years in the ancient world had taught me anything, it was that people rarely did anything for me out of the kindness of their hearts (Vitulus and his family being the rare exception). These guys wanted something from us, and judging by the way the leader had stared at my cap, I began to think they wanted something from *me*.

Whatever it was, they needed us alive...and for the moment that was good enough for me.

I bowed deeply and said, "We accept your generous offer."

Paetus issued a little moan next to me, but at least he didn't run.

The leader smiled widely and then returned his blue turban around his mouth. "Excellent! Our camp is three miles down the beach. We will return within two hours with a cart to carry your wounded man and your possessions."

Then he turned his horse around and trotted back down the beach, his men following. A hundred paces away, they were joined by the two riders from the cliff, who trotted down the hidden trail. Once they were all together, they spurred their horses into a gallop and disappeared around a cliff beside the beach.

I looked at Paetus. "I'll take some wine now."

8

Considering I still hadn't gotten used to telling time by looking at the sun, I couldn't tell if the riders were true to their word of returning within two hours. But return they did and with the promised cart, a simple two-wheeler covered by a thin linen sheet and pulled by a stocky horse. The leader and four of his riders accompanied the cart. They were all still armed with those nasty curved short swords.

And, most importantly, skins of water for all of us. I knew enough first aid to know that you don't guzzle water when you're severely dehydrated, so I took sips, swished the water in my mouth before swallowing slowly. The water was warm and tasted leathery, but it was the most glorious tasting water I had ever drank in my life. Cana and Paetus used the same drinking strategy as I did.

Elissa helped Juba drink, since he was still terribly weak from blood loss and the healing, before she took a sip for herself. Poor little Alishat was the only one who drank too much too fast, despite my warnings, and got sick.

Even though the riders had given us water, none of my companions were happy about going anywhere with these strangers, especially Elissa, Juba, and Alishat. While the riders were their countrymen and shared the same native language, my three Carthaginian companions were thoroughly Romanized. They were just as culturally different from the riders as I was. They had heard all the same tales of barbarian savages as Paetus and thus had the same fears as him. And Cana just didn't trust anybody.

But they all reluctantly agreed that our choices were limited.

After we drank enough to feel human again, I helped the riders carry Juba to the cart. They'd brought a thick wool blanket with them, so we helped Juba onto the blanket and carried him that way. All the while, Juba jokingly complained about the bumpy ride and asked that we step softly on the rocky terrain down to the cart. The riders glared at him while Elissa tried to shush him. I just grinned. His normally brown skin still looked gray, and he could barely move a limb without almost passing out, but I was encouraged by his good humor. I would've been worried if he was courteous or silent.

None of the debris that washed ashore had been ours (Paetus had searched in vain for his trunk of scrolls and books while we waited for the riders), so we didn't have anything else to load onto the cart besides ourselves. Once we got Juba on board, we were ready to go. We all piled in and the cart lurched forward.

The cart didn't move much faster than walking speed, but at least the linen cover kept the blazing sun off us. And we were all still weak from our ordeal. That bumpy, rickety cart felt about as luxurious as a twenty-first century air trolley.

Not that any of us could actually relax. I was just as much on edge as the rest of my companions. When Elissa and Alishat weren't watching Juba, they were casting wary glances at the armed riders next to us. Paetus laid out one of his scrolls to dry, but he kept flinching when one of the horses snorted or knocked a rock loose. Cana, to her credit, had closed her eyes and was attempting to meditate despite the bumps and swaying of the cart, but her fists were clenched white in her lap.

And I just prayed to the Unknowable Will that I hadn't killed my friends by agreeing to go with these riders.

The sun was well past noon when the cart turned right off the beach and headed up a rocky trail between two steep cliffs. The air was far cooler between the cliffs, but had a stale quality to it that seemed to grow more rotten the further we traveled into the twisting crevasse. Along with the increasing odor, the sounds of rustling echoed from up the trail. I realized what the odor and sounds were just moments before I saw the bodies.

Two crosses stood on either side of the trail, each holding a crucified man. Both men wore gray tunicas with "SPQR" stamped on the chest in red. Feasting gulls surrounded the head of one of the men. The second man's head was leaned back, but the gulls had pecked out his eyes. The gulls flew off the first man as we passed by, but I didn't dare look too closely at him.

Alishat vomited over the side of the cart. It was all I could do to keep my own stomach under control.

"Merciful Juno," Paetus moaned, his hand over his nose and his eyes closed tight.

Cana couldn't maintain her meditations and was leaning past Paetus to stare at the dead. She cursed something in her Gallic tongue, and then nodded toward the first man and said, "He is still alive."

Before I could stop myself, I looked. His head was leaning forward, and I now saw that his eyes had also been pecked out. The bloody skin across his face was scoured with gull bites and gouges. He made small strangled, gasping noises as we passed. I didn't think he was actually conscious, though there was no way to tell with his eyes gone.

And that's when I leaned over the side of the cart and vomited all the water I drank.

When I was finished, I looked up to see the lead rider staring at me with hard eyes. He didn't say anything to me, and I didn't say anything to him. I just leaned back into the cart and tried not to look at the crucified men behind us.

The air gradually freshened the further we got from the bodies until we emerged from the crevasse trail into a small valley. At least a hundred linen tents filled the valley along with hastily constructed pens for horses, goats, and sheep. As the cart made its way through the tent city, more armed men strode by us with short swords, spears, and bows. Each one gave us curious stares, sometimes muttering to themselves as we passed. And then, to my surprise, I noticed small children sitting in the tents we passed, regarding us with far less curiosity than the turbaned soldiers. In fact, their blank stares were downright creepy. Their mothers sat nearby, sewing clothes or preparing meals, with the same blank expressions. These people were severely traumatized by something. Given the crucifixions we just passed, I assumed they'd witnessed many other horrors that *weren't* on display.

What was this place? And why were they using two crucified Romans as a "Welcome" mat?

The cart finally stopped in front of a tent made of patched leather and held up by multiple poles and stakes. The flaps on the front of the tent were rolled up to create an entrance, but I couldn't see into the darkness.

"He is waiting for you inside," the lead rider said from atop his horse.

I squinted up at him. "Who?"

The leader's eyes crinkled from the smile beneath his turban-covered mouth, but he said no more.

I looked at my companions and then back at the leader. "My friends—"

"Will remain here until you return," he said. "Upon my honor, they will be safe."

I hated being separated from Paetus and Cana, who both stared at me with clenched teeth, apparently feeling the same way. But I doubted I had any choice in the matter. I moved toward the edge of the cart, my stiff, weary limbs protesting along the way, and stepped down on to the dusty gravel. My gladius was still strapped to my belt. I was surprised that they hadn't asked me to give it up. I hoped that was a good sign.

I gave one last reassuring glance to Cana and Paetus and then entered the dark tent.

It took a few moments for my eyes to adjust. When they did, I saw several men standing around a crude table, five of them in all, and each one dressed in multi-colored tunicas. Their long beards were black and braided with colored beads. They looked more like priests than bandits.

Although dressed the same, one of the men stood out from the others. While he was also black-haired and had a beard with the same braids, his skin was fairer than that of his North African comrades.

When our eyes met, I remembered.

I'd last seen him at Aventicum. He was clean-shaven back then, but this was definitely him.

Centurion Terentius stepped from around the table with a broad smile and strode up to me. He studied me a moment and then wrapped me in a strong embrace. He then backed away, but continued to hold my arms in a strong grip. His eyes had a zealous glint that made me think of the flamens back in Rome...just before they gutted a pig in their sacrifices to Mars.

"Natta Magus," he said in Latin, "I've been expecting you."

9

S o quick review.

    Terentius was an officer at the Roman garrison of Aventicum in Germania Superior. Or at least he was the last time I saw him over a year ago. We met there during some, er, unpleasantness caused by my insane, former mentor, William Pingree Ford. Terentius hated me the moment I entered the fort until the moment we parted ways. Never mind that my friends and I helped the Romans escape slaughter of a most gruesome fashion. Terentius was a patrician of the most noble and, therefore, annoying kind—he was an ardent believer in the Roman Religio. Since my magic did not come from the Roman gods, he considered it blasphemous at best, evil at worst. And he never let me forget his opinion the whole time I was in Aventicum, even when I was saving him from corrupted monster vines ripping apart his fort and rampaging *strix* ripping apart his comrades.

Which is why I stared at him now as if I were seeing a ghost (and trust me, ghosts are even creepier to magi then they are to mundanes).

Terentius continued grinning at me. "Natta Magus, my friend, you don't need to speak for me to know your confusion. You are wondering, 'Why is Terentius leading this band of Carthaginian refugees? How did he get to North Africa? Why would he abandon his oaths to Rome?' Am I correct?"

I nodded slowly. "And the beard," I muttered.

He laughed. "Of course, the most important change. How could I forget? Better to fit in among my new friends, I suppose."

I glanced behind Terentius at his new friends, the four priests or generals or whoever they were. They stared at Terentius and me without saying a word. While they didn't smile, their eyes and postures seemed to hold a lot of respect and reverence for Terentius. I can't really describe their expressions and bearing, but it was more of a feeling I got that they would cut their own throats if he told them to.

"Since you brought it up," I said, beginning to recover from my shock, "how *did* you get here?"

"Ah, now that is a story of much adventure and woe," he said, leaning toward me, his voice lowering. "Here is what happened. I boarded a trireme in Rhegium. I sailed to Carthage. I stepped off the trireme in Carthage. One thing led to another, and now I'm here talking with you."

He stepped back from me with a satisfied smile.

"Some holes in that story," I said quietly.

Terentius's laughter boomed within the tent. I don't think I ever saw him laugh once in Aventicum. The priests behind him didn't even crack a grin.

"And I will tell you the rest later," he said, slapping me on the shoulder. "I have some business to attend to, but I will return tomorrow morning and answer all of your questions. In the meantime, you and your friends will have food, water, and rest. Himilco!"

The lead rider stepped into the tent and then stooped to one knee before Terentius, his head bowed as if he were addressing Augustus. "*Ba'al?*"

"Take Natta Magus and his friends to my tents. Ensure they have all the food and water they need."

"Yes, *ba'al*," Himilco said, and then stood. He looked to me and said, "Follow me, Natta Magus."

Terentius continued to watch me with that same friendly grin. I nodded to him and said, "Thank you for your hospitality."

His smile widened so that I could see his teeth. "I owe you much, Natta Magus. It is the least I can do."

I followed Himilco out of the tent, feeling the stares of Terentius and his silent priests on my back.

When I climbed into the cart, all of my companions gave me questioning looks. Even Juba was awake and his face was serious for a change.

"Later," I muttered, glancing at Himilco who was speaking to the cart's driver.

The cart bumped along over the uneven, gravely path through the myriad tents. I studied the faces of the people that we passed: Men, women, and children alike mostly watched us with curiosity on their dusty, brown faces as they went about the tasks of daily life in the ancient world. Some children played and laughed, while others stared after us with the same shell-shocked faces as their parents, who maintained a protective grip on them. I simply couldn't get a read on this place. Where they glad to be here or afraid? It seemed a genuine mix. And *why* were they glad or afraid? Where did they come from?

We stopped at a large tent made of striped fabric and colored leather. Its back was up against one of the sheer cliffs that surrounded the entire valley. Four blue-turbaned men with spears and short swords guarded the tent. They stood next to the rolled up entrance talking quietly to each other, but straightened when they saw Himilco. Himilco said something in Punic, and two of the men hurried off into the camp while the two who remained came over to the cart.

Himilco gestured toward the tent with a grand sweeping motion of his hand. We climbed down from the cart while the two guards carried Juba on the woolen blanket. Elissa and Alishat stayed beside Juba, while Cana and Paetus followed me with wary eyes. I led the group inside.

Terentius may have left his patrician life behind in Rome, but that didn't mean he'd abandoned his patrician comforts. The entire floor of the tent—about twenty paces long and ten deep—was covered in patterned rugs and blankets so that not an inch of dusty soil or gravel shown through. Several tables stood in the corner filled with scrolls, clay tablets, wine cups, and plates. Three couches that could've comfortably sat ten people were arranged around a brass brazier in the center of the tent. There was an opening in the tent above the brazier, which provided light and fresh air. In the left corner was a single cot of military quality that stood about six inches off the carpeted floor.

The guards carried Juba to one of the couches, laid him down gently, and then left the tent and waited outside. Himilco stood in the tent's entrance, the bright sunshine behind him casting his face in shadow.

"*Ba'al* will return here once he has finished his business with the priests."

"Ba'al?" I said.

Himilco stared at me a moment and then said evenly, "The one you call Terentius. Food and water is being gathered and will arrive soon."

Then he turned and left. The two guards who had carried Juba in followed Himilco away from the tent. We were finally alone.

Paetus cast a wary glance at the guards as they walked away. "Ba'al?" he said in a low voice. "That's the name of a Carthaginian god. Who is Terentius? Who are these people?"

I was about to tell him what I knew when I suddenly felt a humming in my teeth and every cell of my body. It's the way I feel when powerful magic is being used nearby. I shot a look at Cana, who returned my look with a shocked one of her own.

"You can feel that, yes?" she said.

"Oh yeah."

I stared at the opening and then siphoned from my low reserves of cell magic. With magic in my eyes, I could see multi-colored swirls over the tent's entrance, like an oily film on a placid lake surface. It was a magical shield; nothing with magic in its nature could come in or go out.

And that meant Cana and I were trapped.

IO

True to his word, Himilco's guards returned minutes later with sacks of water and trays of hard breads, some kind of jerky that I suspected to be goat, and some pears and dates. They entered the tent, set the trays and water on one of the tables, and then left without so much as flinching when they passed through the magical, filmy shield. Nobody guarded the tent entrance. They knew we couldn't go anywhere.

While Paetus and my Carthaginian companions dove into the food and water, Cana and I walked around the tent inspecting the shield that trapped us. It was pretty damned powerful. It was the kind of containment we used in the twenty-first century when we studied ancient artifacts or magical weapons from the Dark Wars.

At least it wasn't the kind that canceled the use of magic within it, because I could siphon what remained of my cell magic just fine. But when I tried passing my hand through the shield, it was like plunging into ice water: It seemed to suck all the warmth and magic from my body and became excruciating after a second or two. I couldn't tell how thick the shield was since I could barely keep my hand in it for more than a second. Was it no thicker than my hand? If so, could I jump through it quickly if I got a good running start? Or was it so thick that I'd get stuck in the middle, dying from the burning cold as it drained my body of all warmth and magic? In my current fatigue, I had no desire to test it.

No, my biggest desire was to figure out who put it there and how.

I was staring at the shielded entrance and thinking so hard that I didn't notice Paetus approach me. "Eat and drink," he said, handing me a plate of food and a water sack, "or you'll not have the energy to save the world again."

I frowned at him, but took the plate and water. "I don't want to save the world," I said. "I just want to figure a way out of this mess. Every moment we waste here is another moment Helva—" I shook my head and bit into a date, chewing absently.

"She knew what she was doing," Paetus said quietly. "She never asked you to come after her."

"And I never asked her to die for me," I snarled. I glanced at Cana, who was still inspecting an opening between the tent flaps in the back. "Eat and drink something, *leerling*, or we're not getting out of here."

"I know," she said, still staring at the shield, "but the patterns on it show—"

"I said forget it," I snapped. "Eat and drink. You're going to need your energy."

She scowled at me but went to the food table and began picking through it. Once she had some food and water, she sat down in front of the tent entrance and stared at the shield with her back to me.

"So," Paetus said, "who is Terentius?"

I washed down some salty goat jerky with a gulp of warm water. I'd already told Paetus months ago about my adventures at Aventicum: How William Pingree Ford had used a daemonic strix army to destroy the Roman garrison there so that he could reach the ancient temple beneath the fort. All part of his elaborate plan to show me my "destiny," a destiny that involved me abandoning the people I loved—*Brianna,* I thought with a sudden pain in my chest—in twenty-first century Detroit and staying in ancient Rome. I had seen that destiny, too, through a magical artifact that I'd dubbed the Ring of Saturn. I spent what felt like years in that timeless artifact vainly searching for a future that allowed a humanity with magic to survive past the twenty-first century.

I'd only found one among the multitudes, as William had predicted, but it could only come to pass if I stayed in ancient Rome. Of course it didn't tell me what I had to *do* in ancient Rome for that future to exist. No, that would be too easy. I'd been left behind to figure it out myself.

Anyway, I'd already explained all that stuff to Paetus, but I'd never given him the names of the minor players, which, until now, I had placed Terentius.

"I know his *gens*," Paetus said after I told him about Terentius and my surprise at seeing him again. "They are not patricians, but they are wealthy and pious plebeians. His father must be Senator Terentius Lucanus. Though he is plebian, his politics are often more patrician than many patricians."

"Yeah, well that's how this Terentius was back in Aventicum. I felt like I had to keep one eye on him and one on the strix."

"What made him change?"

"That's the big question, isn't it?"

"Maybe," Cana said, her back still toward us, "he is a magus."

"I thought about that, but I don't think he is. I didn't see a magus aura around him when I spoke with him. Granted, I wasn't really looking, but a spell like this shield requires a magus with some serious skills. Aura or no aura, I would've sensed that right away."

"A different kind?" Paetus said. "Like...Helva? You told me she was very good at hiding her power from you."

I nodded slowly, tossing the hard bread that I'd been nibbling onto my plate. "I suppose it's possible. I never thought earth magi like Helva existed until I met her. Regardless of whether he's a magus or has a magus on staff, the point is that he has access to some serious magic. How did he get it? And why did he turn from patrician wannabe to rebel who crucifies his own countrymen?"

"Perhaps he is a prisoner himself," Paetus said. "They may be deferring to him and calling him *'ba'al'* to make you think he's their leader. When in reality they are using him."

Cana turned around. "For what? Carthage has been pacified for two hundred years. They are as Roman now as any tribe in Italia. What would they hope to gain with a hostage? Independence?"

Paetus laughed sarcastically. "They're not rebels; they're pirates! Why have pirates taken hostages throughout time? Money, power, lands. Shall I go on?"

I shook my head. "No, he's not a prisoner. He was in control in that tent. I saw the way the priests looked at him—it was the same way Augustus's followers looked at him. Maybe one or two can fake it, but all five of them?" I clicked my teeth together. "He's in charge and he has magic. And I want to find out where that magic is coming from." Then I glared at the shield. "Because it's making things damned inconvenient for us."

Cana set her plate on the rug floor. "I've eaten my food and drank my water, *leraar*," she said. "May I *now* explain how we can break this shield?"

II

I stared at Cana for a few seconds while her words sunk in. When they did, all I could muster was, "What?"

"I was trying to explain the patterns to you when you ordered me to eat and drink. I have completed that task, so may I now explain my ideas? *Leraar?*"

I sighed. She was mad at me for snapping at her earlier like she was still a slave. I happened to think I was rather easy on her—she should have seen the nuns I had to deal with when I was her age at St. Leo's Academy in Detroit.

But I just said, "Okay, tell me."

She pointed toward the tent's entrance where we could see the filmy, multi-colored swirls the best. "You see how the patterns move across the shield, yes? You said earlier they were like oil in moving water."

The swirls did indeed move across the shield and change colors as they went. I would think they were beautiful if I didn't know they were the bars to my cage. I had noted this in my mind as soon as I saw the shield earlier, but the *leraar* in me was interested to see where my *leerling* was going with this.

"Right," I said, "they move in a random—"

"No," she said, "not random. It is very subtle, but there is order to them."

I squinted at the swirls in the shield. To my eyes they seemed completely random. They moved and changed slowly, but I saw no more of a pattern to them than sand on a beach.

"Okay," I said, "show me."

She frowned. "You cannot see it?"

"All I see are random swirls of color. If you see a pattern, it might just be your mind interpreting one. Like constellations."

She gave an exasperated sigh, stood up, and walked over to the entrance, muttering, "I am not seeing constellations..."

She pointed to one vortex of red swirls that rotated around a green and yellow circle. But as I looked at them, they changed shape and color again, merging with another multicolored vortex of purple and orange. "Red always revolves around green and yellow," she said, and then pointed to the new purple vortex. "Purple will change to pink..."

As soon as she said that, the purple changed to pink.

"And then to blue..."

Pink turned to blue.

"And back to purple." She turned to me with a satisfied grin.

I stared at the swirls and indeed they changed to the colors Cana had predicted. I looked at her. "Okay. You can predict the colors in the swirls. So what?"

I had an idea of where she was going with this, but I wanted to see if she went there. It was quite the effort to contain my excitement.

"It occurred to me that the enchantments on your shop in Rome had the same sorts of patterns, but they were stable and did not change color like these. They were the work of an amateur compared to these, but they were the same basic concept."

I was too excited to be insulted. "Go on."

"In your shop, all I had to do was send a small disruption into one of the vortices and a hole would have opened in the enchantment, yes?"

I shrugged. "Sure, but I never worried about that weakness since the enchantments were meant to turn away mundanes."

"So to break this shield," she said, her Gallic accent strengthening with her own excitement, "we only have to predict where a vortex will show up and then cast a disruption into it. Like knocking one leg out from a stool."

I finally broke a grin. "Damnation," I breathed. "You're an Engineer."

Paetus, as he usually did during these teaching moments, thrust his hand into his pack, pulled out a clay tablet, and began making notes on it with a stylus. He fancied himself my personal scribe, even though I wrote something in my own journals most nights. He hoped that my journeys would constitute the next *Odyssey* and that he would be considered the next Homer once he published them.

I truly prayed they didn't and that he was not.

Cana blinked once at the unfamiliar English term of "Engineer" and her mouth tried to form the word.

"It's what we called magi in my time who had the talent to build new spells," I said. "They can see the patterns and energies that make up a spell better than other magi and then mix and match them to create new ones. They're pretty rare in my time. For this time...well, you have quite the career ahead of you, *leerling.*"

To say the least. Now I *knew* she was going to be more powerful than me someday.

Her face lit up with pride and a little bit of fear. "Excellent. We can escape now if I just—"

"Wait," I said. I glanced at Juba, Elissa, and Alishat, who talked quietly in the corner of the tent. Juba was sitting up now, and his skin tone was a healthier brown than gray. The food and water were already strengthening him. The wounds on his arms were just angry scars now.

"We'll try in a few hours," I said.

Cana followed my glance and then frowned. She came and sat down next to me, and then whispered, "They will slow us down, *leraar.*"

She was very loyal to me, and to some extent Paetus, but I knew she'd leave the Carthaginian family behind in a heartbeat. I realized that over the last two months I'd been so focused on showing her *how* to use her new talents, that I'd completely neglected teaching her the moral responsibilities that came with them. Especially in an era were 99% of the population didn't have those talents.

"In a few hours," I replied in the same whisper, "Juba will be strong enough to run. I will not leave them behind."

"They are Carthaginian," Cana said. "This refugee camp is Carthaginian. They will be fine."

"No," Paetus murmured next to us, "they are Roman citizens with Carthaginian blood. If this camp is made up of bandits and rebels like I think it is, they will most certainly *not* be fine. They might be seen as collaborators or traitors, for whom rebels usually save their most barbaric punishments."

"But we cannot save everyone!" Cana whispered back to Paetus. Then she turned to me and said, "Remember why we are here, *leraar.* Helva."

I gave her a piercing look. "Why do you want to save Helva?"

She shrugged. "Because you want to."

"Is that all?"

"She was a powerful magus. I learned much from her in just the few hours I spent with her. I could learn much more if we found her again."

"Any other reasons?"

"What else is there?"

"*Because it's the right thing to do,*" I said. "Because she sacrificed herself to save us. Because if there's even a chance we can save her from literal Hell, we need to take it." I leaned back from her a bit. "Any one of those answers would've worked, *leerling*."

"Yes, we owe Helva much," Cana said, her whisper getting louder. "What do we owe these Carthaginians? Will you risk Helva to save *them*?"

I was about to snap back at her, but I glanced at the family again. All three of them were staring at us. Heat arose in my face, and I averted my eyes in embarrassment.

"I will understand if you leave without us," Juba said quietly. "I do not want us to be the reason you stay and endanger yourselves or your friend. I will be honest with you: If I and my sisters had the chance to leave without you, we would do so, too."

I stood, walked over to Juba and his sisters, and sat down cross-legged next to them. "I will be honest with *you*. I can't abide feeling regret. And if I left you three behind, I would feel much regret. So, if you think about it, my reasons for staying are purely selfish."

Juba stared at me a moment and then grinned. "Well that makes me feel much better."

Elissa shook her head at the both of us. "I never suspected there was another man in this world with the same strange humor as my brother."

"Now that we are all a tribe," Cana said bitterly from right behind me, "when *will* we try to leave?"

"Tonight," I said. Then I turned to Cana. "Which gives you and me plenty of time to break through this shield and do some snooping."

An eager gleam filled Cana's eyes.

12

ana and I waited until the sun went down before we tried breaking the shield. Two reasons for this: Once we did break out, the concealment spells that we'd cast on ourselves would work better in the semi-darkness of dusk. And second, we wanted to see just how closely our tent was being observed. Nobody came to check on us since the guards had brought food and water. Nor did we see anyone watching us when we peeked through the entrance and the other openings between the tent flaps. Either they didn't care, or they were awfully confident in their magic.

I was betting on the latter. Which meant we had to be extra careful breaking the shield in case there were breaching alarms built into it. Cana stared at the swirling patterns for quite some time before she felt certain that there were no alarms. The patterns still looked random to me until she pointed them out, and even then it took some time for me to "get it." Once I did, though, I was pretty sure we could make a temporary hole in the shield rather than completely take it down, which meant we'd have to jump through fast when it opened.

Once dusk came, we went to the back of the tent and pulled aside one of the flaps. Beyond the swirling shield rose the sheer cliff face about two paces away. Cana concentrated on the moving swirls a few moments and then accurately predicted where a vortex would manifest. I turned my Wolverines ball cap around and siphoned cell magic to the surface of my skin. I pointed at where Cana said the vortex would appear and then flicked a puff of cell magic into it. It wasn't even enough to produce the euphoria that accompanied my magic's release.

The vortex appeared a fraction of a second later, exactly where Cana said it would be. It flashed a bright white and then a ragged hole opened in the shield, its edges blackened but with a white glow like slowly burning paper. The hole widened to about six feet, stopped, and then began to slowly collapse.

Cana and I jumped through the hole. We had to put up our hands to stop ourselves from slamming our faces into the rocky cliff two paces beyond the shield. By the time I turned around, the shield had already reformed itself.

"That didn't last long," I whispered.

I suddenly felt a vibration in my teeth, the kind I always felt when powerful magicks were being worked nearby. At first I thought it was the shield itself, but my senses told me the magicks were coming from the south, beyond the camp.

I looked at Cana. "Do you feel that?"

She nodded, looking toward the south without me prompting her. "What is it?"

"No idea," I said. Then I held my left hand out to Cana. "Ready?"

She nodded and took my left hand in her right. Then she searched the ground at our feet and picked up a stone that fit snuggly in the palm of her free hand. She held the stone out to me. I took out a talc powder vial from my components vest and tapped a little onto the stone. I siphoned some cell magic and then tapped the stone with my index finger.

"*Vervagen me en Cana,*" I said.

I sighed with the pleasant release of cell magic and looked at Cana's hand. It faded until it completely disappeared. However, if I concentrated on it from the corner of my eyes, I could make out a blurry image of her hand. Nor could I see my body when I looked directly at it, only from my peripheral vision, and even then it was more of a shadow than corporeal.

I concentrated on her outstretched hand, trying not to look directly at it, and then I tapped the stone again. "*Zwijgen en mij Cana.*"

My cell magic entered the stone. I exhaled slowly.

I shuffled my feet a bit. Silence. I shuffled them harder, heard nothing, and then tried to speak. No sound came from my mouth even though I felt my throat vibrate with my speaking. However, I could still hear bleating goats and the occasional snuffling horse from within the camp. The *stilte* spell would cancel out any sound that Cana and I made, so long as she held the stone and I held her hand.

Cana held the stone so that I was free to wield my enchanted gladius, which made no sound as I drew it from the sheath on my belt. I'd only had the time and energy to cast one *slapen* spell on it, which should put to sleep one or two full-grown men. The *stilte* and *vervagen* spells would keep us hidden, but my time in the ancient world taught me to prepare for anything.

I squeezed her hand twice. She squeezed twice back, our pre-arranged signal for "okay." I took the lead, guiding her around the back of the tent and into the camp.

I was immediately grateful that the *stilte* spell had worked because without it our movement through the quiet camp would've sounded like a marching legion. Lamps and candles burned inside most of the tents, but I heard no one talking. The loudest sound I heard besides the animals were tent flaps moving in the desert's cool night breezes. It was barely dusk. Did everyone go to bed at the exact same time?

Earlier today I'd seen families with children. Judging by the families that lived around my old shop on the Aventine Hill in Rome, families with kids were never quiet. There was always someone laughing or shouting or whining or scolding. Something.

But as I peeked into every open tent we passed and saw empty blankets, cots, and chairs, I began to suspect the camp was empty.

Where had they all gone? Did it have something to do with the powerful magic being worked nearby?

A blue-turbaned guard charged from around the corner of the tent nearest to us almost running into me. I jumped out of the way and pulled Cana with me. She stumbled a bit, and I squeezed her hand tighter to keep her from falling. I doubted he noticed us in the waning light, for he continued running past us without pause.

After I took a few deep breaths to calm myself from the scare, I watched the guard to see where he was jogging. He seemed to be heading toward the tent where I'd first met Terentius and his priests. He was the first person I'd seen since Cana and I left our tent, so I pulled Cana along and hurried after the guard.

It was no trouble following him through the darkening camp, for his footfalls were the only loud noise there. Sure enough, we followed him to Terentius's meeting tent where he ran inside. We only had to wait a few seconds before the guard ran back out of the tent with a large, rolled up scroll in hand. He charged past us again without sparing a glance in our direction and headed back the way he came.

In the direction of the magicks.

I pulled Cana into a jog and followed.

The guard ran along a path that led away from the camp and toward the cliffs that surrounded us. The path was barely a path at all, and I had to take care not to slip on the uneven rocks and gravel. I even admired the guard's sure feet as he seemed to glide around the rocks and divots. Unfortunately that meant that he was pulling farther ahead of us, and I was afraid we would lose him soon. But he kept running in the direction of the magicks, their vibrations growing stronger the further we ran. I only needed to follow the magicks.

I noticed an orange glow coming from the cliff face toward which the guard was running. As we got closer, I saw there was another crevasse path marked by a torch wedged into the rocks. The guard darted past the torch and into the crevasse. Cana and I followed.

We wound through the crevasse for a minute or so until we arrived into an open area about the same size as the camp. But this one was built like a natural amphitheater—torches and braziers illuminated a tiered bowl with a flat stone floor at the bottom. The rings of the bowl were lined with the people from the camp. It looked like everyone was there: all the soldiers, men, women, and children, and even the elderly. They all sat quietly in the orange light, no one speaking, everyone's eyes preternaturally focused on the center of the bowl.

Terentius stood there behind two Roman legionaries on their knees, their hands tied behind their back. Both wore the same gray tunica with "SPQR" stamped in red on the front, and both looked severely malnourished and dehydrated. Their heads hung low, and they swayed as if they were about to fall over at any moment. Two large braziers stood on either side of Terentius, and a large wicker basket that could've held a grown man sat in front of the two Romans.

That basket was the source of the magicks. My teeth felt like they'd vibrate out of my head if I stared at it too long.

Cana and I tried to make our way toward a corner near the top of the bowl where no one was standing. The guard we had followed weaved in between the crowd down toward a priest standing just outside the light of the center braziers. The guard, head bowed, handed the priest the scroll, which the priest took with great annoyance and a glare at the guard. The priest unfurled the scroll on the ground, produced a stylus with a vial of ink from a leather pouch near his feet, and then looked up at Terentius as if ready to record his every word.

Terentius glanced once at the priest and then raised his hands to shoulder height. Taking in the entire crowd with his zealous eyes, he cried out something to them in Punic. They dutifully chanted something back. About the only word I could understand was *ba'al*. After crying out a few more words and receiving replies from the crowd, Terentius closed his eyes and muttered something.

His entire body suddenly glowed in an aura. A magus aura.

13

Once my brain had accepted what my eyes were telling it, I noticed there was something off about Terentius's magus aura. If it was a normal aura, it would've been a glow containing two or three colors. The colors and how they behaved—sparking, swirling, pulsing, etc.—were as unique to a magus as a fingerprint and never changed.

The aura surrounding Terentius, however, kept changing colors. Kind of like the shield that had enclosed the tent. Their blues and greens shifted to reds and yellows and then to purples and magentas. Every color in nature made an appearance in that aura. A normal magus should not have been able to do that.

Moments after the aura surrounded Terentius, the wicker basket in front of the Romans erupted into the same multi-colored aura. But the basket's aura was thousands of times brighter than the one surrounding Terentius. I had to look away. It was invisible to mundane eyes, but to another magus, it was like looking directly into the sun. Cana's grip on my hand tightened.

But then the aura dimmed enough so that I could cautiously look back. Terentius continued to mutter something that I couldn't hear, his eyes closed and his hands still raised to shoulder height.

The aura around the basket forked out like lightning at the two Romans. The men jerked and screamed as if they were being crucified. The aura encased them...and then began to tear them apart. Their hair was yanked out first, soon followed by patches of skin and chunks of bloody flesh. The men screamed and screamed as the aura flayed them alive, only turning silent when their vocal cords were stripped from their throats. Blood, tissue, and organs swirled into a vortex of gore, funneling into the wicker basket. Once the aura had ripped everything off of their skeletons, it dismantled those piece by piece, the vortex feeding them into the basket. Soon there was nothing left of the

Romans besides the gray tunicas they'd been wearing. They fluttered to the stone ground.

All this time, the crowd sat watching, silent. The only sound I heard was the scribbling of the priest near Terentius as he recorded these events on the scroll.

I wanted to retch. I don't know whose hand was squeezing tighter, Cana's or mine.

A blue glowing mist floated out of the wicker basket, rising into the night air like the smoke from a new fire. The mist coalesced into a large blue globe. Inside the globe, the mists swirled to form shapes...and then people...and then a crowd standing in a circular amphitheater.

It was a copy of this amphitheater as if seen from someone floating above us. I clearly saw the bearded Terentius standing in the center with his arms raised, the silent crowd surrounding him. I even saw the priest scribbling down the events on his scroll. My eyes took in the tiered bowl, the entrance to the crevasse—

And Cana and me standing there, holding hands, as if the *vervagen* spell had failed. But it hadn't. I looked at my hands and couldn't see them at all. I'm glad the *stilte* spell was working because I think my gasp would've sounded as loud as the bell above St. Leo's.

Cana's hand squeezed mine three times quickly, our prearranged signal for "trouble." I couldn't see her, but when I looked up at the blue globe, I saw her looking up at it with wide, fearful eyes.

I turned back to Terentius. He was staring in our direction, a grin slowly materializing on his crazed, blue-lit face.

Cana and I turned and ran. We ran as fast as we could through the uneven, dark crevasse path that was only lit by the moon and stars. The *stilte* spell kept our flight silent, but did nothing to keep us from tripping or stumbling along the way. I slammed my toes into rocks and boulders, my shins scraped against the outcroppings. But we never lost our grip on each other's hands.

We exited the crevasse and bolted toward the camp across the now dark valley. I had to get my friends out of here. I didn't know where we'd go, but any place was better than one where they tore people to pieces with artifacts. Terror fueled my muscles, and my curiosity over Terentius had turned to revulsion. I had no idea what kind of magic he had stumbled across, but it was my ongoing policy to run as far and fast as I could from magic involving human sacrifice.

Halfway back to the camp, Cana's hand suddenly flew out of mine. I could see and hear myself again. I turned and saw Cana, but she was on the ground frantically searching for something.

"I lost the stone," she said in a panic.

"Forget it, let's go!"

She jumped up, and we both ran as fast as we could in the darkness and uneven ground. It wasn't as fast I could run on a flat surface in the sunlight, but at least we were making better time than when we were holding invisible hands. I kept glancing over my shoulder expecting to see a torch-lit mob following us, but all was quiet back there.

Terentius had been looking right at us through the globe. What was he going to do about it?

We arrived at the tent entrance and skidded to a stop in front of the magical shield still blocking Cana and I from entering.

"Paetus," I said in a loud whisper, "we need to leave, now!"

Terentius stepped from out of the tent's entrance as if he'd been there the whole time. I stumbled backward and fell painfully on my ass.

"Calm yourself, Natta Magus," he said soothingly, holding his open hands to his sides. "Come inside and sit. I assure you it will be more comfortable than the gravel."

14

I realized how un-intimidating I looked sitting on my ass. I quickly stood and straightened my tunica. I'd adopted a few Roman mannerisms over the years, especially the one where you never let terror stop you from maintaining your dignity.

I glanced past Terentius. "Where are my friends?"

Terentius sighed. "Your friends are fine." He stepped aside so that I could see the interior of the tent. Paetus sat with Juba, Elissa, and Alishat, all four of them looking from me to Terentius. They all seemed nervous, but okay.

"I am not your jailer, Natta Magus," Terentius said.

"Really? Because this shield makes me think otherwise. Or is this more confusion on my part?"

Terentius nodded slowly. "A regrettable necessity. I didn't want you leaving the tent and possibly witnessing my miracles before I could explain them to you. Alas, I forgot how resourceful you are." He waved a hand in front of the shield as if shooing away a fly, and the shield just disappeared. He turned back into the tent and stopped next to a couch. "Come, sit. Please."

I glanced at Cana, who looked at me with wide eyes. She reminded me of a rabbit ready to bolt from a cat. I wouldn't blame her if she ran, and I wouldn't try to stop her. I just couldn't follow her. I was still as terrified now as ever, but I now had control over that terror. And there was no way I would leave Paetus and the Carthaginian family behind.

I walked inside the tent. Cana followed.

I gave Paetus and the Carthaginian family a reassuring nod and then sat down on the couch across from Terentius. Cana sat next to me. We both stared at Terentius, waiting for him to speak.

Terentius glanced between Cana and me, and then said, "Despite what you saw, I'm not a monster, Natta Magus."

I swallowed a retort about him crucifying and magically flaying people. I was in no position to argue with him at the moment.

He frowned, and his eyes unfocused as if he was struggling for what to say next. "Before Aventicum, I'd been taught all my life that the only way for a proper Roman to gain honor and prosperity for his gens was to appease the gods of the Religio. And I believed it. I made all the proper sacrifices; I obeyed the flamens and the omens. I struck down barbarians who refused to submit to Rome. It all seemed to work, too, as my gens has never been more prosperous."

Terentius stood, clasped his hands behind his back, and began pacing the rugs. I sat rigidly on the edge of the couch, ready to draw my gladius the moment I saw an aura around him.

"I did all that and yet...I never felt a connection to the gods. That sense of divine power working in my life. Sacrifices all seemed so academic, like a judicial proceeding in the Forum: There was a procedure, the procedure was followed, a verdict was reached, and then everyone went home. It was all interesting, but I felt nothing." He stopped and gave me a piercing stare, that zealous gleam back in his eyes. "Until Aventicum. Until I met you."

He sat down on the couch across from me, leaning forward. "You showed me that there *is* divine power in the world. I admit, I denied you at first, for it was hard to overcome a lifetime of teachings and habits. But when I saw how you put out the fires in the fort, how you defeated the daemons and the corrupted vines, how you could disappear and reappear with a thought." He shook his head, his fervent eyes still holding my gaze. "I knew that you held the divine power that I'd been seeking all my life. And that it did *not* come from the gods."

I stared at him. "Is that when you realized you were a magus?"

Terentius chuckled at first, but it soon bubbled up into sardonic laughter. It set me on edge even more than I already was, if that was possible. "Oh, I am no magus. At least not in the way you think." He gave me a mischievous smile and said, "We will save that for another conversation."

"Actually," I said, "I think that's pretty relevant to *this* conversation."

Something ugly flashed in his eyes. I didn't know if it was because I challenged him or because he was losing his marbles. Whatever it was, it was gone quickly and his "friendly" smile returned.

"Not. Yet."

I decided not to push him. He'd just used magic to flay two men and gate himself to this tent ahead of me. I figured it was best to learn a bit more about him before I really pissed him off.

"Fine," I said. "So you saw the light at Aventicum. What *can* you tell me after that?"

"Before I do that, let me ask you something. Do you feel free?"

I glanced around the tent. "You mean now?"

He waved a hand. "No, I mean in your life. Do you feel free to make your own choices? What to do, where to go, whom to love? Do you *feel* free?"

Now that was a strange question. Not to mention a hard one. *Did* I feel free? I supposed I was legally free: I wasn't a slave, and I had citizenship papers signed with Augustus's own hand. I had all the rights of a Roman citizen, such as they were. Was that freedom? In this world, I supposed it was.

But did I *feel* free? Not exactly. A year and a half ago at Aventicum, I learned that I had a destiny to ensure that magic survived. Those events, which I set in motion in this time, would ensure a future where humanity survived past the twenty-first century. I never learned what those events were or what I was supposed to do, but I knew that I could never go home to the twenty-first century in which I was born. In that sense, I was bound to ancient Rome with shackles of conscience. That didn't feel like freedom.

But then I had *chosen* to stay. I could've easily gone home to the twenty-first century with Brianna, lived a few happy decades with her...and then watched our children and world die by one catastrophe or another.

Did that choice make me a coward or a hero?

"The question has given you pause," Terentius said, interrupting my struggle for an answer, "so I will let you think on it. But I can assure you that people who live in this time and place most certainly do not feel free. They are bound by traditions, religions, and the whims of tyrants and senators. By cultures that dictate their professions, or petty functionaries with just enough power to ruin individual lives. They spend their short, miserable existence crying out for something more, whether with their voices or in their hearts."

"Okay," I said. "And you know how to give them that?"

Terentius smiled. "With your help, I can."

"Can what?"

"I can fulfill your destiny," he said, the zealous fervor back in his eyes. "I will make this world like yours. I will give *everyone* magic."

15

Magic in my world didn't become a universal human trait until well into the fourth century during an event called the Great Awakening. How and why that happened was a debate that led to fist fights at faculty mixers at my old university job. But one theory (which happens to be my favorite, considering my time in the ancient world) is that there were always magi among humans, though they were extremely rare. Over the centuries, people moved about the world and had lots of babies. Humanity eventually reached a tipping point where more people with magic were being born—and refusing to hide their talents—than people without.

I always liked that theory since it seemed the simplest to me. Though the tipping point likely occurred over a generation, it might have seemed like an overnight change to the people living through it, especially when it took centuries for cultures to change in the ancient world. Magic didn't come about by ancient Sourcegems, divine intervention, or the experiments of beings from other worlds (none of which had physical evidence to support). It was simply boring, mundane evolution.

So hearing Terentius claim he could give everyone magic *right now* made me first want to laugh incredulously, but then unease quenched my disbelief. After all that I'd seen during my time in the ancient world, my experiences with prehistoric artifacts in Aventicum, with magi like Helva who had powers that I never knew existed...was Terentius's claim all that crazy?

He watched me with that zealous gleam in his eyes as I processed his words.

"Um," I said, "that's probably not a good idea."

His eyes flashed with that same ugliness that made me want to back away from him. He blinked, relaxed, and resumed his normal craziness. "Why?" he demanded. "Every person in *your* world has magic. Why can't people in this time have it too? Why would you deny that freedom to other human beings? Do you think they are better off enslaved?"

"That's not what I'm saying. Look...magic in my world evolved slowly. It came about after centuries. Magi stayed underground slowly figuring out their powers. They passed their knowledge down to their children, who built on that knowledge. Over time, magi finally outnumbered the mundanes and could safely reveal themselves. Magi needed those centuries to cultivate their talent, to discover magic's limits and ethical responsibilities. That time is what enabled my world to handle magic without instantly destroying itself."

Of course it didn't go as smoothly as I was describing to Terentius. My world's history was filled with wars, atrocities, and horror, too. It's just that I couldn't imagine things ending well if everyone in this time suddenly had magic but lacked the generations of guiding wisdom that my timeline had.

I glanced at Cana. Her power grew daily. What if she had to figure it all out on her own? Would she be okay? Or would she kill herself and lots of people around her?

I had a destiny to ensure that magic survived and thrived in the world. And with that, I felt I also had to ensure it survived in a way that didn't blow everyone up.

Terentius just stared at me as if waiting for me to say my peace and then suddenly agree with him.

"Damnation, you just used magic to sacrifice two Romans, your own countrymen. Not to mention the two guys you crucified outside this camp. That's not considered the proper use of magic in my world."

He continued staring.

"That's something *leerlings* do when they realize they have no limits and no responsibilities." *Best not to say* insane *leerlings.* "You can't suddenly drop that kind of power on people without warning or guidance. It would be like giving a toddler a lit torch and telling him to run off and play with his friends."

The awkward silence and staring stretched almost a minute before I finally broke it.

"What do you want from me?" I asked.

Just because I was asking didn't mean I'd go along with whatever Terentius had in mind. He'd just killed two guys in a way that would give me nightmare fuel for years, so I wanted to escape this bughouse camp more than ever. But he had magic, he had a crazy idea, and I needed to know if it was just him talking a big game or if he really did have the power to give the whole world magic.

Terentius nodded once like he'd expected me to ask. "The basket you saw is a bridge to other worlds. The ritual shows me paths. I express my goals to the basket and then it shows me the next step I need to take to achieve that goal."

"After a little human sacrifice?" I couldn't disguise the revulsion in my voice.

He sighed. "We used goats at first. They served me well and clearly showed me the next small step I needed to take. I built this camp and gathered followers who are loyal to me and my vision. But a month ago the revelations became harder to interpret. So we captured a Roman patrol and used them one by one. The revelations became far more precise. Too precise. They all focused on one person: You."

I shook my head and then barked a mirthless laugh. "Of course. Why not?"

That wasn't the first time I suddenly missed the days when I was just an average Joe back in Detroit and not some "chosen one" here.

"Each time we sacrificed a man, the revelations would show exactly what you were doing at that moment and where you were. They would not move past you. So tonight we used two men and yet it still showed only you."

"Terentius, whatever it is you're trying to do, human sacrifice is a horrible way to do it. It only leads you down dark paths you can't imagine—"

"Forget sacrifices!" Terentius shouted. His voice reverberated with a magic that made my bones and teeth hum. The candles dimmed and a cold breeze moved the tent flaps. Cana shifted in the couch next to me. Behind Terentius, Paetus's face grew tight, and the Carthaginians seemed to huddle closer together.

Terentius took several deep breaths and appeared to regain control. "My point is that I cannot move forward without you. You are either my partner...or my obstacle."

"Okay," I said quietly. "Let's figure this out together." I hoped my soothing voice would stop him from turning into a magical supernova. "First, what is that basket, and where did you get it?"

This seemed to calm Terentius, and the satisfied grin returned. "I found the basket in the ruins at Aventicum. Among other things."

It's always nice when your suspicions are confirmed. That feeling of being right never gets old.

Well, except when you *didn't* want to be right.

"Rullus ordered me to oversee the recovery of those things and the rebuilding of the fort," Terentius said.

Marcus Aurelius Rullus was the Aventicum garrison's commander and Vitulus's cousin. He'd been as clear-headed as any Roman could've been when suddenly faced with magic and monsters for the first time. He'd gladly accepted my help despite Terentius's protests, and I had come to respect his leadership as we all fought for our lives.

Terentius, however, didn't seem to have the same opinion of Rullus that I did. His face twisted in bitterness. "Rullus couldn't get his hands dirty with all that mundane recovery and rebuilding, of course. He had to return to Rome for his triumph. But his desire for glory became the greatest thing that could've happened to me. Circumstances caused my...conversion to your way of thinking. I took some of the artifacts and fled here."

"But how did you figure out what the basket could do?"

He grew agitated again. "That does not matter. What matters is how I learn what to do next. I need your help, Natta Magus."

I swallowed once. I had to tell him this eventually, and there wasn't going to be a good time. "What if...I refuse to help?"

That ugly moving shadow passed over his face, but was gone in an instant. His eyes softened to a resigned look that almost made me feel sorry for him. "Then I would be disappointed. And you would be free to go."

I felt my own eyebrows rise. "Just like that. I could say 'no' and you would say 'farewell' and we could just walk out of here?"

He licked his lips and then gave me a wry grin. "One of the things I've come to understand about magic is that I know nothing. I could certainly force you to stay, keep your friends hostage, and threaten all sorts of tortures on them if you did not help me. But that would only make you constantly search for a way to escape. I cannot make my vision a reality if I'm always worrying about you defeating me with some magic that I don't know. Yes, I need you to stay, but I need it to be because you *want* to stay."

Now it was my turn to stare at him. This guy was all over the emotional map. One second he exudes friendliness, the next second I'm waiting for a daemon to pop out of him, and the next he's sounding all rational. Time to test it.

"I think I can speak for my friends when I say that we will be leaving in the morning."

I kept my eyes on Terentius, but I could feel Cana stiffen next to me, ready to defend herself. I felt the worried stares of the others, too.

Terentius regarded me without expression. Then he sighed, nodded once, and stood. "You are not my prisoner nor a slave. You are free to make your own decisions, Natta Magus. It is what I'm fighting for. So if it is your decision to leave, then so be it."

He walked to the entrance and stopped. With his back to me, he said, "I suggest you leave in the morning, for the desert at night is treacherous." He paused. "Before you leave, know this: I liberated an artifact that might aid you in your search for Helva. As payment for your services, I would give it to you."

He left the tent.

16

Juba was well enough to insist he could do something, so I posted him near the tent entrance to watch for anyone trying to listen to us. Elissa and Alishat volunteered to keep watch on the left and right sides of the tent. I figured the cliff wall behind the tent was too narrow for anyone to sneak up on us there, so we left that unguarded. Of course it was likely a moot point anyway, given Terentius had an artifact that told him what I was doing at any given moment. He was probably listening to us right now. But posting the brother and sisters around the tent gave them a measure of control over a situation that could not have been more out of their control.

Once our Carthaginian lookouts were set, I let Paetus and Cana proceed to argue.

"It's a trick," Paetus said in a low tone. "He's saying anything that might get you to stay."

"But how does he know who Helva is or why she is important to *leraar?*" Cana asked Paetus. Before he could answer, she said, "He knows because he used that basket to spy on us. And if he has that kind of power then it is possible he can reach Helva."

"Exactly, he used the basket to *spy on us*. That's how he knows who Helva is and that's why he knows we're desperate enough to listen to his nonsense. He conveniently has the one artifact we need to find her? It's *too* convenient."

"Perhaps it is the will of the gods that we came here," Cana replied. "Until now we had no idea how to enter the underworld and find Helva. Until now we had rested our hopes on this philosopher friend of yours in Alexandria. If Terentius has an artifact that can help—"

Paetus barked a laugh. "Are you saying you want to help this murderer? This traitor? And you heard what Natta just said: Giving magic to the world would be a disaster."

Cana sneered. "So freedom is a dangerous thing for anyone who is not Roman, yes?"

"I'm not talking about *freedom*," Paetus said, his face reddening, "I'm talking about giving everyone in the world a torch and a barrel of liquid war fire."

"If every person had war fire, then I think people would be less likely to use it on each other."

"Or maybe insane enough to try!"

Cana's voice turned to ice. "So you think magi are insane?"

"Stop putting words in my mouth! You always do that when you're losing an argument..."

I listened to Paetus and Cana argue for a long time. Over the last few months, they'd become the little devil and angel on my shoulders, trading places depending on the situation. Overall, Cana was the voice of my conscience, while Paetus tended to be my voice of practicality. Cana helped me see right and wrong, while Paetus helped me see the best way to get things done. Sometimes Cana's definition of right and wrong were a bit skewed (she believed that leaving Juba, Elissa, and Alishat behind was the "right" thing for us to do), and Paetus had his own definition of morality that sometimes didn't match mine, either. But they gave me differing perspectives on a situation that I usually didn't see. I considered myself very lucky to have them with me.

"I'm not going to help Terentius," I said, interrupting them. They both looked at me. Paetus gave me an approving nod, while Cana gave me a suspicious stare. "But I cannot ignore the possibility that he has an artifact that will bring Helva back."

"He's not going to just give it to you," Paetus said. "You heard his price."

"And it's a price I won't pay. Sorry, Cana, but the world's not ready for magic. Not yet."

She frowned at me, but said nothing. She refused to look at Paetus.

"And Paetus, you've never been a slave. You don't know what liberty feels like when it comes to you for the first time. Cana just wants to give that to other slaves."

Neither one of them seemed happy with my words.

Cana gave me an accusatory glare. "You have said you wanted to end slavery in this world."

"Of course I do," I said. "But I don't want to destroy the world in the process. Look, magic will bring indescribable beauty and freedom and equality to the world someday. But it will also bring unimaginable death and horrors. The only way my world was able to fight that darkness was because we had acquired the tools and wisdom to do so *over generations*." I shook my head. "This world, at this time, is not ready."

Cana's frown deepened, if that were possible.

"Very well," Paetus said, "you won't help Terentius but you still want his artifact. Are you proposing we steal it?"

I looked at him as he smiled at the absurdity of his last question. I didn't say anything and got somewhat of a guilty pleasure at watching the smile melt from his face.

"You *are* proposing we steal it."

This time *I* smiled.

Paetus glanced warily at the tent entrance, through which night still reigned. "Aren't you worried he can see us talking about it right now with that basket artifact?"

"He's not. I could sense it pretty well when he was using it, and I don't feel it right now."

"But what if he does use it?"

"Then we'll improvise. If we keep worrying about that thing seeing everything we do, it'll paralyze us and we won't do anything."

Paetus sighed and then shrugged. "What's your plan?"

I felt a twinge of guilt about lying to Paetus and Cana. But despite my recent dismissal, I did fear Terentius could use the basket to spy on us right now. Best to keep my real plan to myself for the time being.

"First I need to find out if he has something worth stealing," I said. "I could sense the basket, but I haven't felt any other artifacts nearby before or since."

"If we can sense them at all," Cana said.

I gave her an approving nod. "You're right, *leerling*. Artifacts were poorly understood even in my time, so the one we want could be sitting in this tent for all we know." I exhaled and spoke even softer. "So I need to convince him that I'm with him. And then he'll take me to it."

"And then what?" Paetus asked. "You grab it and run?"

I grinned, hoping my guilt over this lie wasn't showing through. "*We* grab it and run."

17

When Terentius came to our tent the next morning, I gave him my conditions.

"I understand your need for verification," he said with an approving smile. "I would ask the same if I were in your position. Come, I'll show you."

"Can I bring Cana and Paetus?"

Terentius glanced at them and shrugged. "All great teachers have students, and all great leaders have scribes. Of course they may come."

He walked out of the tent without turning to see if I followed.

That was...easy.

As we agreed last night, Juba, Elissa, and Alishat would remain in the tent. Juba was back to full health and looked resolute standing in front of his sisters. We traded knowing glances, and then Paetus, Cana, and I left the tent.

The post-sacrifice party must've gone deep into the night, for there was hardly anyone outside their tents running about like when we arrived yesterday. The few people I saw were mostly blue-turbaned guards walking unhurried to whatever tasks rebel soldiers do. For a chilling moment, I wondered if Terentius had somehow sacrificed all the civilians to the basket, so I peaked into each tent we passed. I grew relieved as I saw families either sleeping or sitting on rugs talking quietly. Everyone, however, looked tired and depressed and barely spared me a glance as we walked by.

Even for a refugee camp, this place was a downer.

Terentius led us out of the camp and back in the direction of the crevasse path leading to the basket's altar. In the light of morning, I could plainly see the opening between two cliffs only a hundred paces from the camp. It was unguarded and looked like the kind of place that didn't need to be guarded: Approaching it felt like walking into the maw of an ancient leviathan. The closer we got, the more I had to fight the urge to flee, until I realized the path was enchanted with a crude turning ward. Once I realized the ward was the source of my fear, its effects seemed to dissipate entirely.

I turned to Paetus and Cana, who had slowed the closer we got, fear contorting their faces. "It's just a ward over the path. Your fear isn't real. Terentius likes to lock his doors."

Terentius chuckled up ahead of me, but didn't turn around. Paetus and Cana stared at the opening a moment, and then they both seemed to relax. Except for Paetus, his perpetually anxious face returned to its normal anxiety.

The path wound its way through the rock. Though blue sky hung over us, the narrow, uneven path produced shadows that seemed to move when my gaze passed over them. I couldn't tell if it was the lingering effects of the turning ward, my own imagination, or if there really were intelligent shadows flitting around us. I was pulling for the imagination scenario.

When the path opened up into the bowl-like altar, Terentius strode down to the center where the wicker basket sat all by itself, its lid slightly askew. I didn't feel the tremendous artifact magic emanating from it like last night. For all the world, it looked like an old basket in which someone would throw their dirty laundry.

I instinctively siphoned my cell magic, felt the icy tingle across my skin, and then put a hand on my enchanted gladius. Had Terentius brought us here to sacrifice us? If two Romans hadn't given him the vision he wanted, what about two magi and a Roman?

"If I had wanted to sacrifice you, Natta Magus," Terentius said as he walked toward the basket, "I would've done it last night while you were here spying on me. The artifact I spoke of is down here, if you want to see it."

I glanced at Cana and Paetus. Cana's teeth were clenched with resolve; Paetus was pale and sweating, but stood his ground while holding the clay tablet he used to chronicle my actions. I shrugged as if walking into the potential trap of a potentially evil magus was no big deal and then strode down the bowl toward Terentius.

Terentius had already removed the lid on the basket and was peering inside when we arrived next to him. He pointed his chin inside. "It's the red cloak. Think about Helva and then put it on."

I hesitated at first, still suspicious of Terentius, but then looked inside the basket. A red cloak lay at the bottom, neatly folded. Next to it were several other items: two torches made of wooden clubs but with golden bands near the top; a right-handed glove made of evergreen needles that seemed to glow with its greenness; and, I kid you not, a light brown teddy bear that looked as if it had been plucked from the hands of a sleeping child.

I was relieved when I didn't see the gory remains of Terentius's sacrifices.

"You found these at Aventicum?" I asked.

"Indeed," he said, staring at the items. "Strange, are they not? Do they come from some ancient past? Or perhaps from your future?" He shrugged. "All I know is that each one contains tremendous power. With your help, we can use them to make the world a fairer place. And by the way, if you touch anything other than the red cloak, you'll find that you and your friends will be the basket's next sacrifice."

I looked a little closer at the artifacts with my cell magic enhanced eyes and noticed a multi-colored, swirling aura around each one, including the red cloak. More wards, and powerful ones at that. I had no idea what they did, and I certainly didn't want to test them right now.

Even if I had wanted to steal the cloak, there was no way I could've done so with those wards. And I think that was the idea Terentius was trying to convey.

I looked at him. "When are you going to tell me how you learned to use magic?"

I tried not to glance up at Cana and Paetus, who still stood at the top of the bowl. That question was my pre-arranged signal to them that the "theft" was off. I made sure to say it at a volume they could hear. Now my goal was to see if the artifact could do what he said.

He arched an eyebrow. "After you agree to help me."

"Is it a natural ability? An Aventicum artifact you're wearing?"

"Are you going to put the cloak on? If not, then I've told you before that you are free to go whenever you wish."

I reached into the basket and grabbed the folded red cloak. I exhaled softly when I didn't blow up.

I unfurled the cloak and held it up. Compared to all the other artifacts that I'd seen in the bowl and Aventicum, this cloak looked brand new, like something I would've found in the twenty-first century. The fabric was thick but light, soft but strong. It felt like silky cashmere. The stitching around the edges was modern and precise with golden frills that you'd see on American Union flags in the President's House. It also had a hood and a drawstring made of a thin, silvery rope that seemed far too delicate to be used for anything besides decoration. I assumed the rope, like the cloak, was far tougher than it looked.

"Think of Helva," Terentius said, repeating his earlier instructions, "and then put it on and raise the hood. Remove the hood once you're satisfied I'm telling you the truth."

Visualization is one of the key skills of any magus, so it wasn't hard for me to pull up a mental picture of Helva: her short dark hair, olive skin, sharp cheekbones. The scents of lilies and cinnamon in the oils that she used in her hair and on her skin. The way she looked up at me from beneath lidded eyes...

She was the granddaughter of Cleopatra and had certainly inherited the Egyptian queen's legendary beauty.

But there was far more to her than that: her fierce pride that refused to let her give up on anything she set her mind to; the power in her exotic earth magic that she siphoned from the world's geomagnetic forces; her loyalty to me, and even to her brother and William. I'd only known her for such a short time, and yet she had become someone that I'd risk dying for.

She once told me she loved me, though her pride had made her deny it later. I didn't know how to feel about that at the time, and I pretty much had no clue now. I was certainly flattered—who wouldn't be?—but I still missed Brianna, my fiancé in the twenty-first century and the love of my life. I knew there was no way I could go back to her, but what if I was wrong? The magical laws that I'd known in the twenty-first century had turned upside down in ancient Rome. What if I *had* pursued something with Helva and then discovered a way to go back home without destroying the world in the process?

Damnation.

I was letting my mind wander, which was why I tried not to think about these things too much. I hadn't even verified that Helva was still alive, and there I was imagining a soap opera love triangle.

I had a pretty good visualization of Helva in my mind, so I wrapped the cloak over my shoulders and pulled on the hood. Much to my surprise, it actually fit me. For the first time since I'd arrived in Rome, I found a garment that was made for someone my height.

When I looked up, I found myself standing in the middle of a thick forest of evergreen trees. It was night, and I could barely see the stars and the moon through the pine branches above me.

Then from behind me came a loud crash like a tree falling. I whirled around, and though I didn't see anything right next to me, more crashes came from that direction. And then came a gibbering, maniacal laughter from something that I knew in the depths of my soul I did *not* want to meet.

I was about to sprint in the other direction when two figures charged from out of the forest and skidded to a stop in front of me.

One of them was Silanus, the magus who I'd stopped from killing Rome's firstborn several months ago. His terrified eyes took me in with the same shock that I felt.

The other was Helva.

18

The three of us stared at each other for no longer than an instant. If this were an old cartoon from my time, our jaws would've been on the dry needle ground.

But the crashing and gibbering laughter behind Helva and Silanus was getting closer.

"Run or get out of our way, Natta Magus!" Silanus snarled, and then took off past me.

I tried to grab Helva's hand, but my hand went right through hers. We both used another precious moment to gape at that twist.

Which gave me a chance to see the thing chasing them when it burst through the trees.

Even now, while writing this journal entry, I still can't quite remember what that thing looked like. What I remember most is how it made me feel: more terrified and revolted than I'd ever been in my life. Fragments of visual memory tell me that it was all slime, teeth, and a billion coarse-haired centipede legs. It had joints that moved in the wrong directions, a stench that would make a hardened medical examiner gag, and a gibbering cry that made fingernails on a chalkboard sound like birdsong. Imagine the things you feel crawling up your leg in the middle of the night, the horror of fearing for the life of a loved one, or the sickness of witnessing a deadly trolley accident, and you wouldn't even come close to how it felt to be in the same continent with this thing. It was reserved for torturing the souls who had been judged on the scales of Ma'at and been found *extremely* wanting.

I have no idea if it had an official name. The Thing With a Hundred Eyes, the Brown Goo Thing, or the Thing That Smelled Like Rotten Socks would've all been accurate. For simplicity's sake—and to help dampen the nightmare fuel—I'm officially naming it Gibber.

Before I could move my frozen limbs, Gibber took a swipe at me with misshapen claws...and like Helva's hand, they went right through me.

Needless to say, Helva and I ran.

Silanus was already far ahead of us carving a path through the evergreens, bushes, and soft forest floor. My cloak didn't catch on any of the pine needles or branches, and my footing was as sure on the uneven ground as if I were running down Woodward Avenue in Detroit. '

I heard Gibber behind us, giggling and squirting fluids as it crashed through the woods. But we seemed to be building our lead, for it was no longer on our heels.

And then Silanus was suddenly in front of me. Instinct took over and I skidded to a stop in front of him as if I were sliding into second base.

I jumped back to my feet and said, "How about a little warning before you—!"

"End of the path," he said, looking down.

I followed his gaze and saw that, yes, this was literally the end of the path. We stood on the edge of what I first thought was a mountain cliff that descended into a misty valley, kind of like what I saw north of the Alps in Germania. But when I looked closer, I saw that the edge of the cliff descended into...nothing. The space beyond was completely black: no horizon, no mist, just oblivion. I looked left and right and saw that the edge of the forest bordered the nothing-ness as far as I could see. It was as if this forest had been sliced out of reality by a cosmic cookie cutter and then made to float here by the Unknowable Will.

"I hate this part," Helva said as she looked down into the blackness.

"Why?" I asked in a tight voice. It was a struggle to keep my wits as Gibber got closer.

"We must jump," Silanus said. "If the daemon catches us, our bodies and souls will stay here. We will *truly* die."

I stared at Silanus, but Helva said, "We have done this before, it is the only way to escape Invidia's games."

"Is that Invidia chasing—?"

"No!" Silanus snarled, and then grabbed Helva's hand. He was about to jump, but she pulled him back. He growled something at her in Coptic, but she ignored him and looked at me.

"I do not know how you came here," she said, "but I do not think you can come with us."

"I figured that," I said, "but I need to know if this is really you. Tell me something only I would know. No time to explain."

She took a precious moment to think, despite the thing getting closer and Silanus pulling her toward the edge of nothingness. Then she gave me a quick smile. "I will reform the ground around your neck and leave you for the crows if you tease me about what I told on the beach."

I remembered the Egyptian coast on the Mediterranean, a deserted beach covered in sand dunes, rocky outcroppings, and...smoking craters. Helva had blasted the beach with her earth magic after some frustration with me. She'd told me she loved me that day, but then her pride—and my needling—forced her to deny it: *"If you tease me one more time about a moment of weakness, I will rip the ground apart on which you stand and reform it again so that you are sunk up to your neck. And then I will leave you there for the crows to pick out your eyes."*

It was her.

"I will find you again," I promised.

"See that you do," she said.

"Come on!" Silanus yelled, and then pulled Helva over the edge with him. They disappeared into that infinite darkness.

The thing burst into the clearing behind me, all insane titters and cracking bones and the stench of garbage juice at the bottom of a trash can in summer. It took all my will to keep my back toward it—by all the gods, I did *not* want to see it again. I pulled the cloak's hood down from my head...

I stood in the crevasse bowl again facing Terentius. I gasped several times, my muscles still quivering from the terror that I'd felt while fleeing the daemon. All I wanted to do was sit down, think happy thoughts, and purge my memories of that thing.

But as the fear drained away, a quiet elation filled my heart. Helva was alive. She was in hell, yes, but she was still alive. And against all odds, she seemed to be surviving it with Silanus. This was the first confirmation I had since she followed Invidia and her captive brother into that underworld gate on the Capitoline Hill.

She was alive.

Terentius gave me several moments to regain my wits, and then asked, "Satisfied?"

I turned my head to Cana and Paetus at the top of the bowl. Both gave me questioning looks: Paetus with his stylus hovering above his clay tablet, Cana with one hand tugging on her long brown braid. I nodded to them. Paetus grinned and began scrawling something on his clay tablet. Cana gave a quick sigh and released her braid.

I turned back to Terentius. "Yes."

"Then you will help me."

I swallowed once. "No. I won't. And we'll be leaving in the morning."

That ugly flash exploded in Terentius's face, and for a moment I thought it would burn me to ashes with its rage. But he closed his eyes for a second, opened them, and it was gone.

"Why?" he asked through clenched teeth.

"Look, I admire you for wanting to set people free and to empower them with magic. That's my goal too. But your way is far too dangerous. It will happen someday, but not now."

"'Someday.'" He sniffed. "So say all who fear freedom when the oppressed cry out for it. 'It'll come,' they say, 'but not now. *Someday.* Be patient.'"

One of my policies was never to argue with a fanatic. You're never going to persuade them no matter how much logic and facts you possess.

So I simply said, "We'll be leaving in the morning. I'm sorry, Terentius."

He clenched his teeth a few moments and then said, "Very well. I'll see that you have food and water for your journey to Carthage."

I nodded my thanks, turned around, and started back up toward Paetus and Cana.

"Natta Magus," Terentius said behind me. "I can't help but think you used me just now. You just wanted to make sure Helva was still alive. You never intended to help me."

I didn't turn around and continued up the bowl. I had a hard time feeling guilty about lying to a murderer.

When I got to the top of the bowl, I smiled at Cana and Paetus. "I saw her," I said. I quickly described my encounter with Helva, Silanus, and the daemon thing. "Tomorrow we'll leave for Carthage. When we get there, we'll ensure Juba and his sisters are safe and then book passage to Alexandria."

Paetus nodded with relief and put his clay tablet back in his shoulder pack.

Cana eyed Terentius behind me. "He will just let us go then?"

I looked behind me. Terentius reverently replaced the lid on the basket and then began climbing the bowl up to us.

"I guess we'll see," I said.

19

"Natta Magus!"

I jumped up off the couch on which I'd been sleeping, my heart pounding and icy cell magic rising to my skin. It took me a moment to focus on where the voice came from and who was calling me.

It was Terentius standing next to my couch.

"You must go, my friend," he said. "The camp is under attack!"

"What? Who?"

"Romans," he said, his voice tight. "They've found us."

Or maybe they found me.

I still assumed the attack on our galley was a hit on me ordered by Augustus. Had the Romans tracked me to this camp and sent a legion to finish the job?

Screams started to arise from outside. It was still dark, though the purple light of dawn was creeping along the tents just outside the entrance. Dark forms ran by in different directions.

"Where can we go?" I asked, glancing at Paetus and Cana who stood next to me looking as confused and terrified as I felt. Double that for Elissa, Alishat, and Juba.

Terentius hurried to the entrance and looked in both directions. "The Romans have blocked off the beach crevasse and have surrounded us on the high ground. We will head to the altar were I performed the sacrifices. We can use some of the artifacts against them." He looked back at us staring at him. "Gather what you need and let's go!"

We all jumped toward our packs that we had fortunately readied last night for our morning departure (I also grabbed some water skins off the nearby table). I motioned Juba and his sisters to follow Terentius, and then Cana, Paetus, and I followed them.

The camp was in chaos. Blue-turbaned men with short swords and round shields ran by in different directions. They were not the disciplined squads and cohorts that I'd seen in Roman camps mustering for battle; these guys seemed just as confused as to where to run as I was. Mothers and fathers carried young children with older children running beside them, but each family ran in all directions.

Nobody knows where to go or what to do, I thought. *They're going to be slaughtered.*

I glanced up at the tops of the cliffs around the camp. In the purple light of dawn, I could make out human figures moving around up there. Some were on horseback, but most were standing. The figures surrounded the crevasse valley. There must have been at least a thousand soldiers up there.

Paetus had followed my eyes to the tops of the cliffs. "Looking for their lost patrols, I'd wager."

I'd been so worried that this was all my fault, somehow, that I hadn't even thought that it might be Terentius's. It made far more sense that they were here to put down a rebellion than hunt down one magus.

I ran up to Terentius who was jogging toward the back of the camp and toward the path that led to his "altar."

"Shouldn't you be leading them or something?"

"My captains are coordinating the defense," Terentius shouted at me over the panicked cries. "They will delay the legion so that we may escape."

"But your people—!"

"Are far less important to our cause than you and me."

Some of the fleeing people had spotted Terentius and began to follow us. By the time we'd reached the edge of the camp, we had a dozen people on our trail, most of them women and children.

That's when the archers at the top of the hill opened fire. Arrows rained down on us from the dawn sky like hailstones. Most struck the ground with heavy *thunks*, either bouncing off rocks or embedding themselves in the gravel. We raced across the open field, about a hundred paces. We'd almost made it to the crevasse path without losing anybody.

But then arrows hit two children.

The kids screamed in that awful way they do when they're in true pain. Not that fake temper tantrum scream, but the scream that all parents hear in their nightmares. I turned to see their mother crouching over them, trying to shield them from the hail of arrows striking around them. Two arrows struck her back, and she slumped over her crying kids.

I stopped just outside the crevasse and was about to run back, but Terentius put two powerful hands on my arms and held me. "If you go out there you'll be killed too!"

"The kids are still alive!" I screamed into his face.

"They are not," he said.

I turned around and saw several more arrows sprouted from the bodies of the children lying near their mother. The archers had found the range and poured down arrows on the prone family as if making them pay for losing the rest of us.

A boiling, magma rage stirred in me: at the Romans, at Terentius, at myself, at my whole godsdamned life. I recognized that rage. It was the same one that tempted me back on the galley, and it was the same one that tempted me every time I felt like things were hopeless.

And it was the same one I could never indulge, even if it meant my death. The problem, though, was that my greatest temptation to indulge was the imminent death of others.

Paetus was suddenly next to me. "They're gone, Natta! We must flee!"

My friend's voice more than anything helped me stamp down that rage that threatened to loosen on Romans and refugees alike. I clenched my teeth, closed my eyes, and took one deep breath. I exhaled, opened my eyes, and turned away from the innocent deaths outside the crevasse.

I followed Terentius down the winding path. The remaining refugees had flooded past him when we'd paused and were already beyond my sight. Paetus, Cana, and my Carthaginian friends stayed close to me, and we made up the rear guard.

Once we arrived at the bowl, we found the refugees huddled under a stone outcropping on the other side. The terrified parents were trying to calm their crying children. Terentius raced down the bowl toward the basket, its wicker glowing orange in the sunlight rising over the cliffs above us.

"Natta Magus, bring your student," Terentius yelled from the bottom, "she can use the—"

An arrow buried itself in the back of Terentius's neck almost to the fletching. Blood sprayed from the severed artery in a red cloud around his head. He tumbled to the bottom of the bowl and lay motionless in front of the wicker basket. Blood pumped out of the wound in huge gouts.

I looked up to see more archers on the cliffs surrounding the bowl, all of them aiming drawn arrows at us. *They're going to murder everyone. Even the kids.*

The thought of that was enough for me to give the rage permission to explode. I couldn't let more kids die. And it would only cost a *little* bit of my soul...

I turned to Cana while I still had control. My face must have conveyed what I was about to do, for her eyes widened and she nodded once.

But then a Roman saved me from myself.

"Hold your fire!" came a yell from atop the cliff. "Any man who looses another arrow without my order will pray for crucifixion before I'm done with him!"

My eyes were pulled to the top of the cliff where I saw a Roman wearing the classic red cloak, a red plumed helm, and a hard leather chest plate.

My confusion and curiosity were enough to stop my rage in its tracks. I closed my eyes a moment and regained control with a great effort of will.

When I looked back up at the Roman commander, silhouetted in the dawn sky, I watched him step forward...and jump off the cliff.

But he didn't fall. He floated above the bowl and then descended like a hot air balloon that I'd once seen at the Detroit Fair. An aura of shifting, multi-colored magic surrounded him, the same one that had surrounded Terentius.

Once the commander had set foot in the bowl, he strode over to me, his armor creaking.

Marcus Aurelius Rullus, former commander of the Aventicum garrison, stopped in front of me and scowled. "Well you've made a damned mess of things, Natta Magus."

20

Did the gods give magic out to *everyone* in Aventicum last year? First Terentius and now Rullus?

But my surprise was again overwhelmed by anger bubbling back up through my gut and into my limbs. It wasn't the rage that made me reach for soul magic—not yet, anyway—but the kind where you have to grab your pant legs to keep from punching someone in the face.

"*I've* made a mess of things," I snarled. "Why did you attack this camp, Rullus? Why are you killing innocent people?"

Rullus snorted. "Terentius is hardly innocent—"

"I'm not talking about Terentius, gods damn you! I'm talking about the children you slaughtered just outside this path! Not to mention the others still in the camp! You're a murderer, Rullus! I thought you had honor!"

I was screaming in his face at the top of my lungs, and yet he didn't flinch away. He just regarded me like a father waiting out a toddler's tantrum. That patronizing look infuriated me even more. I couldn't decide whether to reach for soul magic or the gladius on my belt.

Before I could go either way, Rullus motioned with his chin behind me and said, "Do you mean *those* children?"

I whirled around. The mother and the kids that I'd just seen shot down with arrows were being escorted out of the crevasse path by a squad of Roman legionaries. In fact, they still had the *caccing* arrows sticking out of their bodies. But they were walking with sullen expressions as if their tutors had caught them passing notes in class. Even their mom, who had heroically shielded them with her own body—the six arrows in her back proved it—looked more annoyed than, well, dead.

The Romans prodded them with wooden batons that, to my shock, glowed with the same multi-colored aura that surrounded Rullus. The legionaries pushed the mother and kids toward the other refugees, who also regarded the Romans with the same sullen expressions. There was no more fear, no more crying or screaming. It was as if a great play had been going on and the director had just yelled, "Cut!"

Cana murmured something in Gallic as she stared at the kids and their mom, while Paetus reached for his clay tablet and began scribbling on it with shaky hands. Juba just stared at the unhurt family, while Elissa held Alishat tightly with both arms.

Another cohort of Roman legionaries filed into the bowl from the crevasse. Rullus said to them, "Secure the basket and Terentius."

"Yes, sir," the centurion said, and then led his men down into the bowl.

"I...I don't understand," I breathed.

"Of course you don't," Rullus growled. "If you had, you wouldn't have put on any old artifact that Terentius told you to."

I turned back to him. "What's going on here? And how do you have magic, too?"

"A war and Aventicum. I don't have time to explain further."

He glanced behind me, and I heard footfalls echoing from the path. I turned to see a Roman scout run down to us and stop, breathless.

"Give me good news, son," Rullus said with fists on his hips.

"Centurion Seius wishes to report," the scout said through heavy breaths, "that Himilco and the other priests have escaped, along with about thirty daemons."

"Daemons?" I said.

Rullus ignored me and let loose a string of Latin curses that I didn't understand. "Did Seius deploy his auguries?"

"Yes, sir, as soon as he entered the camp. We missed them by moments, sir. Centurion Seius is rounding up all the daemons he can find and is searching the tents for magic."

Rullus ground his teeth and then said, "Good. Inform Seius we'll be returning soon. Dismissed."

The scout gave a Roman salute and then ran back up the crevasse.

"Daemons?" I asked Rullus again.

"Daemons," Rullus said, walking past me down the bowl. "I assume you're familiar with the term, Natta Magus."

"Well, yeah," I said, and then followed him. Cana and Paetus were close on my heels.

Rullus stopped in front of the legionaries surrounding Terentius's body. Two men had already picked up the basket and were carrying it up the bowl past us.

"Get up, Terentius," Rullus boomed. "You're not fooling anyone, you sack of vinegar."

The legionaries parted to let Rullus in, but they continued to aim those strange aura batons at Terentius's body. Bright red arterial blood still pumped from the arrow wound in his throat and pooled around him in a wide circle.

Terentius shuddered, gave a heavy sigh, and then sat up. He glared at Rullus, grabbed the arrow in his neck by the head, and yanked it all the way through. A spurt of blood came out with it, but Terentius didn't flinch. He just flung the arrow aside. Then he leaned back on his hands in the blood pool and closed his eyes as if taking a tan from the dawn sunlight now hitting the bowl.

"Where did Himilco and your other priests go?" Rullus demanded.

Terentius grinned, his teeth bloody. He didn't open his eyes when he said, "They will come back for me. You may have me and the basket now, but it's a long way back to Carthage."

Rullus did something inhumanly fast: He grabbed a baton from one of his men and struck Terentius in the chin. The blow was so vicious and powerful that it knocked Terentius flat on his back, and then he literally *bounced* back up into a sitting position.

A horrible, inhuman screech arose from the "refugees" near the top of the bowl. They stared down at Terentius with impossibly wide eyes as if they had felt the blow themselves. It sounded as if a nest of baby eagles was having their talons ripped out one by one. It was awful. Paetus had dropped his tablet and put his hands over his ears, while Cana shut her eyes tight and winced.

Curiously, neither Rullus nor the legionaries holding the magical batons seemed affected.

Terentius looked dazed a moment, but then grinned again and spat some blood onto the ground at Rullus's feet. The screeching from the refugees stopped, and they returned to their quiet, sullen postures as if nothing had happened.

No mundane human could've delivered a blow like that, and no mundane human could've survived a blow like that. *What in damnation happened to these guys at Aventicum?*

"I'm not going to ask you again, Terentius," Rullus said quietly, his voice like ice. "Where are Himilco and your priests?"

Terentius laughed. "We both know you can't kill me."

"True," Rullus said, eying the baton, "but I can make you wish I could."

Terentius considered that and shrugged. "They're in the underworld. And you'll need Fortuna's blessings if you ever hope to find them."

21

Paetus, Cana, and I stood near the crevasse path above the rock bowl watching the Romans use their batons to prod the refugees toward the bottom. Six men dressed in black tunicas, who I guessed were Rullus's "auguries," took up positions surrounding the bowl. Juba, Elissa, and Alishat were behind us talking quietly to each other.

"I think I know what they are," Paetus said.

"You mean refugees?" I asked.

Paetus nodded absently. "They're sycophant daemons."

A vague memory from my old daemonology classes in high school came back. "A 'yessir' daemon."

He raised an eyebrow. "I don't know what 'yessir' is."

"You know, 'Yes sir! Right away, sir! What a great idea, sir!'"

"If that's what you call daemons who worship you and give you temporary magic in exchange for blood sacrifices, then yes."

I stared at the compliant refugees below us. "I knew there was something off about them." And then things started to click in my mind. "*That's* what the basket really does. It's a vessel from which the yessirs get their blood. And that's how Terentius got his magic: He feeds the vessel blood sacrifices, out pop the yessirs, and instant magic for Terentius. If I remember my high school daemonology, he can make them take any form he wants." I snorted. "I guess Terentius wants to be a hero to the downtrodden—"

The yessirs began their horrible shrieking. It was like two metal cargo ships from the twenty-first century grinding against each other. I slapped my hands over my ears and looked back at the daemons. Each Roman augury had unfurled a scroll and was reading aloud in a language that sounded Greek. As I don't know a lick of Greek, I glanced at Paetus who was grimacing from the shrieks.

"Banishment," he yelled to me.

I could banish one daemon, but several dozen was beyond my ken. That's probably why it took six mundane auguries (I saw no auras around them) to do the job. Their words hummed with power, and I could feel them more than hear them.

And whereas I felt simple humming, that same humming was ripping the daemons apart. Their bodies, including their clothes, shifted and cracked and melted, their screams becoming higher pitched. After a few excruciating moments, the screams died away as each daemon lost its mouth and transformed into a brown, hairless slug. The slugs were the size of a person and writhed about in the humming banishment spell. And then each daemon, one by one, exploded into a purulent goo that coated the rock bowl. The pus sizzled on the ground a few seconds and then evaporated into wispy smoke that quickly dissipated.

With the banishment spell's conclusion, the scrolls in each augury's hand burned in a cold, magical fire, vanishing with that same wispy smoke. The auguries turned away from the rock bowl as if they'd just finished a chore and joined the other soldiers forming up to leave the crevasse.

"That was disturbing," Cana said, her nose upturned.

"Death ain't pretty," I said. "Even for daemons."

"Technically they're not dead," Paetus said. "They've simply returned to the spirit world from which they were spawned. Daemons use temporary bodies when they enter this world—"

"We know," Cana and I said at the same time. We grinned at each other. Paetus sprouted a sideways grin as well.

A horn blew from the front of the column already inside the crevasse path. The fifty or so legionaries began marching in two-man columns through the path. Rullus was at the head of the column two dozen paces away; I couldn't see him, but I saw his standard, a golden "III" on a red field, swaying with the march. A cohort with magical batons prodded a bound, yet disturbingly confident, Terentius along the path. My friends and I let another cohort of legionaries pass us before we merged into the middle of the column. A rear-guard cohort of about a dozen legionaries followed us.

"What about the pictures in the air that we saw of ourselves?" Cana asked as we marched. "If the basket was used to feed the daemons, then how did he make those pictures?"

I shrugged. "Once the yessirs gave him some magic after the sacrifices, he could've conjured that image of us in the air. He must've seen through our *vervagen* spell. It's not that hard with the right magic, which is why nobody used it in my time to spy on one another."

"Then how did he learn the 'right magic'?" Paetus asked.

"And the arrow in his neck," Cana said. "What kind of magic stops death after losing that much blood?"

"Both good questions," I said. "I don't know." I stared at the backs of Rullus and the bound Terentius. "But I'm going to find out. Wait here."

I weaved my way through the cohort ahead of us and past Terentius. I found him staring at me with a smirk. His wrists were bound in front of him by a tight cord that glowed with the same multi-colored aura as the batons of the men surrounding him.

I jogged up to Rullus, who walked alone at the head of the column.

"*Now* can you answer some...?"

My voice trailed off when I noticed his eyes were silver. They scanned the path ahead, moving from left to right. He blinked once, and then his eyes returned to their normal brown. He looked at me with the same scowl as earlier.

"Ask," he said.

"First, what was that just now?"

"I was scanning the path for magical residue. Terentius loves his traps."

"I can scan for magic, too, but my eyes don't turn silver."

He sniffed. "That's because you are a magus."

"Then what are you?"

"I am the general of Legio III Augusta, tasked with maintaining the security of North Africa and Carthage."

"Come on, Rullus!" I said, my voice rising with my anger. "I'm tired of all these games from you *and* Terentius. *What have you two become?*"

His jaw moved back and forth, and his gaze returned to the path. He seemed to consider his words carefully. "I swore an oath to Augustus, before the very altar of Jupiter Optimus Maximus on the Capitoline, that I would not reveal my purpose to you. Interpret that how you will."

"To me specifically?"

He didn't say anything, but I got his message loud and clear. Whatever it was that he was doing here—not to mention how he had come to wield magic—was a secret that Augustus knew and wanted kept from me.

"Are you here to kill me?" I asked hesitantly.

"I have no such orders."

"Then why did a Roman trireme sink my galley just off the coast?"

He looked at me sharply. "When?"

"Two nights ago."

"You're sure they were Roman?"

"The sailors were Carthaginian, but I saw Roman officers on the deck and the bow had a Roman eagle at the head. They rammed the galley and sank it. We floated to shore where Terentius's men found us."

His face hardened. "Terentius."

"You think he had something to do with it?"

"Roman patrols, along with a trireme, have gone missing over the last two months. He wanted to shipwreck you so that he could use you to..." His words trailed off as he refocused on the path.

"Damnation, Rullus! You need to decide which oath you're going to keep: that stupid secrecy oath to Augustus or the oath you took to maintain peace in North Africa. I can help you if you let me!"

He continued struggling with the conflicting oaths. *Damned Romans and their damned honor and pride.* They took their oaths as seriously as we took our magically constrained Oaths in the twenty-first century.

Wait...

"Your oath to Augustus was sealed with magic," I said. I purposely phrased it as a statement of fact rather than a question, for a question implied that I was asking him for verification. A statement, however, implied that I *did* know, which would release him from his Oath to keep a secret from me.

Rullus gave me a sharp look as if urging me to go on. "Yes."

"You're hunting Terentius because he stole the basket and the artifacts within it."

He frowned in disappointment. "That much is obvious."

"Augustus created this legion to secure the artifacts we found at Aventicum."

Rullus sighed and turned away. We had just left the shelter of the crevasse and began marching in the sun-blasted valley. The temperature must have risen fifty degrees. Sweat sprang up on my back.

So while the march was getting hotter, my deductions regarding Rullus's purpose were getting colder.

The artifacts at Aventicum were potentially destructive weapons. I knew Augustus had ordered them secured after Vitulus and I had eliminated William and his strix. But the underground temple in which we'd found them was completely destroyed, so it was likely the Romans had missed a few, which would necessitate the creation of a specially trained legion to hunt them down.

If that wasn't the purpose of Rullus's legion, then what else could've made Augustus create a magically empowered...?

Oh.

"You were created to kill me," I said.

Rullus slowly turned his head to me and grinned. "Now we can talk."

22

"Then Augustus *does* want to kill me," I said.

"Not at the moment," Rullus said. His silver eyes had returned as he scanned the hot valley around us. "But once Salvius Aper told him about you two years ago, he began to plan for ways to stop you if he had to."

It didn't surprise me that Salvius Aper, Rome's Praetorian prefect, had given Augustus all the details about the supernatural jobs I'd taken for him. In fact, I had suggested to Aper a year ago that he create a special Praetorian cohort to deal with the daemons and beasts that Vitulus and I encountered on a seemingly monthly basis. Aper seemed to shrug at the idea and nothing came of it.

Apparently they *had* thought about that. And long before I suggested it.

"So did he think I was going to start laying waste to Rome or something? Do you know how many times I've stopped people and things from doing that?"

"I know every one of those times. At least the incidents that Aper knows. From the day you rescued his breastplate from that 'imprint daemon', as you called it, to your fight on the Capitoline two months ago. I saw you firsthand at Aventicum, so my appointment to command Legio III Augusta was obvious. It was part of my commission to study your battles. Just in case, one day, I had to fight you. He fears you still, Natta Magus."

And then I remembered whom we were talking about here: Augustus didn't become "First Citizen" of Rome by ignoring potential rivals. Of course he would try to come up with a way to counter me. He saw me as a threat to his position and power, never believing for once that I didn't *want* his position and power.

"But I turned him down two months ago," I said. "He offered to adopt me and make me his heir. I refused. What more assurance does he want?"

Rullus chuckled. "That just made him distrust you even more. What man would turn down an offer like that? Only an insane one...or one who wanted to take that power for himself."

"Or someone who knows the fates of the men who held that job and wants nothing to do with it."

"Augustus does not think that way."

"Wait a second," I said. "You've been around for over a year, and you couldn't lend a hand two months ago when Rome was under attack by daemons, a dark magus, and a revenge goddess?"

Rullus grimaced. "I wasn't in Rome two months ago. I was here searching for Terentius. Eight months ago he stole that basket and the artifacts within it. I've been chasing him ever since." He eyed me sourly. "Now that I've found him and the artifacts, I should be celebrating. Instead I have to prepare for an even greater battle to come, thanks to you."

"What are you talking about? Everything that's happened has been out of my control. I've only tried to protect my friends since that *caccing* shipwreck."

Rullus's eyes had turned back to their original brown, but there was an anger in them. "And that is why you've made things worse. How could you use the cloak artifact without knowing anything about it? You're from the future where you supposedly studied those things! And for a woman! You were thinking with your manhood and not your mind."

A twinge of rage bubbled to the surface of my skin, bringing a fire that had nothing to do with pain. It was, oh, so tempting to siphon soul magic and rip this pompous, lecturing—

I took a deep breath and released it slowly. "I had to know that Terentius was telling the truth. And I had to know that Helva, who, by the way, helped save Rome's collective ass, was still alive somewhere in the underworld. Now that I know she is, I can figure out a way to get her out. You can keep your cloak artifact."

Rullus gave a growling chuckle, which just made him sound more angry than amused. "If only that was *all* you did. We recovered hundreds of artifacts and items from Aventicum after you destroyed the underground temple. Most of them do nothing—that we know of—but a few of them...well, they are very powerful. That cloak was one of them. From what our auguries could determine, it's not just a way to communicate: It opens doors. By using it to contact your Egyptian princess, you opened a door to the underworld."

"Okay," I said slowly. "I get that's not a good thing, but what does that mean?"

"It means that Terentius's fanatics can bring in an army of creatures that you cannot imagine."

I *could* imagine. I'd been to the underworld, and not just the evil forest through which I'd fled with Helva and Silanus. Helva had opened a door to the underworld two months ago that we had used to find Silanus. We had encountered things there every bit as awful as Gibber.

"But to what end? I mean, death, destruction, mayhem, I get that. But *why* do they want that? The creatures of the underworld are mindless, chaotic monsters. They cannot be controlled and would just as likely turn on Terentius's fanatics as they would anybody else."

"They can be controlled," Rullus said, glancing once behind us. "But only by the lord of the underworld."

"The lord of the..." I looked back at Terentius and saw him staring directly at me. He winked once. "You're joking," I said to Rullus. "That's not really—"

"Natta Magus, meet the avatar of Pluto," Rullus said grimly.

I slowly turned to Rullus. "And who are you?"

"I'm the avatar of Vulcan. And I'm here to bring my brother back home before he destroys this world."

23

Back in the twenty-first century, I believed in the Unknowable Will, a Creator who made the material universe and the spirit worlds. Then it pretty much let you do what you wanted. Of course there were consequences to your choices, which were reflected in whatever afterlife you found yourself in upon death. I still believed that.

So I certainly didn't believe Rullus was possessed by Vulcan and Terentius by Pluto.

Yes, two months ago I'd met "Invidia," the supposed Roman revenge goddess. She'd forced me to pull together a team of nascent Roman magi to call "Jupiter" to fight her. But they were just aspects of the myths, powerful constructs that we'd built with magic and elements from the spirit world to match our preconceived notions of what those deities would be. I did not believe we had called *the* Jupiter to fight *the* Invidia.

That said, it was obvious Rullus and Terentius *were* possessed by some magic that I'd never seen before. My understanding of auras—not my specialty back home, by the way—said that they symbolized a magus's personality and talents. They may change subtly over a lifetime, but such a gradual change only came after life-altering events. The ever-shifting colors I saw around Rullus and Terentius implied that their talents and personalities were changing before my eyes. How was that possible? Just what kind of artifacts had they found at Aventicum?

"Okay," I finally said, "let's say that's true—"

"It's not," Terentius called out from behind us. "Don't believe a word he's saying, Natta Magus."

Rullus rolled his eyes. "Centurion," he said.

One of the Romans surrounding Terentius jabbed him in the back with a baton. Terentius grunted in pain. He said no more, but maintained that creepy grin as he stared at me. I turned away.

"Let's say that's true," I continued. "Roman mythology"—a sharp look from Rullus—"I mean, the Roman *Religio* says that Pluto's more of a judge than a villain. Why would 'Pluto' want to destroy the world? And why does 'Vulcan', the god of metals and blacksmiths and such, has to be the one to stop him?"

"First, Terentius is not Pluto and I am not Vulcan. We are the *avatars* of each god, which means we are aspects of their natures on earth. *Pluto* doesn't want to destroy the world, but *Terentius* does. Just like *Vulcan* is not standing here before you, but I am imbued with some of his powers and his personality. As to why Terentius wants to destroy the world, you'd have to ask him, though I doubt he'd speak the truth. All we have are his actions. And his actions since he stole the artifacts tell us he is trying to bring the denizens of the underworld to the earth. I need not tell *you* how such a thing would be undesirable."

I shuddered again thinking of Gibber chasing Helva, Silanus, and me through the forest or the things I'd met in the Egyptian underworld with Helva.

"I'm sure there's a good story behind how you became avatars..." I prodded.

"I'm sure you've already guessed that Aventicum artifacts were involved."

I shook my head. "Of course they were. So if you and Terentius have godlike magic now, then why did he need the magic of the yessir daemons?"

"He didn't. But his priests did. Which is why we need to find them, because they are every bit as dangerous as Terentius now. Maybe even more so, for they are fanatical in their loyalty to him and will do *anything* for him."

I turned and looked at Terentius again. He shrugged at me.

"He told me," I said to Rullus while staring at Terentius, "that he wants to give magic to every human being. He said he wants to *free* them."

Rullus stopped. I almost ran into him, and the legionaries behind us almost ran into me. But we all stopped in time to avoid a pileup on the cross-valley highway. He slowly turned to me, and I saw the silver instantly cover his eyes. His multi-colored aura flashed around him.

"And what did you say?" he asked quietly.

"I told him no," I said. "And why are you looking at me like that?"

He stared at me for several moments. I tried to be the fearless magus and return that stare with a defiant one of my own, but inside, my bowels were doing that thing again where they cramped up when I'm terrified. I hate that thing. Almost as much as I hate being intimidated.

"You speak the truth," Rullus finally said. The silver faded from his eyes like clouds on a breezy day, and the brown came back. He began walking toward the camp again, and the legionaries behind us streamed around me to follow. I got the feeling Rullus would've solved the problem that his legion was designed to remedy—me—if he'd thought I was lying.

Did I have any Roman friends left? It was times like this when I really missed Vitulus.

I hurried back up to Rullus. "So how do we stop Terentius from unleashing the dregs of the underworld upon the earth?" I asked.

"*We* don't do anything. *You* have to stop it now."

"And we're back to this being *my* fault again."

"Yes," he said. "You're the one that was tricked. *You* opened the door to the underworld with that cloak. Therefore *you* are the only one that the cloak will let go back into the underworld to close the door."

More clicking and clanging in my head as the gears shifted into place and plans began to form. If I was the one who opened the door *and* I was the only one who could close it before all the nasties from the underworld flooded in...it meant I could reach Helva and pull her out before I closed the door.

And before you stare aghast at the selfishness I'm writing here, no, I did not consider Saving the World a sub-plot to rescuing Helva. But you have to admit that it was damned awesome that the method to achieve both goals was the same.

"I'll do it," I immediately said.

Rullus had been about to say something else, but clicked his teeth and regarded me suspiciously. "Do not make this a personal task, Natta Magus," he warned.

"Hey, I want to save the world just as much as the next guy," I said. "Which means saving all of it...including my friends."

Rullus licked his lips. "Becoming the avatar of a god gives you a certain perspective on the world. The good of *all* must outweigh the good of a *few*."

"Damnation, you sound like an old mirror drama," I said. "I've saved the world before. I know how to take down daemons."

"I don't think you do," he said, silver flashing in his eyes. "I've come to understand how the three realms of existence—the heavens, the earth, and the underworld—maintain a balance. There are few laws that the gods of all the realms obey, and maintaining that balance at all costs is one of them. For if that balance is overturned, then all realms will fall. You saw how we just banished those 'yessir' daemons, as you call them, right? Well imagine their fate upon *all existence*. It is what will happen if Terentius's fanatics overturn that balance. That includes all timelines...like the one your beloved Brianna went back to."

That made me pause and gulp down the sudden lump of responsibility that stuck in my throat. Along with it came a bitterness that had slithered into my heart since Aventicum. My experiences in the Ring of Saturn—my name for it, by the way—showed me an infinite number of worlds and timelines. But only one timeline contained a world where magic thrived *and* humanity lived beyond the twenty-first century. That was the one Brianna had gone back to.

The catch was that I had to stay in ancient Rome for reasons I still did not know. Was it one big crisis that I was destined to stop, or was it the multitude of crises that I had faced since Aventicum? Would my entire life be filled performing magical damage control on the ancient world? Would I ever know peace or have the love I once had with Brianna?

I've found that when the bitterness began to rise so did the rage that tempted me to use my soul magic. *Go away bitterness and let me think.*

It was obvious there were things Rullus wasn't telling me. Damnation, I couldn't even be sure he was telling me the truth about Terentius. But one thing I did know for sure was that the cloak got me into the underworld and had brought me to Helva. That was reason enough for me to sign on to another world-saving mission.

"I get it," I said to Rullus firmly. "I will use the cloak to close that door. But can you tell me one thing?"

He raised an eyebrow at me. "If I can."

"You're the avatar of a god so you probably know some history. Just who in damnation were these ancients who created these world-ending artifacts?"

Rullus smiled. "If I told you that, you'd go mad."

24

By the time we reached the outskirts of the camp, I had filled Paetus and Cana in on the situation. Paetus scratched notes into his clay tablet, a skill that I always admired considering how hard I found it to dig into the clay when I had it flat on a table. Cana's eyes gleamed like a green soldier who'd trained long for battle and had just received her orders.

"There's only room for one passenger on this wagon," I said, trying to forestall any notion she had of following me into the underworld.

Her gaze turned stony. "How am I to learn from you if I cannot see you in battle?"

"Like on the galley?"

"That was against mundane pirates. I want to be there when you face *real* magical threats, like daemons and other magi."

"Like on the Capitoline Hill?"

"You are insufferable," she growled.

I glanced at Terentius as the legionaries herded him past us. He grinned at me, and then he was pushed into a tent. He was either really insane or really confident, and I didn't know which made me more afraid. Rullus strode by as well, leading the Romans who carried the basket of artifacts toward a different tent several paces away.

The Romans who had remained in the camp searching for daemons and other artifacts had already put the daemons they found into a goat pen. The same six auguries that had banished the yessirs in the crevasse stood around the daemon pen with fresh scrolls, waiting for the legionaries to finish moving them all in. The yessirs, about two dozen taking the forms of children, women, and the elderly, stood sullenly and watched their brethren file towards them without a sound or a drop of sweat on their brows.

"I'm sure you'll get your chance for battle, *leerling*," I said. "But for this one, I have to go alone. The cloak wasn't built for two."

She frowned and was about to say something, but I countered, "Besides, you need to make sure Juba, Elissa, and Alishat get home to Carthage." The three Carthaginians had found an empty tent nearby and were sitting in the shade after the terror of battle and the walk along the scorching valley floor. Juba had somehow made Alishat giggle, while Elissa shook her head with disapproval at yet another one of his terrible jokes.

"Why?" she asked harshly. "They can take care of themselves."

"Because it's the right thing to do. Look at them, *leerling*. They've lived in cities all their lives. They don't have the survival instincts that you do."

"But what makes them different from any other person in this—"

"Just do it, please!"

She ground her teeth and then nodded once. She looked at Juba, Elissa, and Alishat as if they were the pigpen that I'd just ordered her to clean.

Yeah, that lesson on a magus's responsibilities was long overdue.

The yessirs chose that moment to begin their unearthly shrieks. The auguries surrounding the daemons had unfurled their scrolls and begun their chanting. I turned away. Yes, they were just daemons, but watching what looked like children melt away into yellow-white goo was not something I wanted to see twice. Cana averted her eyes, too, but Paetus watched with the fascinated curiosity of a daemonologist.

As soon as the screams and pop-splatter of each daemon exiting the world ended, I turned to Cana. "Look, I wish I could bring you into the underworld with me but...what, Paetus?"

He was staring at the goat pen where the daemons had been. His eyes had gone from curious to terrified within a heartbeat. When I looked at the pen, I understood why.

The pus that the daemons had devolved into was not sizzling and evaporating like it did when a daemon was banished. This time, the pus was slithering about the pen as if it were alive. It slithered toward the center, where it began to gather into a slimy pool. The yellow-white pool bubbled and boiled, then began to rise into a mound that sucked into it all the daemon pus still left in the pen.

The auguries stared at the rising mound as shocked as I was. This wasn't supposed to happen. The daemon elements were temporary and could not hold together without the daemon spirit to bind it.

Unless another daemon spirit was binding the leftovers.

The mound of yellow-white pus continued to rise until it was almost twenty feet tall. Then it darkened and writhed, forming into something else.

I felt a familiar fear rising from my gut. It was the same fear that had made me want to run until my legs fell off when I encountered Gibber in the underworld with Helva and Silanus.

Oh no.

The Gibber daemon took shape, which was thankfully obscured by a swarm of brown locusts. As horrible as that swarm was, I felt like it was a blessing: The daemon's true shape must have been awful enough to drive even the earth mad.

It released that insane laughter and the auguries ran, leaving Cana, Paetus, and I standing alone in front of it.

I couldn't blame the auguries. Every daemon has a specialty, and Gibber's happened to be a terror that made my heart want to claw its way out of my chest and run for the mountains. Most people can't deal with that kind of terror. Running is smart. It's how people survived the savannas of Africa and saber-toothed tigers and all the predators and natural calamities since then.

But sometimes terror makes people freeze, unable to move or even blink. That's what happened to the three of us. All we could do was stare at our approaching deaths.

The locust-swarmed monster lurched forward, one slimy hoof or tentacle stepping toward us over the small goat pen's fence.

And then it strode past us as if we weren't there, its hoofs making impact tremors that I felt in my knees. It left terror in its wake, a couple of locusts flapping against my face, and that week old garbage smell.

When I could finally think, I turned my head to watch Gibber march toward the tent where Terentius was held. A huge arm—more like a tentacle crossed with a limb that had been chewed to the bone—reached out of the locust cloud and tore the tent off its stakes. Several legionaries stood in the center of the tent surrounding Terentius. They raised their batons, more to defend themselves than to attack. Another tentacle shot out from the locusts, this one more like a snaking spear. It spun through the air like a corkscrew, slammed through the chest of one legionary in a spray of blood, and then flew through the backs and chests of the remaining legionaries. Gibber lifted the skewered Romans off the ground and flung them off into the middle of the camp as if they were ants on a branch.

Terentius stood in the middle of it all, unharmed. He looked up at Gibber with the approving gaze of a master to his dog. He lifted his magically bound hands above his head. Another tentacle shot out of the locust swarm and sliced through the bindings. Gibber released a yelp in between its insane giggles, and I somehow had the wits to notice that the tentacle sizzled when it touched the bindings.

Terentius looked at me and shouted, "My offer still stands, Natta Magus. Expect a letter from me soon."

Then he stepped into the locust swarm and disappeared.

The swarm shifted, seeming to turn toward me. I couldn't tell for sure, however, since the cloud of locusts thankfully obscured Gibber's face. But three large tentacled arms rose up from the top of the swarm, the appendages all slimy and bloody and lined with purulent wounds.

Then the arms crashed down on the tent in which Juba, Elissa, and Alishat had been sitting, crushing everything inside.

25

Gibber's smashing tentacles reduced the tent to ragged canvas covering irregular mounds (supplies, furniture, *bodies?*). For good measure, Gibber hit the mounds several more times, producing sickening crunches with each strike.

Something like a groan and a sob escaped my throat, the kind that awakens you from a nightmare. I hadn't seen my Carthaginian friends leave the tent. But then my focus had been directed elsewhere the last few minutes. Were they dead? Had I failed them?

The familiar rage boiled inside me.

But Rullus forestalled my damnation by one more day.

"Natta Magus!" he cried from behind me.

I took two heartbeats to bring my soul magic under control and then turned around. Rullus was running toward me, his gold-tinted armor gleamed in the sun, his red cloak flared behind him, and his silver eyes sparked with electric energy. In one hand he held a gladius that shimmered with that multi-colored, shifting aura.

He literally looked like the hero from all the mythologies I'd ever read.

"Use this!" he yelled, and then threw something at me. I caught the item before I realized what it was.

It was the teddy bear from the basket.

"Seriously?" I asked.

"Put your cell magic into it, fool," he growled. As if that was so obvious.

Gibber gibbered insanely, and then its tentacles fell toward me. I jumped out of the way of one, then had to dive to my right to escape a second one. Paetus and Cana had to dodge tentacles, too, but they quickly fled while I remained. I had a moment of relief when I saw them run out of Gibber's range. I tried siphoning cell magic into the teddy bear, but lost my focus when I had to dive away from another tentacle that whipped out horizontally from the side of the locust swarm.

One also came at Rullus, who by that time was near me. He swung downward with his glowing gladius, severing the tentacle with an easy swing. The thing screamed. Another tentacle whipped out and knocked Rullus ten feet into the air. He landed on top of a tent, which collapsed under his weight and covered him.

A cohort of archers had formed behind Gibber and began firing multi-colored arrows at it. The arrows sank into the locust swarm with angry hisses. Gibber screamed. In retaliation, it sucked in a huge breath, and then a stream of brown liquid shot out of it toward the cohort. The Romans had no time to dodge the stream before it sprayed them all. The liquid sizzled upon their armor and skin. The men screamed as the liquid ate through armor and skin, leaving horrible blackened holes. Some of the Romans hurriedly shed their armor before the liquid could reach their skin, but Gibber simply shot more at the naked Romans. The entire cohort was now down and writhing upon the ground with ragged shrieks as they all seemed to melt from the inside out.

Our survival now seemed to rest on a teddy bear and me. I siphoned as much cell magic into the stuffed bear as I could.

I felt a *whump* in my chest as a blast of magical energy exploded from me in a heated wave that knocked down the tents near me.

The first thing I noticed was that I was no longer afraid. In fact, I felt calm and at peace. Even safe. I couldn't remember the last time I'd felt so secure and...loved. All I wanted to do was lie down on the ground, curl up, and fall asleep, dreaming about rainbows, unicorns, and puppies.

I refocused on Gibber...but it was gone. Well, not gone. Where a nightmarish swarm of locusts with gruesome tentacles had been standing moments ago, now stood a small jack-in-the-box that I'd actually owned when I was kid. The little clown had already popped out of the box, its white gloved hands spread wide. The bobbing clown seemed to give me a reproachful look, though there was no malice or fear in it.

"That's why Terentius stole it," Rullus said. I glanced at him and saw he didn't look hurt at all from his tent dive. "The bear destroys fear when wielded by a magus. And fear is Terentius's greatest weapon."

Gibber had been fear incarnate. No wonder it had been destroyed; or at least turned into something that generated anticipation rather than terror. I looked down at the plush bear still in my hands. It felt warm as if it had been hugged all night. For the first time I noticed its multi-faceted brown crystal eyes. They were really out of place for a bear that looked like it had been picked out by a child at a rummage sale.

I breathed a contented sigh, not wanting this feeling of peace to end. "How long does this last?"

Rullus strode up to the jack-in-the-box, raised a sandaled food, and smashed the toy with several powerful stomps. It issued a small gibber, but I wasn't sure if that was from Rullus's stomping or Gibber releasing a final gasp. Once Rullus had flattened the toy, it dissolved into a purulent ooze that sizzled and then evaporated.

"Not long enough," he said.

Upon hearing those words, I felt a mild concern rise in me. It slowly turned to worry. When I turned to the tent in which Juba, Elissa, and Alishat had been in, my worry gave way to outright horror.

I handed the teddy bear back to Rullus and ran over to the tent. I began pulling at the thick canvas, afraid of what I would find underneath. Paetus and Cana arrived shortly thereafter and helped me find a way beneath the tattered canvas.

"I am sorry, *leraar*," Cana said, her voice cracking as she helped dig through the tent debris. "I did not stand with you. I...I do not know what came over me..."

"Stop it," I said. "Everyone has a breaking point. Everyone. Only reason I didn't join you was because it had broken *me*. I couldn't move because I was so—"

"Natta Magus!"

I looked up to see Juba running toward us from the center of the camp. I choked out a relieved laugh and stood to meet him. He stopped short, and I gave him the manly Roman wrist clasp, which he returned with a grin. He glanced warily behind me.

"The monster?" he said.

"Gone for now," I said. "Are your sisters safe? Where did you go?"

"Just before the daemon people in the pen began their screaming again, I decided to take my sisters to the center of camp. They did not want to see those people...explode again. When I heard the other monster, I had to come back."

"You came back here? Weren't you afraid?"

"Of course not," he said, his eyes twinkling. "I have killed many locust monsters. They constantly infest my family's private gardens."

I grinned and put a hand on his shoulder. "Well I'd love to know which bug sprays you use, my friend."

Rullus came over to us, still clenching the teddy bear in one hand. He'd already sheathed his gladius. His eyes had gone back to brown, but there was a smoldering anger in them that made me flinch.

"You smile and jest after watching twenty of my men burn to death?" he said quietly.

My relief melted away. I glanced at the gruesome, blackened remains of the Roman archer cohort that had bravely tried to take down Gibber. They'd all been burned alive. Not one had survived. Those guys had stood their ground and tried to fight an unwinnable battle. And they'd all known it.

I didn't know what to say to Rullus. Even then I could smell the scorched flesh of the dead men. What could I *possibly* say to that?

"I'm sorry, Rullus," I managed.

He moved his clenched jaw back and forth. "This is only a taste of what Terentius will unleash upon the world. Do not be distracted by his lies, for he wants only one thing: to watch the world burn like my brothers over there. Once he gathers his forces in the underworld, they will swarm the earth. And no banishment spell will stop them." His eyes moved across all of us standing there. "So go ahead. Smile and jest while you can. The *real* trial approaches. And I fear you will all suffer greatly before it is over." Then he shoved the teddy bear into my hands. "You're the only one who can use it anyway."

A centurion with a red-plumed helm and segmented armor jogged up to Rullus. Behind him by a dozen paces was a cohort of spearmen in formation wearing mail shirts and their shields held chest high.

"General," the centurion said, breathless, "we formed up as fast as we could. Are you all right?" His eyes found the remains of the Roman archers and his face hardened.

"I'm fine, Seius," Rullus muttered. "Place a guard on the tent with the artifacts. Have your auguries found anything in the camp?"

"No, sir. It's clean."

Rullus nodded. "Have the men ready to march within the hour."

Seius glanced again at the remains of the Roman archers. "Shall I form a funeral detail?"

Rullus stared at his dead legionaries. He paused a few moments, spat into the dirt, and said, "There's nothing left to burn. Have the auguries say a few words though."

"Yes, sir," Seius said, and then left to carry out Rullus's orders.

Rullus turned to me. "Get as much food and water as you can. It will be a fast march to Carthage."

He whirled about, his red cloak billowing, and strode back toward the tent from which he had emerged when the fear daemon appeared.

"Grim fellow, that one," Juba murmured. He then stared at the teddy bear in my hands. "What is that?"

"Our secret weapon, I suppose."

"Looks like a toy to me."

"It is to you and me. To that daemon..."

My eyes were drawn to the spot where Gibber had been turned into a toy, and then beyond it to the tent in which Rullus had entered.

The darkened entrance was glowing with a solid aura that I did not recognize. More ominously, I sensed soul magic wafting from the tent. Having siphoned my own soul to cast magic, I knew the feeling well: an emptiness that swallowed all empathy, love, and every other good feeling you ever had.

Before my mind could register the danger, I heard a clash of steel come from inside the tent. And then Rullus's gurgled scream.

26

I ran toward the tent, drawing my gladius as I went. I sensed Cana running beside me. My first instinct was to tell her to stay put—I didn't want her anywhere near someone using tainted soul magic—but then I figured she'd ignore me and keep running anyway.

And if someone was throwing soul magic around in there, I worried that I might get tempted as well. I'd need her help if I wasn't strong enough to resist.

I charged through the dark entrance and cursed. My eyes took several precious seconds to adjust to the darkness after being in the blinding desert sun. Once they did, I saw Rullus on the rug-lined ground, blood streaming from punctures in his breastplate. His eyes were open, but I couldn't tell if he was dead.

Cana noticed the man next to the artifact basket in the tent's corner before I did.

"*Slapen!*" she screamed. A wave of cell magic blasted past me and hit the man.

The man raised a curved short sword at the exact moment the spell hit him. Cana's sleeping spell dissipated when it hit the sword. The spell did absolutely nothing to him.

I saw him more clearly now that my eyes had adjusted. It was Himilco. He raised his short sword and did a downward swipe. A blast of soul magic—empty, cold—flew past me and hit Cana. She screamed once and landed on her back as if someone had pushed her. Her eyes were wild and blood seeped from the corner of her mouth and from her nose.

Before my own rage could take over, I turned and aimed my enchanted gladius at him and yelled, "*Slapen!*"

Himilco again raised his sword, and the sleeping spell once again fizzled when it hit the sword.

But I figured it would. And I figured his raised sword would distract him long enough for me to charge the three paces forward and stab at him with my outstretched gladius. My numerous sparring sessions with Vitulus had not made me a sword master, but one of his lessons had sunk in: *Distract, then strike.*

And by Fortuna's own luck, it worked. My sword buried itself into his chest up to the hilt. I was close enough to see his eyes widen and feel his final hot breath on my face as it left his lungs. I yanked my sword from his chest. Himilco slumped to the ground lifeless.

I turned back to Cana. She was already sitting up, but she looked unsteady.

"Easy, *leerling*," I said, kneeling next to her. "Where did he get you?"

She wiped the blood from her nose and mouth with her sleeve, and then winced. "My ribs," she gasped. "I think he broke some."

"Anywhere else?"

She paused to take an internal inventory and then shook her head. "My nose hurts and I bit my tongue when his magic hit me. Other than that—"

"Not dead," Rullus said weakly from behind me.

He was still lying on the ground, blood now trickling from his mouth. I got up and stooped next to him. His wounds looked far worse and were pretty obvious. The punctures, as I feared, came from a sword, and I counted at least six of them in Rullus's chest. I had no idea how Himilco had surprised the avatar of a god so thoroughly, but I figured it had something to do with the soul magic blast that I had felt outside.

I grabbed Rullus's hand. "Yeah, you're still with us, general. I'm going try and heal you—"

He pushed my hand away and gasped more forcefully, "Not...dead...!" His teeth were bloody and bared, and he was looking behind me.

To where Himilco had fallen.

I followed his gaze back to Himilco. The "dead" man's eyes were fluttering and it looked as if he were trying to rise. Well then. Most normal people die when you stab a gladius through their hearts. So Himilco was either a daemon or was being reanimated by magic.

Both of which can be solved with a beheading, I thought grimly.

I started to rise, my gladius up, but Rullus grabbed my arm with a strength that belied his condition.

"No," Rullus gasped, blood gurgling from his mouth. "Put on...the glove."

My first impulse was to chop off Himilco's head before he had the strength to rise, but Rullus was telling me to use the glove artifact. If I did that, however,

I'd need precious seconds to run over to the artifacts basket and find the glove. Himilco would be up and ready to blast me again if I did that. Chopping off Himilco's head seemed more prudent than putting on another artifact that I had no idea how it worked.

But something told me to trust Rullus's wisdom over my own bloodlust.

I leaped up and took four quick strides to the artifact basket. Out of the corner of my eye, I saw Himilco get to one knee and then stand on shaky legs. I looked into the basket, found the evergreen glove on the bottom. I picked it up and shoved it onto my right hand. The needles gouged into my fingers and hand, and I winced with the pain.

Himilco charged toward me with his curved sword raised. I shifted my gladius to my gloved hand, winced at the needles digging further into my skin, and brought my sword up to block Himilco's strike.

And block it I did, which surprised both of us.

Himilco pushed me away and sneered. "Your magic has not worked on me, magus. You think your sword will?"

He swung again, and I blocked that strike almost as if I knew where he was going. I realized he was off balance so I pushed him back with my gladius...but then I saw he happened to be off balance at the *exact* moment that I pushed him. He regained his balance and took another swing at me. I blocked it as if he'd showed me exactly where and when he was going to swing before he actually did it.

Damnation, I thought. *I have foresight.*

I didn't think about how the artifact glove worked or what the cost would be, I just pressed my advantage on Himilco. He seemed to be a very experienced swordsman, but all he could do was defend against me. If he even thought about an attack, I countered it with either a defensive move or stance. Even his defense against my attacks was faltering. I attacked low, *knowing* that he would slice down to push my sword to the ground and thus leave his face unguarded for me to punch him in the jaw with my left hand. I'm a righty, so the punch was weak, but it was enough to surprise him. I ducked beneath a swing that I saw coming from Monday. I plunged my gladius into his chest again in virtually the same place as before.

"You cannot kill me," he snarled. "I will come—"

I yanked the sword out of his chest and decapitated him with a spinning back swing. Which again surprised us both.

Though not as much as when his body and head exploded into daemonic pus that seemed to coat everything in the tent. After a moment, however, the pus sizzled and evaporated.

I stared at the evergreen glove. Even now it felt like a thousand needles stabbing into my hand. Foresight was some seriously powerful magic; at least it was in my time. The future was always changing, which made it impractical to pin down. It was possible but only with an industrial-sized effort. Some nations in my history had tried it, but then other nations developed magicks to counter it, thus making foresight a waste of resources.

Once again, the ancients had done something that not even the twenty-first century with all its arcane wisdom could do.

I heard Rullus grunt behind me and then remembered that he and Cana were wounded. I whirled around and went over to them. Cana had already laid her hands on Rullus's face and I saw her cell magic's aura glowing about her—misty green of the Gallic countryside, flecked with red sparks—as she tried to heal him. When I stooped down next to her, she blinked away the healing trance and gave me a frustrated look.

"I tried healing him but I cannot see inside his body—"

"I said it won't work on me, girl," Rullus said, blood flowing from his mouth. "Save...your strength."

I grabbed Rullus's muscled forearm, siphoned my cell magic, and tried entering the same healing trance that Cana had used. When I had first arrived in ancient Rome, it had taken several minutes for me to enter the trance, but with plenty of practice of the *heal this guy now or he dies* variety, my timing had become almost instantaneous. My magical senses tried to enter Rullus's body to mend the muscle and organs that Himilco had severed, but they were blocked at the surface of his skin by that multi-colored aura. No amount of pushing could break through.

I broke out of the healing trance and looked down at him desperately. "You're supposed to be a god. How did Himilco get you?"

Rullus barked a laugh, which came with more blood than air. "Told you...not a god..."

There was a commotion at the tent's entrance. I looked up to see Centurion Seius charge in, his sword raised. Three other legionaries came in behind him. Seius scanned the tent, his eyes adjusting, and then finally saw me...kneeling over his bloody commander with a sword in my hand.

Thank the gods I still had foresight, because I raised my gladius in time to block a thrust that would've surely gone straight through my eye.

"Seius!" Rullus gasped. "It wasn't him!"

Rullus coughed up another gout of blood. Seius gave me a wary glance and then knelt down next to Rullus. He studied his commander with grim frustration. It was obvious that he'd seen men with wounds like this and knew the inevitable outcome.

Seius exhaled once. "What are your orders, general?"

"Stop...Terentius." His fading eyes took in Cana and me as well. "Together..."

Those words had taken all of Rullus's strength. His eyes rolled up into his head, and his breathing came in more gurgling wheezes. He exhaled one more time and then was still.

27

I sat on the ground outside Rullus's tent staring at the evergreen glove on my right hand. I flexed my fingers. The needles dug into my flesh, but I had no desire to take off the glove despite the pain. I wondered if that was a symptom of the glove's power or the desire was my own.

Damnation, I was wondering a lot of things at that moment. Was Himilco really a daemon? How had he surprised Rullus? Was that his soul magic I sensed just before his attack? As far as I knew, only human magi could use soul magic. What did it mean that Himilco died like a daemon?

And don't even get me started on my questions regarding Rullus's powers. Those could've filled a whole new scroll tube.

I felt the same way I did when I woke up in ancient Rome: lost, confused, and scared. Just when I thought I knew my way around the place, when I assumed I was the only magus in the ancient world who knew the rules of magic, destiny had to throw in gods and artifacts and daemons that didn't play by those rules. And now I was tasked by a dying man/god/avatar/whatever to save the earth from a magical apocalypse.

The Unknowable Will had a grim sense of humor.

Paetus sat down next to me. He didn't say anything for several moments, but then asked, "Does it hurt?"

I looked at the evergreen glove again. A trickle of blood seeped from out of the glove and down my wrist. I clenched my fist, feeling the needles pierce deeper into my hand.

"Yeah," I said. "But I don't want to take it off."

He was silent a little longer. "Isn't that some kind of warning that maybe you should?"

Just to prove to him—and myself—that I wasn't under its control, I yanked the glove off my hand. As I suspected, it was covered in tiny dots of blood where the needles had penetrated. My hand seemed to sting even more now that the glove was off.

Paetus grimaced. "There's always a cost to using these artifacts, isn't there?"

I snorted, but didn't say anything.

"Cana told me it helped you kill Himilco."

I nodded.

"What does it do?"

"See the future. Read my opponent's mind." I shrugged. "I'm not sure, exactly. I don't even sense any magic on it."

"What are we going to do now?"

I wanted to laugh and yell that I had no *caccing* clue what to do next. Rullus was supposed to have told me all that, but now he was dead and I had possession of these artifacts that could either blow up the world or help me. I had no idea where Terentius or his priests were going to strike next or even how to find them besides some vague notion to *use the cloak*. Use it to do what? I mean, I had to think of Helva and then I found her. Was it the same with Terentius? And what happened if I did? I certainly didn't want to pop into existence right in front of him when he'd have all his daemons ready to turn *me* into human pus.

But I didn't say any of that. It wouldn't be very heroic or leader-like.

"We're going back to Carthage with Seius," I said. "Where's Cana?"

"She's gathering our things. Natta, I don't think Seius is pleased with Rullus's final orders to work with you."

"Whatever gave you that idea?" I asked. I'd seen the way Seius frowned at me as he left Rullus's tent and how he eyed me while he spoke quietly to his auguries and his men.

Paetus apparently didn't hear the sarcasm in my question. "When he ordered his men to take the artifacts out of the tent, he told them to separate the artifacts throughout the wagons. He didn't want them in one place, he said."

"Seems prudent, considering what just happened."

"Then he told them to kill you if you didn't give up the glove and the bear."

"Seems suspicious." I shook my head. "It doesn't matter, anyway."

Paetus raised an eyebrow. "It doesn't? I thought you needed the cloak to—"

"Maybe, maybe not. Look, I've just realized something that I should've realized a long time ago: No matter where I go or what I do, these crises always find me and force me to act. So I'm not going to worry about it anymore. I'm just going to do what I planned on doing to begin with. We'll go to Alexandria, find your scholar friend, and figure out a way to rescue Helva. If it is my destiny to stop Terentius and his world-ending madness, then destiny will find me again and force me to act. Until them, I'm not going to worry about it."

Paetus nodded slowly. "That seems an awfully...passive way to live. You've always been so eager to jump into the middle of things."

"No I haven't, and it's not passive at all. I have a goal that I'm actively pursuing: Rescue Helva. Anything other than that, well, I'll deal with it when it happens. That's the way these things keep happening, so why should I worry about it anymore? If Seius doesn't want my help, fine. I'm not going to badger him or force him to accept it. I'm tired of being the one who always has to save the world."

And there was the crux of it all. I wasn't a god, or a hero, or even a "chosen one," never mind what the Ring of Saturn implied. I was just a regular guy from the twenty-first century who was in the wrong place at the wrong time. Why was it up to *me* to take on every magical catastrophe when there were so many other *powerful* people in my time who could've fixed every injustice in the ancient world during their first week here? I was happy helping everyday people like I had back on the Aventine Hill in Rome. Now that Augustus had his eponymous, anti-supernatural legion to fix the world, he didn't need me anyway. Hell, he didn't even *want* me around.

So it was time I obliged him.

Cana returned then with our packs and sat them down on the ground next to Paetus and me. She glanced around and then said in a low voice, "I do not believe Seius wants our help with—"

"He knows," Paetus said dryly. "So we're not going to help him."

She looked at me, a smile playing at the corner of her lips. "Right. So we will do this thing on our own?"

Paetus stood up and said, "Apparently we're not going to help at all. From now on, Natta Magus is going to let the world save itself."

I glared at him. "Geez, when you say it like that..."

"I do not understand," Cana said, looking from Paetus to me. "What of Terentius and his plans? Should we not do *something, leraar*?"

Paetus shook his head as he checked his packs. "Apparently it's now the task of the Roman legions fight—"

"Paetus, I can speak for myself," I growled. I turned to Cana. "Here's the short version that I just explained to Paetus: Destiny always finds me no matter what I do. So we're just going to continue on our way to Carthage and then Alexandria like we planned. Seius doesn't want us around, fine. We're going to let him and Augustus solve this crisis. You guys packed?"

They glanced at each other again, and then back at me.

"Come on, what's with you guys?" I said. "Paetus, you hate fights and anything to do with possibly dying. Cana, you were ready to abandon Juba, Elissa, and Alishat at the first opportunity. Now you both want to stay and help the Romans fight a daemon army?"

Paetus shrugged. "Yes, I hate fights. Any sane person does. Since I've met you, I've been in more fights with daemons than even Homer could've imagined." He looked me in the eye. "But each one has made me stronger and smarter than I ever thought I could be. I may seek to avoid them, yes, but when they're over, I thank Juno that you dragged me into them. Why? Because you made me better. Right now, I feel like you're doing something that *I* tried to do whenever a fight came up."

"Paetus speaks truth," Cana murmured before I could reply. "I have learned so much in the last two months, and it is the times when you infuriate me with your ethics where I learn the most. When you force me to use my magic creatively rather than as a bludgeoning tool. When you try to explain the 'right thing to do.'" She waved a hand at our packs. "Leaving does not seem like the right thing to do. It does not seem like the thing *you* would do."

I sighed. "Okay, guys, I get it. I rarely run from a fight, so this worries you. But sometimes there are fights that are beyond even me. I mean, we plan on breaking into the *caccing* underworld to rescue Helva! Paetus, that means lots of fighting to come. Cana, I *guarantee* you and I both will learn more creative ways to use our magic." I swept my gaze around at the mustering legionaries, all moving with purpose and the tight discipline that enabled them to conquer the Mediterranean. "Augustus has a *caccing* army with artifacts, specially trained to deal with the likes of Terentius. They've got this. Speaking of which..."

I noticed Seius marching toward us flanked by two auguries in black tunicas. I wondered how many archers he had hidden among the tents ready to fire at me if I turned my ball cap backwards. I stooped down next to my pack and pulled out the teddy bear. When I stood back up, I saw that Seius had stopped about five paces away, his stance wary, and his hand on his gladius hilt.

I tossed the teddy bear onto the rocky ground next to the evergreen glove. "I believe these are yours."

Seius looked from the artifacts to me, wariness still apparent on his face and in his stance. Then he nodded to one of the auguries, who reverently picked up the glove and the bear. The augury then hurried back into the camp with the artifacts to presumably hide them from me, leaving Seius and the second augury to continue to eye me with suspicion. I held my hands out at my sides, palms open, to show that had I no other artifacts stashed on me.

"Natta Magus," Seius said slowly, "I thank you for your...assistance today. I know you heard my general's last order—"

"The words of a dying man are not always the wisest," I said, "even from a man as great as Rullus. I will defer to your wisdom, Centurion, in the best way to interpret that order."

Seius seemed to relax a fraction, though he kept his hand on his gladius. "I am happy to hear that. In this circumstance, I believe the Legio III is more than capable of meeting and defeating the threat that Terentius poses. Your further assistance is not required."

My first impulse was to snort, but that would've been bad manners. And worse, it would've been me admitting to myself that Paetus and Cana were right. *Cannot have that.*

"Sounds good to me. I only ask that my friends and I march with your column back to Carthage. Then we will go our separate ways."

Seius stared at me a moment longer, and then nodded. "Of course. We leave presently." He backed away several steps as if expecting me to throw a knife into his back or something, and then strode off in the same direction as the augury with the artifacts.

Damnation, I wish I were as powerful as these guys think I am.

I slung my pack over my shoulder and looked at Paetus and Cana. "See, it's all good."

They exchanged doubtful looks and then picked up their own packs. I walked past them and toward the sounds of the mustering horns, thinking that I liked it better when Paetus and Cana fought rather than agreed.

28

Once Seius was confident that his men had looted Terentius's daemon camp of anything valuable, he ordered them to burn it all. My friends and I—along with the rest of the legion—were already on the beach outside the crevasse entrance when we saw the first plumes of black smoke rise inland. I glanced at Seius, who sat upon his horse watching the smoke rise. He stationed himself between the covered wagon that carried Rullus's wrapped body and me.

Several more wagons were scattered throughout the 500-strong legion. I idly wondered which of them carried the artifacts or if Seius had packed them on the backs of random legionaries. Either option was risky. Put them in one place and you risk a daemon attack that collected them all in one swoop. Scatter them about the legion and you risk having a clumsy soldier lose them. I hoped Seius gave the artifacts to soldiers he knew to be competent.

I shook my head. No, it wasn't my responsibility. This was something the Romans had to do. I had my own problems.

As soon as the scouts returned through the crevasse after setting fire to the camp, the column got underway. Since Seius seemed awfully jumpy around me, my friends and I picked a spot far away from him—the back of the column. It meant we had to put up with all the dust and dirt kicked up by the marching men ahead of us, but at least I didn't have 500 swords pointed at my back. Plus, I didn't like the way some of the legionaries were staring at the women in our group. Cana could more than take care of herself, but Elissa and Alishat...well, they were patrician in every way but name. Patricians tended to frown on teaching their daughters how to take care of themselves. Juba noticed the Roman stares as well, and was far more anxious than he'd been even in Terentius's daemon camp.

Yeah, best to cough on some dust than to put this lot at our backs.

There were few armies in the ancient world that could outmarch the Romans, but even they had to bow to geography. It was only twenty miles or so to Carthage, well within a legion's daily march capabilities on European terrain. But the terrain between here and Carthage was rocky, hilly, and mountainous. Loose gravel and rock could break an ankle without warning or send a man tumbling down a hill or off a cliff. Throw in a 100-plus degree sun that fire-blasted the armor each man wore, and the march turned into a crawl. The men had started the march talking and cracking jokes, but after a few hours, they quietly concentrated on keeping pace with Seius atop his horse at the front of the column.

We stopped after about four hours of brutal marching. I collapsed onto the ground in the shade of a large boulder, and Paetus and Cana sat next to me. Juba, Elissa, and Alishat leaned against a boulder about ten paces away looking as sweaty, exhausted, and dirty as I felt.

I gave Paetus a chagrined look. "Now I get why you wanted to take galleys to Alexandria."

Paetus leaned his head against the boulder, his face sweaty and his cheeks flushed beneath his blond beard. He regarded me through barely opened eyes and gave me a smile that seemed more like a snarl.

Cana wrung out the gray headscarf she'd been wearing. Sweat dripped from it as if she'd dunked it in water. Brown strands of hair that had escaped her tight braids were stuck to her head.

"I miss green," she said wearily. "Even Rome was greener than this place, and I thought Rome was too dry. I miss thick forests and grassy hills covered in mist."

I swished some warm water in my mouth from the skin I carried, and then asked, "Where in Gaul did you grow up?"

She rarely spoke of her homeland, and she shifted uncomfortably after my question as if she had revealed too much without thinking. She shrugged. "A village east of Cenabum."

When she noticed my blank stare, she said, "The center of Gaul."

I nodded. "Is that were you were captured?"

She studied her headscarf for a while. "I was not captured. My family gave me to a Roman publican as a tax payment."

I stared at her. *Damnation, what do you say to that?*

She shrugged again as I struggled to say something. "It is a common thing. We had two poor grain harvests in a row. The Romans did not care; they demanded the same amount in taxes. My parents had four children including me. They could not feed us all, so..." She looked at me with a sad grin. "I was odd, even then. So I was the one they sold to the publican. The Romans must always have their taxes."

"I'm sorry," I murmured.

"It is a bitter thing to be abandoned by one's family," she said, looking at me. "But I would not have had the chance to develop my talents if I had *not* been sold. I would not have met you, *leraar*. In my village, I would have become a priestess." She upturned her lip. "And I do not have the stomach for staring at entrails all day."

I barked a laugh. "No 'stomach for entrails.' Good one."

She grinned, this time more genuine. "I thought you would like that."

"Maybe I'll write that down," Paetus said. He still leaned his head against the boulder, his eyes closed. "So far my journals are less Homer and more Plautus."

"You wanted to come," I said. I leaned my head back against the rock and closed my eyes.

I dozed a little and dreamed. I was an actor wearing clown makeup doing a slapstick routine on a stage in front of 'yessir' daemons, who dutifully laughed at every joke.

The Roman mustering horn jerked me awake. I opened my eyes and saw the legionaries nearby cursing and standing up. They slung their packs over their shoulders and got back into line. I was half-tempted to rest for a while more and let the column advance ahead of us—it's not like Seius would care if I disappeared into a crevasse. But then Terentius's minions had a bad habit of popping into existence at the most inconvenient times. Better to have a legion nearby that was trained to deal with those surprises.

So I stood up with only a slight groan, gave Paetus a hand up, and slung my own pack over my shoulder. Cana had already stood and was wrapping the headscarf over her hair again. I glanced at the boulder were Juba, Elissa, and Alishat had been sitting, but didn't see them there. I scanned the forming lines of grumbling legionaries, but didn't see them there either.

"Where's Juba and his sisters?" I asked Paetus and Cana. They looked around just as I had.

"Relieving themselves?" Paetus said. But his worried expression suggested even he didn't think that was true.

I strode over to the boulder and felt the niggling tug of recently used cell magic upon my skin. It was coming from beyond the boulder, from an alcove in the cliff wall next to which we had stopped. My stride turned into a jog. When

I rounded the corner, I stopped in my tracks and could only stare. The seconds stretched into that eternal moment that only happened in nightmares.

Juba lay in one corner of the alcove, his throat cut and a pool of blood seeping into the ground beneath his head and unseeing eyes. Elissa and Alishat lay on the ground next to him, their eyes wide, but they appeared frozen. It was unnatural stillness, which made me think magic was involved.

Finally, I saw the three Roman legionaries. One held a glowing, multi-colored baton pointed at the two girls. The other two were just about to drop their tunicas.

We all met each other's eyes for another eternal nightmare moment.

After two years of swearing I'd never do so, I unleashed my soul magic.

29

Mostly what I remember is the uncontrollable fury that rose in me. I couldn't have stopped it even if I'd wanted to. The red-hot fury exploded across my body and then dissipated into emptiness. After that, things got hazy, so I'm relying on the witness of Paetus and Cana for what you're about to read.

I killed the Roman holding the baton first, quickly, by using soul magic to twist his head all the way around and practically off his neck. As he fell, the other two Romans tried to pull up their tunicas, but I never gave them the chance. I sent a wave of soul magic at them that picked them up, slammed both of their bodies into the ceiling three times. Blood splattered all over Elissa and Alishat. I flung the Roman bodies over my shoulder. The armored foot of one legionary struck Cana in the face as the body flew past her. She went down, stunned and half-unconscious.

Apparently I didn't even notice.

But two legionaries behind me did notice. Paetus said they must've seen me run off and wanted to find out what I was up to. Well, they did. When I turned toward them—my eyes completely white at this time, according to Paetus—they tried to run. I caught them in a wave of soul magic that twisted them both in half at the waist, each half flying in different directions. Both men were still alive and screamed until they died.

I strode calmly from around the corner of the cliff and came face-to-face with Legio III. They'd heard the commotion behind the cliff. Cohorts formed in front of me with their shields raised and linked, spears poking from between them. The spearheads glowed with that multi-colored aura and then fired bolts of magic at me. I had raised a black, misty bubble around me, which flashed whenever a multi-colored bolt struck and dissipated into mist. Arrows arose from behind the front lines and fell on the bubble, but most flared in a white fire and turned to ash. Some reversed direction and shot right into the eyeballs of the men in the front lines, felling them with instant death.

Nevertheless, whistles blew and the cohorts advanced toward me. Men in the back took the place of the men who'd died from the arrows, their shields linking so that the cohort was one armored organism. That sight had made many armies run throughout the centuries.

But I stood before them, watching them curiously as they approached as if I were inspecting a bug that I was about to step on (Paetus's words, not mine). When they got within ten paces, I crouched down like I was protecting myself from incoming blows. The cohort's centurion seemed to think that was so, for another whistle blew, and the cohort surged forward as one with bristling spears.

Before the spears could run me through, I stood and waved my arms in front of me like I was parting a curtain. Wherever my hands pointed, the legionaries began screaming. Their armor, swords, rings, pendants, and anything else made of metal lit up like they had just been pulled from the forge. The metal burned, branded, and sunk into the bodies of each man as if its weight had increased tenfold. They all dropped their weapons and struggled with the fastenings on their armor, only to burn their fingers on the metal buckles. Their screams turned inhuman and ragged. They all fell to the ground, twitching and spasming even after their bodies had blackened and shriveled from the heat.

The next cohort stepped forward with linked shields and bristling spears. They at least had the sense to pause, though they advanced as one when their centurion blew his whistle.

I burned them, too.

The third cohort behind them had linked their shields and pointed their spears, but they didn't advance. Arrows and bolts from their spears crashed harmlessly into the black misty bubble around me. This time I didn't wait for them to advance; I walked toward them. Whether it was courage, training, or shear frozen terror that kept them in place, they stood their ground. Even as I waved my hands at them and burned them alive.

That did it for the final two cohorts in Legio III. They broke and ran up the beach, leaving behind their weapons, shields, and supplies. Riders on horseback raced ahead of them up the beach. Paetus said later that he could spy Seius leading them.

One of the things I do remember about that battle is running along the beach after the legionaries. I didn't feel angry, only a sense that I wasn't finished killing and that it would be folly to let any one of them escape.

Another thing I remember was hearing Cana yell from behind me. "Natta Magus!"

I stopped, turned, and began to wave my hands to burn her just like the Romans. But before I could release the spell, she screamed in heavily accented English, "Warm milk!"

And then I don't remember anything else until I awoke an hour later.

30

I smelled cooking bacon when I came to, and my stomach actually growled. Then I opened my eyes and saw an army of blackened corpses about fifty paces away. I was smelling burnt human flesh.

My stomach lurched, I rolled onto my side and dry heaved. When I got my gut under control, I lay on my back. My mouth was dry and tasted of salt. My whole body felt wrung out as if I were a sponge that had dried in the sun all day. I stared up at the deep blue, cloudless sky.

Because I certainly didn't want to inspect my handiwork.

Cana leaned over me. "*Leraar?*"

"Yeah," I said, "I'm me again. Water?"

Paetus sat down next to Cana and handed me a water skin. I sat up slowly, hoping to keep the heaves away, and took the skin from Paetus. I took several gulps of warm, leather-tasting water and swished them around before swallowing. I kept my eyes on the skin, for I was aware of all the dead men just down the slope from us. I didn't want to think about them right then.

"Where are Elissa and Alishat?" I asked.

Cana nodded behind me. I turned and saw them sitting cross-legged in the shade of a boulder, staring at a pile of rocks at the top of the hill. Elissa held a wooden figurine. She quietly chanted something, and then Alissa repeated words in the same quiet tone. I looked back at the pile of rocks. A cairn. For Juba.

I swallowed once, not really wanting to know the answer, but I had to ask. "What did I do?" I still refused to look at the blackened shapes beyond them.

Paetus and Cana glanced at each other, and then she asked, "What do you remember?"

Fury and emptiness...

"I saw Juba. I saw Elissa and Alishat. And the Romans." I shook my head. "After that..."

Paetus bit his lip and then proceeded to tell me everything he saw. From the moment I released soul magic on the Roman murderers/attempted rapists to the moment Cana cast the "warm milk" spell that she and I had worked out to put me to sleep for this very situation. She would've cast it sooner, but had been stunned after I hit her with the first Roman body that I had flung over my shoulder.

"We buried Juba while you slept," Paetus finished, giving Elissa and Alishat a worried glance.

"They are strong," Cana said. "They gathered every stone and placed it themselves. They only let us carry Juba to the top of the hill."

After hearing that, I allowed myself to look at the legion that I had single-handedly decimated. It was exactly as Paetus had described: hundreds of blackened, skeletal bodies wearing blackened Roman armor. Some had even been reduced to ashes in the shape of a body. I could even see where each cohort fell, for each group was about ten paces behind the other. Swords, shields, spears, and other legionary detritus lay strewn about the battlefield.

I had done that. With soul magic.

And at that moment I felt nothing.

I had killed hundreds of men for the crimes of three. I should've felt some guilt or perhaps anger. Maybe even satisfaction that I'd achieved *some* justice for Juba. I knew the emptiness that I felt should've worried me, but I couldn't even muster that.

I had stolen so much of my own soul to fuel my vengeance that I was already beginning to lose my empathy. At a detached and academic level, I knew that meant I was sliding into Darkness. If that trajectory continued, I would burn up my entire soul, go mad, and then destroy myself, and those around me, in a final conflagration as I used up the last of my soul. The Dark Wars in the early twentieth century almost destroyed the world that way, and it was only the combined strength of Allied magi from across the world that stopped it. The Allies had cast the Aether, a magical shield around the Earth that stopped the use of soul magic and the daemons it spawned. The Aether was so successful that my twenty-first century civilization took for granted the peace and safety it had provided for a hundred years.

Who would stop me here?

I glanced at Cana. *And would I bring my* leerling *down with me?* It had been far too common for *leraar* to tempt their *leerlings* into soul magic. Damnation,

I didn't even have to actively tempt her into it. What if she desired the power that she saw me wield against the legion? In most cases, that was all it took for the Dark armies to swell.

Again, thinking all these things should've come with horror and shame over my own actions. But I couldn't muster any of that as I scanned the dead.

You did this! part of me screamed. *Feel something!*

To which I mentally shrugged.

"Augustus will come for me now," I murmured. "I bet Seius is already sending couriers to Rome about me. There's no going back from this. You two will take Elissa and Alishat to Carthage."

"'You two'?" Cana repeated. "What about you?"

I shook my head. "Staying near me is a death sentence. If the Romans don't kill you then I..."

I felt a twinge of horror over what I might do to my friends. That brought me a bit of relief. Perhaps I wasn't too far gone yet?

Cana abruptly stood and glared at me. "You are a fool, *leraar*, if you think we are going to let you wander the world without us. You need us more than ever. You feel guilty over what you did here today, yes?"

I stared at the carnage and whispered, "I should."

"How much worse would it have been if I was not here to put you asleep?"

I closed my eyes as one of the few memories of my soul magic madness came back to me: readying a spell to rip Cana in half.

Oh, gods.

"I was about to kill you, Cana," I choked. "And you, too, Paetus. And then I would've gone after Alishat and Elissa—"

"But I stopped you," she said, "just like we practiced. If you leave, who will stop you next time?"

I desperately wanted to tell her there would be no "next time." But I knew that was a crock, so I wanted to tell her that none of them should be around me *when* there was a "next time."

But she was right, who would stop me? I needed another magus to put me to sleep if I lost it again. Where was I going to find another magus who I didn't care whether or not I killed in a fit of soul magic madness? Who I trusted not to simply put me to sleep for the hell of it? Or worse, learn how to wield soul magic by my example?

The fact that I struggled with this, however, began to hearten me. It meant that I still cared what happened to the people around me, especially my friends.

If I had shrugged and said without any worry "Yeah, sure, come along. I may kill you in the morning," then that would've been a huge warning sign.

I still had some control. I hoped.

I glanced at Paetus. "What do you think, old friend?"

He sighed. "Your abilities have always frightened me, Natta Magus, even your cell magic. This new power frightens me even more. But I know you are a good man and will do everything you can to control it." Then he surveyed the carnage I'd left behind with a worried expression. "What frightens me is Augustus. You're right; he will not forgive this, no matter how many times you've saved the State in the past. This is a challenge to his power, a challenge to Rome. He *will* come for you."

"And what will you do?" I asked. It was a logical question, but rather insulting to a man who said he was my friend. I didn't realize this until I watched his expression turn from worried to wounded. Had my question come from my normal obliviousness to Roman honor, or was it my empathy seeping away?

"I am a Roman," Paetus acknowledged, "and that means I am loyal to my friends. I may not be useful in battle, but you have my services nonetheless. Such as they are."

I grinned at him. "And I am truly grateful for that. It's your wisdom that keeps us on track." He nodded, lifting his chin a little higher.

I looked at Cana. "And your tenacity."

"Flattery will not stop me from knocking you senseless the next time you wield soul magic," she said.

"I should hope not."

I lifted my ball cap off my head and wiped the sweat from my brow. I set the cap firmly back on and then stood on shaky legs. After a moment of vertigo, I felt like my normal self—albeit thirsty and tired as hell.

"Okay, guys, let's gather what supplies we can from..." I waved my hand at the battlefield, not relishing the grim task of searching it for water and food.

"Done," Cana said, standing. She pointed at a bunch of packs sitting in the shade behind me, each one bulging with contents. "You slept, so we worked."

"Well, then." The fact that I wouldn't have to pick through blackened skeletons lightened my mood considerably.

Skeletons that you created.

I still couldn't muster any sympathy or guilt over the men I'd killed. Right now, all I cared about was that I still cared about my friends. That was enough.

"Good. Let's go to Carthage, then..."

I paused. *Ah, damnation.* Seius was heading to Carthage. We'd walk right into his highly pissed off hands.

Paetus nodded knowingly. "Yes, Seius might be waiting for us there. We thought of that, too. Elissa said her family can arrange discreet sailing passage for us from Carthage to Alexandria. They will be more than happy to do so after what you did for them. All we have to do is get to Carthage unseen."

"Which gives me more chances to practice my camouflaging magic, leraar," Cana said eagerly.

I licked my dry lips. Walking north to Carthage and the dangers it posed were more preferable to walking east across hundreds of miles of desert to Alexandria. It seemed we had no choice.

"Well, then," I said again. "Seems you guys have thought of everything."

"You slept a long time," Paetus grinned.

I went over to my pack to find it filled with excess ration pouches and water skins. I hoped my other things—Lares' statue, spell components—were buried in there somewhere.

I slung the pack over my shoulder and then noticed Paetus giving me an indecisive look.

He turned to Cana and said, "We should tell him."

Her lips thinned and her eyes scanned the valley, the battlefield, Juba's grave. Anywhere but my eyes.

"Tell me what?" I asked slowly.

She scowled at Paetus, but he said, "He'll figure it out sooner or later. It's a long way to Carthage."

"*What*, guys?" I asked.

Cana exhaled and then picked up one of the packs. She opened it and showed me the contents.

"The Romans were so eager to flee that they left a few things behind," she said.

They had gathered some of the Roman weapons that still glowed with a multi-colored aura: two batons, a dagger, and an arrow. But it was the contents at the bottom of the pack that really got my attention: a teddy bear, evergreen glove, red cloak, and the two bronze torches.

31

We searched the rest of the battlefield for the basket, but couldn't find it. I assumed Seius took it when he fled. His idea to spread the artifacts throughout the legion to "protect" them from me was silly to begin with. Now my impulse was to giggle at the irony of me having them in my hands anyway. The only thing stopping me from giggling was that I worried it would sound mad.

We then followed the detritus of a legion in flight—a helm here, a shield there, empty water skins everywhere (no more weapons with auras, though). It meant we were on the right path back to Carthage. After a few hours, the trampled path and debris field eventually merged onto a well-traveled road. We decided to rest a while and then walk the road at night to avoid the Romans and the baking heat of the sun. We had plenty of food and water, so we took it slowly. In the morning, we collapsed into sleep in an alcove among the cliffs about a hundred paces from the road. We set a watch schedule; besides the occasional merchant wagon, we saw no one else traveling the road. When the sun began to set, we cautiously left our shelter and started our journey again.

Our first sign that something was wrong was the trickle of people who were hurrying south along the coast road from the city. A few carried shoulder packs, but most barely had the clothes on their backs. We were still trying to keep a low profile, so we tried hiding from the first few people we saw. But the trickle became a torrent, and hiding became impractical. Besides, no one was paying attention to us. Everyone seemed to stumble ahead with haunted eyes. When anyone did look at us, it was not out of curiosity; it seemed more like surprise that we were heading in the direction they were fleeing.

I traded grim looks with Paetus and Cana, but we continued on.

If the increasing refugee traffic—for that's what I assumed it was—didn't confirm my suspicions, then it was the angry orange glow upon the northern horizon when we got within two miles of Carthage. The acrid smell of a burning city hit us and made my eyes water. When we rounded a cliff on the coast road, we beheld the full awful site of Carthage engulfed in flames. Even from over a mile away, I could feel the heat on my face from the fires.

When most people in my time thought of Carthage, they only thought of the Punic Wars, where Rome eventually triumphed, razed the city, enslaved its citizens, and salted the earth so that nothing would ever grow there again. A lot of that happened, but the three laws of real estate still applied in the ancient world: Location, location, location. The city's location as a port on the Mediterranean was far too primo for it to remain down for long. Within a hundred years after Scipio Africanus crushed the final Carthaginian armies, Roman merchants and wealthy Carthaginians farmers had turned the city into one of the Empire's most cosmopolitan and prosperous. Carthage would've rivaled Rome again if it was not so thoroughly Romanized.

So it was with all that in mind that I stared at the city with as much shock as my companions and the refugees streaming around us. How...why...what...? Fire and smoke covered the entire *caccing* city. Almost 500,000 people lived there. Carthage had newly organized fire brigades stationed throughout the city, modeled after Augustus's reforms in Rome. How had a fire so thoroughly engulfed the *entire* city? Were the fire brigades asleep?

I felt a tug on my left arm and looked into the resolute face of Elissa. Alishat stood close to her, her gaze transfixed on Carthage.

"The way to my uncle's farm is at the last crossroads before the city," Elissa said, holding my gaze and ignoring the flames. As if refusing to believe her city was dying. "We should leave this road."

Her words broke the frozen shock that had descended upon me. I nodded and tried to copy her resolve. "Right. Yes."

I glanced at Paetus and Cana who still stared at the city. "Let's go, team."

They nodded absently and followed me.

Many of the people who stumbled past us were either burned or had traumatic wounds. Many had open slashes on their chests and backs as if something with claws had attacked them. I saw one guy jog past me whose right arm ended in a bandaged, bloody stump at the elbow. My first instinct was to stop and heal them, but I didn't think any of them would stop for me to try. They all seemed maddened with fear, gibbering and cursing and crying as they ran.

I asked Elissa what they were saying, but she said they weren't speaking Punic at all. "It is as if they are babbling like a baby trying to talk for the first time."

Which was pretty much what they sounded like to me.

Paetus agreed, saying they weren't speaking any language he had heard before.

Regular human armies can certainly cause maddening fear just fine, but this seemed different. This seemed supernatural. I couldn't sense any magic nearby, but this had the feeling of daemons.

Had Terentius started his world-ending with Carthage? Rullus had said that he still needed the artifacts and me to do it. So had he simply decided to end the world one city at a time?

The closer we got to Carthage, the fewer refugees we had to weave around. I figured that those who could get out had already fled. The one's who couldn't were now part of the funeral pyre in front of us. We saw numerous bodies along the road, mostly elderly and—heartbreakingly—small children.

The crossroads that Elissa had mentioned was about a half-mile from the city walls. Even that far away, the heat, smoke, and stench were overwhelming. We had to tear off strips from our tunicas and wrap them around our mouths and noses. It didn't eliminate the smells and the smoke, but it did make breathing go a bit easier. I wasn't sure if that was true or just psychological. At that point, I would take any relief I could get.

Once we reached the intersection, we were all alone, which made me even more uneasy. We took the west road, which skirted the edges of the city's suburban tenements, taverns, and way stations.

I drew my gladius and said, "I probably don't need to mention that you should keep your eyes open for anything."

Cana had taken her headscarf off and wrapped it around her mouth and nose, so all I could see were her eyes. "I have held my cell magic for the last hour, *leraar*," she said.

I hadn't even noticed Cana's aura until now. Just shows how distracted I was by all the destruction and death around me.

Paetus drew his dagger, and his eyes crinkled with the smile hidden beneath his own mouth cover. "My dagger shall strike fear into the black hearts of any daemon."

"That's the spirit," I said.

"My uncle's home is just over this hill," Elissa said. She and Alishat had taken the lead and quickened their pace now that they were so close to family. I couldn't imagine what it must've felt like to see all this, especially after what they'd been through over the last several days.

Considering the deserted road and farms that we passed, I wondered if their uncle was even home. What would they do if he wasn't?

Damnation, what was *I* going to do? I had come to Carthage because it was the only port within a hundred miles where we could book passage to Alexandria. Even the docks and ships in the harbor were burning. I ground my teeth. I did *not* want to accept that this was destiny backing me into the same corner it had ever since William abandoned me in Rome.

Elissa and Alishat were a dozen paces ahead of Cana, Paetus, and me and had stopped at the crest of the hill. When we joined them, I stared in the direction they were looking. A farm complex surrounded by stucco walls stood about a hundred paces away. Within the walls were a house, a barn, and a couple of other buildings. The entire complex was completely dark, and we could only see it by the hellish light of the burning city to the east. A small river wound its way through the valley about a hundred paces behind the farm. The land within the river's floodplain was verdant with stalks of wheat.

Elissa and Alishat began running down the road toward the dark farmhouse.

"Hey, wait—"

They ignored me. I didn't try to shout again and simply ran after them. Cana and Paetus followed.

Thank the gods for well-made Roman roads, for we ran down the sloping road with barely any light to illuminate the way and didn't sprain an ankle in any potholes or ruts. I kept an eye on the sides of the road for any trouble. All I saw were the vague shapes of wheat fields swaying in the hot wind generated by the burning city. Or at least I hoped it was wind. Images of the wounded people I saw on the main road, and the possible creatures that made those wounds, made me whip my head left and right whenever I noticed movement in the fields.

I saw the first body when we got within twenty paces of the farm's walls. I could barely see the face in the dim light, but I did see an arrow shaft protruding from the man's neck. Three more men lay in front of the heavy wood gates, all of them with arrows in their chests, backs, and necks. I didn't know whether to be relieved they were simply men and not monsters or worried that someone on the wall was going to put an arrow in my jugular as I approached. A spark globe would've made it far easier to see, but I didn't want to startle any jumpy archers on the wall with magic...nor alert any daemons to my presence. So I scanned the top of the wall for movement, but didn't see anything. Of course, the damned fires a half-mile away made it hard to distinguish real movement from the flickering light.

Elissa and Alishat stutter-stepped when they noticed the bodies, but they continued running toward the gate. They skidded to a stop at the gate and began pounding on it with their hands.

"Uncle Danel!" they both cried. "Please open! It is Alishat and Elissa! *Uncle!*"

Their cries filled the entire countryside. I nervously glanced at the fields surrounding us. I didn't have to tell Paetus and Cana to do the same, for their heads were constantly moving like mine.

"Uncle Danel, please let us—!"

Elissa screamed. I turned back to see one of the bodies filled with arrows crawling toward her. A second body was lurching to its feet. The third one had sat up and was turning its head slowly toward the sisters. The motions of the bodies were horribly jerky and unnatural as if they had to break their bones in order to move each limb.

I was about to charge forward, my gladius raised, but a heavy weight slammed into my back from behind. I stumbled forward several paces, dropped my gladius, and broke my fall with my hands. I turned over just in time to see a body jump on top of me. I recognized it as the body of the first man that I'd walked past. An arrow protruded from the center of his neck. Black blood glistened upon his entire neck and chest.

This close now, I could see his eyes. And they were completely white.

He opened his mouth in that horrible jerky fashion—cracking, crunching—and lunged for my neck.

32

I 've faced death many times during my stay in the ancient world, and each time seems to come with a semi-detached, instantaneous evaluation of how I will die. I suppose it's some kind of defense mechanism to help me accept my end.

In this case, with a daemonized human trying to rip out my throat with his teeth, my first thought was that someone had figured out how to make more strix. You remember those guys from Aventicum, right?

But I dismissed that idea because this creature didn't seem self-aware; more like a twenty-first century golem that did what it was programmed to do. It didn't gloat or smile at me or seem to take any pleasure in killing me like the strix did. This thing just killed, and that was that.

So not a strix. Undead then. A corpse reanimated by magic. Undead had been used by soul magi during the Dark Wars as a twisted form of soldier recycling: If a human soldier's body was not too damaged, then why not reuse it rather than let it go to waste? But undead had not been seen in my world since the Aether went up, so my assessment was based on history books and embellished illustrations. If these were undead, then that meant this was Terentius's work.

All of this ran through my mind before it got to the time sensitive topic of what to do about it. My mind had nothing. The thing had me pinned. I couldn't raise my arms to fend off its bite or squirm out of the way. I couldn't use a spark globe like I had with the Dea Tacitas because this thing was still partially human; spark globes only destroyed pure daemons.

This thing was going to rip my throat out. I was going to see my windpipe dangling from its bloody mouth before I finally—

A flash of steel in the hellish light of the city fires, and then the creature's head was gone. A black, glistening stump remained, and the undead slumped on top of me. With the head gone, the body seemed absurdly light, like a blanket

I could throw off any time I wanted. Its magic must've given it strength and weight.

Cana stood over me, holding my enchanted gladius in two hands, her eyes glittering in the orange light. Elissa screamed again, and then Cana ran toward her. I threw the undead body off me, jumped to my feet, and raced toward Elissa.

She was pinned down by an undead like I had been. Alishat was cornered by two undead, which jerked toward her in those awful, cracking motions. Cana was several paces ahead of me, the gladius raised. She paused momentarily when she neared the gate, and I could sense she was wondering whom to help first.

She ran for the two that had cornered Alishat. Cana swung my gladius at the neck of the nearest one. The sword embedded itself into the undead's neck, but then got stuck halfway through. The monster whirled around, wrenching the sword from Cana's hands. Its head swung to the left, gruesomely flopping around on the muscles that still kept it on its neck. But its jaw and teeth continued snapping as it jerked toward Cana, who had nothing to stop the creature but her bare hands. She backed away from the oncoming undead. The monster moved surprisingly quick despite its jerky motions.

Strix and undead were kind of the same creature: They were both essentially reanimated corpses. Apparently you could kill them by decapitation. So in theory, the potion that I had developed two years ago to stop the strix should also stop the undead. In theory.

I dug for the potion in one of the pockets sewn into my component vest, uncorked it with one hand, and tossed its contents into the face of the undead that chased Cana. The droplets coated the creature's face, and at first I thought it didn't do a thing because it kept lurching after her. But that was only forward momentum. The undead jerked forward two more steps, stumbled, and then fell flat on its face. My gladius fell free of its spinal column. I grabbed it and then swung down on the creature's neck to finish the job. When the creature's head rolled free of its neck, pus boiled out of the stump as if it were a daemon trying to escape the body it possessed. The pus spilled onto the ground and evaporated within seconds.

Paetus screamed a string of curses and nonsensical words. I turned to see him on the back of the last undead that was attacking Elissa. He plunged his dagger into the creature's back over and over again, but it didn't seem to have any affect. The creature reached for Paetus with two cracking, powerful hands in a horribly unnatural angle and flung him off it. He landed on the ground on his back next to Elissa, and I heard the air burst from his lungs ten paces away. He was stunned, gasping for breath, and completely defenseless. The undead reset its limbs and lurched toward Paetus.

I gripped my gladius and charged toward them, but knew I wouldn't get there in time before the thing was on top my friend. I prayed that Paetus could fend it off for just two seconds. But the way he landed and didn't move...I only hoped the monster needed time to open its mouth wide like it had me, rather than immediately rip out Paetus's throat with its ragged hands.

An arrow appeared in the monster's neck, then another in its ear. The undead stopped its shamble toward Paetus and swatted at the arrows as if they were bees. Two more arrows sprouted from its chest, and one ricocheted off the gravelly road near its feet.

The arrows didn't kill the monster, but they gave me the two seconds I prayed for. I wound up my gladius swing like Gaius Blohm in the '11 World Series. The undead turned to me the instant I brought my swing around. That made me miss its neck but I sheared off the top half of the creature's head in an explosion of black blood and pus. The undead crumpled to the ground, and the daemonic pus sizzled and evaporated from its half-head.

I stood staring at the undead creature's remains with clinical detachment. So it wasn't magic that animated them, but daemon possession? That was interesting; I had always assumed undead were magical constructs. They weren't completely like the strix then—

Alishat cried out from behind me and rushed over to Elissa, who still lay on the ground breathing heavily and staring at the undead that had attacked her. Both girls hugged each other tightly. Paetus had already caught his breath and was sitting up. He grimaced at his black blood covered hands and wiped them on his tunica.

I blinked. My first thought should have been to see if they were all right, and there I was contemplating the engineering aspects of undead.

Where was my empathy?

The heavy gates shuddered and began to creak open far enough to allow four men to hurry out. They wore tunicas and carried short swords, but none wore the armor of legionaries. The man in the lead, with a balding head and a steel-gray beard that hung over his neck, ran over to the girls.

"Alishat? Elissa?" he cried, and then scooped them up in his large forearms. All three of them clutched each other, crying their tears of joy and relief. They spoke mostly in Punic, but I got the gist that this man was Uncle Danel. Yes, my powers of perception are boundless.

One of the men behind Danel eyed the road warily. "Dominus, we should get inside," he said with a shaky voice.

Danel nodded abruptly and said, "Come, come, my dears." He led them toward the open gate.

I helped Paetus up off the ground with one hand. Then Cana, he, and I followed the rest of them toward the gate.

But the three men with swords barred our entry.

"Hey," I said.

Danel turned to us, and his eyes turned from joyful to cold in an instant. "These are evil times," he said in the same accented Latin as Elissa and Alishat. "I do not know you, so I cannot let you into my home. I am sorry."

"Uncle," Elissa said, shocked. "We would not be alive if not for these three. You must let them in!"

Her uncle pointed to the decapitated bodies of the undead creatures. "The se...things were my friends. They came here tonight. I was about to let *them* in before I saw what they had turned into." He shook his head sadly as he stared at me. "I do not know you. I must protect my family and my property. Go inside and— Ali!"

Alishat slipped through Danel's grip, ran between the surprised slaves, and toward me. She slammed into me and wrapped her arms tightly around my waist.

Well I was just as surprised as everyone else.

"Ali," Danel said sternly, "you must come inside. It is not safe out here."

"If they cannot come in, then I will not go in," she said fiercely.

Danel glared at me and gripped his sword dangerously. The last thing I wanted now was to fight this guy. Not because I might die, but because I would win. My hold on my soul magic was tenuous at best. All I needed was the pain of an arrow in my shoulder by one of his archers—which, from experience, hurts a lot—to distract me enough to release it.

I hugged Alishat back and said loud enough for her and Danel to hear, "Thank you, Alishat. But you should listen to your uncle. Go inside where it's safe. We have things to do anyway."

"No," she said, and hugged me tighter.

Elissa pulled away from Danel too, and strode to Cana, Paetus, and me. She turned back defiantly to her uncle. "They are our friends. We will not leave them behind."

Danel exhaled with frustration. "I am your dead mother's brother. Your father is also dead, so that makes me your *paterfamilias*. You will obey me, girl."

Elissa shook her head. "I love you, uncle. But I will not obey you in this matter."

Danel shifted his eyes to the sky and muttered something in Punic.

A mournful cry arose from beyond the hill that we had crossed to get to this farm. At first I thought it was someone crying out their grief over dead loved ones or the burning city. But the cry turned into an inhuman shriek that could not have been made by a human throat. The shriek was answered by several more from the hills in the opposite direction. The entire valley seemed to echo with answering shrieks. It raised the hairs all over my body.

The wary slave next to Danel said, "Dominus, we must—"

"I know, Pilo!" he snapped. Then he turned to us. "Fine. They may enter, but they will be locked in the wine cellar until dawn. That is my only off—"

"We'll take it," I said, hurrying toward the gate. I let Elissa lead the way into the complex. Alishat walked beside me holding my hand. Their protection was stronger than any armor I could've worn against the armed slaves and Danel's smoldering glare.

33

Danel was true to his word: He locked Cana, Paetus, and me in the wine cellar as soon as we entered his villa complex. The horrible shrieks continued outside the stucco walls and were getting closer. Once we got inside, I noticed a couple dozen archers manning the ramparts surrounding the interior of the walls. Each archer had a long spear nearby, leaning against the wall, and I saw the glint of swords at their belts.

"We can help," I told Danel as he marched us toward the cellar.

"We do not need your help," he growled.

"Uncle," Elissa said, "he is a magus. He can—"

"*We* know how to fight these creatures," Danel said firmly. We arrived at the wine cellar door. It was basically a heavy wooden door fastened at a forty-five degree angle to a small hill. He swung open the door and motioned us inside. Sandstone steps led down into pitch-blackness.

"Get in. Now." He held is curved short sword at his side, but its tip was pointed at me.

"Uncle, please," Elissa said again.

He glanced at her, then back to me. In a less gruff tone, he said, "If you are what my niece says you are then I will accept your help. But not until the morning. Not until I am *sure*. Do you understand?"

I nodded once. He was trying to protect his family and his people. I got it. Didn't mean I liked being treated like a daemon, but I got it.

I turned and tentatively took each cellar step by feeling it with my toes and holding my hands out to either side of the cement walls. Cana and Paetus followed me down. As soon as Paetus's head had cleared the door, it slammed shut behind us, and I heard a heavy bar slide into place on top of it.

As soon as the door shut, I siphoned a small spark globe above my right hand. In the ethereal white light, I saw that the bottom was three steps away.

I stepped down into a typical wine cellar: a ten by ten foot room with labeled wooden barrels stacked against each wall.

"Well it's better than sitting outside," Paetus said. He went over to one of the barrels and read the label. He snorted. "I know this brand. An excellent rose wine, among Africa's best."

"Perhaps we should open a barrel," Cana said, leaning against one and slipping down to the floor. She looked exhausted. "We will have our drinks and then spill the rest onto the floor as payment for his hospitality."

More inhuman shrieks came through the barred cellar door. My whole body was tense and hummed with a desire to *do something*. The daemons—whatever they were—must have been attacking the farm's walls by now. I prayed that Danel was right and he did know how to fight the creatures.

I glanced at Cana and Paetus in the spark globe's meager light. They too stared nervously at the cellar doors.

"I don't blame him," I said, even though I wasn't feeling magnanimous at the moment. "We don't know what's happened over the last few days. It must've been awful."

Paetus sat down across from Cana and leaned his head against the barrel. "I don't know how we'll get to Alexandria now. The harbor was filled with wrecked and burning ships. And smoke obscured the docks. I couldn't see if any galleys still survived."

I was too wound up to sit down, so I paced the floor. "We have the cloak," I muttered. "We may not even need to go to Alexandria now."

A man screamed, and then his scream ended abruptly. Several shrieks arose which sounded disturbingly like daemonic celebration. Then that was cut short, and a cheer arose from the men lining the walls. The daemons must've either been defeated or ran away. Regardless, the battle sounded over.

Paetus and Cana stared glassy-eyed at the cellar door as if they hadn't heard me. We all needed sleep if we were to survive the next few days, but we sure weren't going to get it while listening for another daemon attack.

I took off my pack and pulled out the teddy bear artifact. Its stone eyes glittered in the light of my spark globe. I got the sense they would've glittered even in the darkness. I didn't know how far its effects would reach, but I figured it was worth a try.

I siphoned a healthy dose of cell magic into it...and the fear and worry drained from my body. Comfort, warmth, and an absolute certainty that I was safe replaced it all. I hadn't known how scared I was until that artifact took it all away. I wanted to weep at how peaceful I suddenly felt.

I saw that Cana and Paetus felt the same. They both leaned their heads back and closed their eyes, their breathing slow and relaxed. In an instant, their expressions had gone from wide-eyed terror directed at the cellar door to the contentedness of a sleeping infant.

I figured they had the right idea. I slumped down against another barrel and cradled the teddy bear in my arms like a toddler. I heard an occasional, far-off inhuman shriek outside, but I didn't care. With all the worry drained from me, my body had nothing to keep it wired and pacing.

I was asleep in moments.

34

The cellar door flung open, startling me awake. Instinct rather than conscious thought made me jump to my feet. I squinted in the brilliant daylight flooding down the steps and then extinguished my spark globe, which was still hovering in the middle of the cellar. Cana and Paetus had also jumped up by the time my spark globe dissipated into dim vapor.

Several men came down the stairs with swords pointed at us. One of the men, the wary slave that didn't like being outside the gates last night, motioned me up the steps with his sword.

"Come," he said. "Now." The slave and his men backed up the steps with their swords still pointed at us.

I raised my hands and then followed them up with Cana and Paetus behind me.

The brilliant daylight actually wasn't so brilliant once my eyes adjusted. I couldn't see the flames of Carthage to the east over the villa walls, but I did see the black, smoky pall covering the eastern horizon. The dawn sun shone through the smoke as a weak, pale orb. The stench of a multitude of burning things—wood and flesh—hung in the air.

I did get a better look at Danel's villa. The courtyard was about fifty paces wide and long with stucco walls about twelve feet high surrounding the entire complex. I counted six archers standing on the rickety wooden ramparts along the walls. The men looked fairly relaxed, though watchful. To my right was a stable and storage barn for farming equipment. To my left stood the main family residence, a two-story building with a nice columned porch at the front. Behind the residence I noticed a long building with several doors, which I figured to be the slave quarters. All the buildings had the classic red tile roofs of ancient Rome.

The slaves prodded us to the center of the courtyard. Danel strode between his men and stopped within three paces of me. He inspected me as if I were a cow in the forum. Then he studied Cana and Paetus the same way. Cana returned his stare defiantly, while Paetus's eyes were on a small building behind Danel.

Danel turned and looked at the pale sun in the east and then looked back at us with narrowed eyes. He grunted once, and said, "Forgive me my caution, Natta Magus. The creatures do not like daylight. You have not burst into jelly yet, so you must be human."

"Lucky me," I said. "But how did you know Elissa and Alishat weren't 'creatures'?"

"I did not."

"What would you have done if—?"

"I would have killed them," he said simply. "But they survived until the dawn locked in comfortable rooms in my house. They are still my beloved nieces, and you are now my guests. I only wish I could give you better accommodations. My wife usually..." He trailed off and his tired eyes wandered to the eastern horizon. He sighed once and then said, "Come, I have food."

He turned and led us toward the main residence.

I smelled fresh bread over the ever-present smoke as soon as we entered Danel's house. He led us through an atrium that was decorated with a mishmash of Roman and Carthaginian styles. Ceramic tilework on the walls depicting lions and ostriches competed with geometric Roman tilework on the floors. A stone goat's head sat in an alcove next to another alcove, where there stood a painted statue of a goddess dressed in a multi-layered stola and braided hair. Like most wealthy Roman homes I've visited, a circular *impluvium* pool sat in the middle of the atrium with a tiled bottom beneath the clear water.

I saw an open doorway off the atrium. The room beyond held shelves of books, scrolls, and tablets illuminated by a brazier upon a writing desk. Paetus noticed it at the same time as me, and his eyes alit with interest. "You have many books, sir," he said to Danel.

Danel lifted his chin. "I have the largest collection outside of Carthage. They are mostly histories and religious practices of Rome and old Carthage. I am a recognized priest of Jupiter *and* Ba'al."

It was still strange for me when I heard someone say they followed two different religions. In the twenty-first century, this was highly contradictory behavior, to say the least. Here, nobody even shrugged. The Romans never disputed the *existence* of foreign gods and were even fine with conquered peoples retaining their religious practices. Just so long as they paid their taxes on time.

I saw Alishat at the same time she saw me. I must've looked and smelled like I'd just crawled out of the Cloaca Maxima, but nonetheless, Alishat ran over with a large smile and hugged me the same way she had last night. Elissa walked behind her with a smile of her own. Both had changed out of the dirty, bloody clothes they had worn since the shipwreck and now wore vibrantly colored stolas.

"I knew there was a kid somewhere under all that dirt," I said, grinning down at her.

"I am glad to see you all well," Elissa said to the three of us. She gave her uncle a matronly frown. "And I am relieved that my uncle declared you human."

One corner of Danel's mouth upturned in a smile, but he said nothing.

"We made bread," Alishat declared. "And my uncle has dates and olives and cheese, too!"

My stomach rumbled with undignified passion. "Sounds glorious," I said. Alishat turned and tugged my hand toward the kitchen.

A long wooden table with benches on either side took up most of the kitchen. A brick oven occupied one corner while workbenches topped with cooking tools and basins sat beside the oven. Several loafs of Alishat's fresh baked flatbread sat on a platter on one end of the table, along with small platters of olives, dates, and cheeses. Little bowls of olive oil sat next to pitchers of watered down wine.

"Please sit and eat," Danel said. "I will have baths prepared for you." Danel then left the kitchen through a door that led outside.

At that moment, I didn't know which I wanted more, the food or the bath. Well, the food was in front of me, so I dug in.

After days of eating legionary hardtack, just about anything fresh would've tasted like ambrosia. This food may have been simple fare, but by all the gods, I'd never tasted anything so good. The flatbread was warm and soft, the dates were sweet, the olives salty and spicy, and the cheese was soft enough to spread.

"I am sorry we could not make more," Elissa said, as if this feast were scraps from the gutter. "Uncle Danel says we must conserve food if the legions do not come and drive away the creatures soon."

"How did the battle go last night?" I asked through mouthfuls of bread.

"Uncle barred the door to our room on the second floor the whole night," she said. "But we could still see the battle through the window. I could not see the creatures clearly, but they had a long reach and even grabbed one of the men off the ramparts." She shuddered. "We did not watch after that. I did not think we would ever fall asleep, but soon after the creatures took the man...Alishat and I suddenly felt very content. We both fell asleep quickly after the battle. I cannot explain it."

Cana gave me a sharp look. Paetus did, too, while he shoved more dates into his mouth. It seemed my new teddy bear had a considerable range. I had wondered belatedly this morning if the bear's magic would've taken away the fear—and thus the fighting spirit—from the men on the ramparts. Apparently, that didn't happen, considering we were still around.

"Uncle woke us both up at dawn and brought us down into the sunlight," Elissa said. "After ensuring we were human, he asked us to bake some bread."

"And thank Fortuna he did," I said, swallowing a piece dipped in olive oil. "It's excellent."

Danel returned through the kitchen door and sat down wearily. He put his elbows on the table and leaned on them, and I expected him to fall asleep at any moment. "Your baths will be ready soon," he muttered. He stared at the food without any hunger in his eyes, as if it were a pile of gravel.

"When did all this begin?" I asked him.

He continued to stare at the food. I was about to ask him again, but he said, "I first knew something was wrong a week ago. I found slaughtered sheep within their pens, but no evidence that an animal had broken through. And they were not just slaughtered—they were chopped to pieces. Barely recognizable but for their wool mixed in. I had heard nothing in the night, nor did any of my slaves. So I set a watch the next night, two men I trusted. The next morning, I had lost six sheep, and the two slaves were gone. I thought they had stolen the sheep and killed the first few, so I was going to send for the legionaries the next day, but the slaves came back that night...as the creatures who attacked you last night."

He plucked an olive from the platter, but he just studied it.

"We beheaded them after they attacked and then burned their bodies. The next night, more creatures arrived wearing the faces of my neighbors to the north, the *paterfamilias* of the Iuventii. He was with his wife, two young sons, and three slaves. He begged to be let inside my gates. So I let him and his people in."

Danel squeezed the olive, crushing it between his thumb and forefinger.

"They had looked normal when they were outside. But after they entered, they all changed. They all became monsters. I lost six more men to their teeth and claws. We killed all but one of the boys. We chained him in the courtyard, for I wanted to question him to find out what he and his family had become. But when the morning sun arose, he made screams and sounds that could not have come from a human throat. And then he melted before our eyes. As did the bodies of his family who we had not yet burned."

He looked up at me with eyes that had seen far too much of the unbelievable in too short of a time.

"So you see why I did not trust you last night."

All I could do was nod. Elissa and Alishat had watched their uncle while he told his tale with wide eyes.

He picked up another olive and stared at it. "Carthage began burning two nights ago. And more creatures came, more frightening and terrible than the night before. Some did not even look human anymore. Like the ones we fought last night."

"Last night," I said, finding my voice again, "did anything seem different about the battle? Like the way you felt while fighting? Or perhaps a difference in the monsters?"

He crushed the second olive again and dropped it on the platter. "Yes. After the battle where Pino was killed, we all regained a sense of courage that we had not felt since this all started. At least that is what I felt. I have not questioned all my men about it, but I could see it in their eyes. A few more monsters attacked the walls later, but my men did not waver or recoil. I do not know if we had found strength or the strength of the monsters had diminished, but we won the night. After Pino fell, I thought the gods had abandoned us. But looking back, perhaps Pino's sacrifice gained the favor of Mars, who gave us the resolve we needed to prevail."

I'd been so focused on Danel's story that I hadn't even noticed when Paetus had pulled out his clay tablet and was scribbling notes. Cana listened to Danel as intently as I had. When Danel described his sudden "resolve," she raised an eyebrow at me.

That teddy bear did have a considerable range, and it seemed to affect people in different ways. Last night my team and I—and apparently Elissa and Alishat—had needed sleep above all else, and it gave it to us. Danel and his men had needed courage, so that's what they got. And the monsters attacking the walls had been diminished enough for the Carthaginians to push them back. They must've been made from earthly elements, for they had not withered to something playful like the fear daemon.

Regardless, I was hanging on to that bear.

"My nieces have told me what you did for them. They also told me of Juba."

I nodded, my full stomach rising as I remembered his body and what I did after. "I wish I could've saved him."

Danel sighed. "He fought to save his sisters from those Roman pigs. His death was honorable. My nieces say you have powerful magic."

I glanced at them warily. Elissa quickly said, "We spoke of how you can heal with a word and a touch. And how you hid us from the pirates in the water and during our escape from the Romans."

Whew. If Danel knew that I could snap at any moment and kill everyone here, he'd probably cast me outside no matter what I'd done for his nieces. And I really wanted that bath.

"I must ask a great thing of you," Danel said. His exhausted eyes held my gaze in a firm, desperate grip. "I must ask that you protect my family when we flee this farm tonight."

35

I sunk up to my neck in the warm bath water and let a week's worth of grime and tension float away. Danel's bathhouse had a ten-by-ten foot smooth stone tub set into the ground. Submerged stone benches lined the walls of the tub. I sat at one end while Paetus sat at the other, sighing with the same contentedness that I felt. I was almost as relaxed as with the stuffed bear.

Cana was next door in the women's bath with Elissa and Alishat. Most baths and lavatories were mixed gender in Augustan Rome, but Danel's house was built for the more traditional separation.

I kept my Wolverines cap, gladius, and components vest within arm's reach.

"What are you going to tell Danel?" Paetus asked, his eyes closed and his head leaning on a towel propped against the edge of the pool.

"Can't I just soak here a few minutes before thinking about work?" I grumbled.

"Work?" He snorted. "Have you reopened your 'magus-for-hire' shop? Are you a merchant now?"

"You know what I mean. I just want to take my bath and think about it later."

"Your decision won't be any easier after this bath."

"Paetus."

"Yes."

"Shut up."

He closed his mouth.

I soaked and tried clearing my mind so I could meditate for the first time in weeks. I needed that fresh mind for the decision I had to make. But every time I closed my eyes, I saw the fear daemon chasing Helva, Silanus, and me through the underworld forest. Then I caught glimpses of Rullus's stabbed body. And what I did to his legion.

I sighed. "Okay, you saw what I did to the legion. I could snap at any moment and do that same thing again. In fact, leading a group of people through the hell out there almost guarantees that I *will* do it again. There are plenty of daemons out there to trigger me. So how can I protect these people if I'm the one most likely to kill them?"

Paetus looked at me, his head still leaning against the towel. "What chance do they have if you do *not* help them? Their fields are destroyed, their flocks scattered. They lose at least one man each night. Their food won't last another two weeks. It could be months before Rome sends a legion here to restore order. They are leaving, whether you help them or not."

"Danel wants to walk to Utica. It'll take us at least a day and a night. Who's to say Terentius's daemons haven't destroyed that city, too? Or if they're lurking in the shadows along the way until the sun goes down?"

Paetus shrugged. "Nobody. I certainly don't relish walking all that way. Nor do I relish staying here, for that matter."

"And what about Helva? My focus was to rescue her. I was getting out of the 'save the world' business."

"Why don't you ask *her* what you should do?"

I opened my mouth and then shut it. Why *didn't* I ask Helva? I had the cloak. I could find her again in the underworld. I couldn't bring her out because the cloak was only a communication artifact. But I could give her the situation and ask her what I should do.

Which was absurd. *Hey, Helva, how's the running for your life thing going? Say, listen, should I focus on getting you out of this hellish underworld where you could be flayed alive at any moment, or should I save a bunch of Romans you care nothing about?*

When I first met Helva, she hadn't given a wit about Roman lives. In fact, she was mighty bitter toward Romans considering Augustus had had her family assassinated. But in the end, she had come to learn how to separate regular Romans from the Romans who had wronged her. And had learned that protecting innocent Roman lives was a noble and honorable thing. That's partly why she had rushed into the underworld after her brother during the battle atop the Capitoline.

How could I put that decision on her shoulders? How could I force her to take it off of mine?

Out of all the shameful things I'd done in my life, that would be near the top of the list. Even considering it made me feel like I needed another scrubbing in the bath.

"No," I said. "I have to take responsibility for this one, no matter what I decide."

"Very well. Then what do you think she'd want you to do? I didn't know her as well as you, but I think you know."

I knocked my head gently against the towel with frustration. The bath water was cooling, and I glanced at the fire in the corner that was warming another barrel of water. I knew I could've called one of Danel's slaves to dump the hot water into the tub for me. But I wasn't some patrician dandy who couldn't take care of himself. If I wanted the hot water, I'd feel far more comfortable getting it myself.

And that was what got me into trouble. When I saw that something needed to be done, I couldn't stand around and wait for someone else to do it. My big talk a few days ago about focusing on Helva to the exclusion of all else was just big talk. I'd always known it was, but didn't want to admit it. I had known even then that I'd get involved with stopping Terentius, even if it meant delaying my efforts to help Helva.

Because Terentius had already killed thousands of people and was going to kill many more with his underworld daemons. I was physically incapable of ignoring—

And then one of those moments came upon me when things clicked into place, and I berated myself for being too stupid to notice it before. I loved those moments.

"I know that look," Paetus said. "You're going to do something foolish."

I frowned at him. "I have a look?"

"Yes. You do this thing with your jaw where it moves side to side. You purse your lips, too."

"I had no idea."

"What are you planning?"

I stood up, stepped out of the bath, and used a towel to carry the hot water over to the tub. "First, I'm going to warm up this bath. Then I'm going to sit in it for a few more minutes."

I poured the hot water into the tepid pool and returned the jar to the fire. I slipped back into the tub and sighed.

"And then I'm going to talk to Helva."

36

"So now we *are* going to help?" Cana asked, her hands on her hips. Her hair was still wet from her bath and hung unbraided over her left shoulder.

We had just returned from the baths and were in a spare room in Danel's house. He'd also had our clothes washed, for which I was thankful, but my tunica and breeches were still a bit damp in some uncomfortable places.

I was searching through the artifact pack for the red cloak amidst the aura weapons and various knick-knacks that I'd thrown in with them since the battle with Legio III. I found the cloak at the bottom of the pack below the teddy bear and evergreen glove. I still had no idea what the two bronze torches did and didn't want to mess with them until I could properly study them.

"Will this decision change by dusk?" she asked.

I looked up at her. "I know I've been all over the board lately, but you know I was going to do something eventually."

"Of course. I just hoped that you would come to your senses after we were far away from here and there was nothing you could do. Then you would feel guilty and responsible, and be so distracted that you stop giving me boring magic lectures."

"I don't do that...do I?"

"When was our last lesson?"

Damnation. Some *leraar* I was turning out to be. I *had* been distracted lately, but running for one's life doesn't excuse slacking off from magic lessons.

"When I get back we'll make up for lost time," I promised.

I pulled the red cloak out of the pack just as Paetus entered the room, his curly hair also wet and hanging in his face.

"Do you think Silanus will be with her?" he asked. He said that with a small growl, which coming from Paetus didn't sound all that threatening, but I understood his hatred for Helva's brother. He had, after all, trapped Paetus in his own home with a Dea Tacita daemon.

"If he still lives."

I held the red cloak up by the shoulders, still marveling at its craftsmanship and delicate, but strong material. As with all the Aventicum artifacts, I could only guess at its origins.

"Let's hope not," Paetus murmured.

"And you will not be harmed?" Cana asked me. She was already re-braiding her hair in a jerky, nervous fashion.

"I don't think so," I said. I draped the cloak over my shoulders, which fit like it was made for me. I wondered if it felt like that for everyone who put it on. "My gut tells me this is just a communications artifact, albeit the most powerful one I've ever heard of."

"What if your 'gut' is wrong?"

I thought about Gibber and felt my knees give a little, but I gave her what I hoped was a confident grin. "When has that ever happened?" Before I could work myself up into a nervous frenzy, I draped the hood over my head and said, "See you guys in a few seconds."

Then I closed my eyes and visualized Helva.

I immediately felt a change in my surroundings. I prepared myself to run and then opened my eyes.

I stood in a temple. Around me were shoulder-high pedestals with lamps that burned sweet, flowery incense, the smoke rising to the high ceiling. Rays of sunshine illuminated the temple floor from rectangular openings near the ceiling. The walls of the temple were covered in Egyptian hieroglyphs and colorful paintings. The floors were polished smooth and gleamed in the sunlight.

Helva stood next to me staring straight ahead. She looked exactly the same as when I last saw her running for her life: She wore a black tunica cinched at the waist, a dusty black scarf wrapped around her neck, her soulful brown eyes and high cheekbones tense.

I turned to where she was staring...and wanted to roll my eyes. Silanus sat upon a throne at the front of the temple. He wore the blue and gold headdress of an ancient pharaoh and looked as serene as every pharaoh painting I'd ever seen. He held a curved scepter in his right hand and a ceremonial whip in the left. A man and woman stood near the dais, both wearing lesser crowns, but elaborate nonetheless. They stared up at Silanus with proud, adoring faces. A couple dozen Egyptian priests with shaved heads and white linen tunicas bowed before Silanus.

"You've got to be kidding me," I murmured.

Helva looked sharply at me and her eyes widened. She stared at me for many seconds, a smile gracing one corner of her mouth. She tried to hug me, but she went right through me as if I were mist. I didn't feel anything and silently cursed the cloak's protection. The way she looked at me with that runway model face that she'd inherited from her legendary grandmother made me *really* want to feel that hug.

She cursed once when she went through me and then motioned me behind a smooth stone column. She glanced nervously at Silanus and his worshipers, and said, "I did not think you would return."

"I told you I would. Are you okay?"

She looked at me for what seemed like minutes, and then whispered, "No."

"What's wrong?"

Helva half-turned her head toward Silanus. "I am losing myself. The longer I stay here, the more I forget who I was." She turned back to me. "For a moment, I did not even know who you were, Natta Magus."

To see Helva like this, after knowing her in the real world as strong, resolute, and unflappable, was disturbing to say the least.

"Invidia's tortures grow more awful with each passing year—"

"Year? You've been here for two months. I just saw you a few days ago."

She shook her head slowly. "To me it has been years."

I was an incorporeal being here, but I felt sick. *She had been stuck here for years?* Damnation, it was a wonder she was still sane.

I glanced at Silanus. "Looks like your brother is doing just fine."

Helva stared at him sadly. "No, he is not. *This* is his greatest torture."

As soon as she said that, dozens of armed Roman legionaries burst into the temple, all of them helmed and wearing mail shirts. The kneeling priests cried out and jumped up, but the invading Romans stabbed and hacked at them all. At the throne, Silanus stood and screamed at the Romans, "You are defiling my temple! Stop this at once!"

They didn't listen. In fact, several Romans charged toward the throne. The crowned man and woman who were standing near Silanus stepped in front of the Romans. But the Romans stabbed them several times until their bloodied bodies slumped to the floor without a sound.

Silanus stared at the man and woman, his mouth open in a silent scream. He didn't shy away from the Romans when they strode up the dais. They pulled the scepter and whip from his limp hands and threw them into the pooling blood on the floor. One soldier knocked the headdress off him with a backhanded slap. Then they put his hands in shackles and a steel collar around his neck. They led him away from the slaughter, the entire floor of the temple covered in blood as if it had been painted that way.

The Romans strode past Helva and me like we weren't there. Silanus continued to scream his madness and grief as they pulled him through the temple's dark exit. As soon as they disappeared, a hissing sound slithered from the darkness as if someone were laughing through sharp teeth. The hissing laughter turned to a throaty chuckle and then became a mad sound that nobody could mistake for real laughter.

Shudder was not a strong enough word for what that laughter did to my incorporeal body

I looked back at the terrible slaughter, but didn't let my eyes linger on any of the bodies. However, my gaze stopped on the man and woman near the dais. "Were those your parents?" I asked Helva.

She watched the dark exit into which Silanus had been led. "Not their true souls. Only shades. This is Invidia's work. And it will break Silanus soon."

"Why didn't they take you?"

She blinked away tears. "Because this is *my* torture: To watch my little brother go mad and be unable to stop it."

The horror of all this was so overwhelming. On a conceptual level, I certainly knew that Invidia was the underworld's lead torturer. But to see her work in action...especially on someone I cared about...

The anger swelled in me, but I did not feel the soul magic rise. In fact, I couldn't even feel my cell magic. I didn't know if it was the cloak inhibiting me or whether human magic didn't work in the underworld. Whatever the reason, a part of me was thankful that I could get angry without worrying that soul magic would take over my senses. That alone seemed to relax me enough that I remembered why I was there in the first place.

"Helva," I said firmly.

She turned to me slowly. "Natta Magus? You came back! I did not think you would."

She tried to hug me again, but with the same results as before. And like the first time, she reeled back in shock.

Damnation, I thought as my heart began to break.

"Helva," I said again, "I'm going to get you out of here. You and...Silanus. But I need your help, first. Can you leave this place? Can you go to other places in the underworld?"

She nodded absently and then glanced at the dark exit through which the Romans had taken Silanus. The chilling laughter still echoed from the impenetrable gloom. "But I cannot leave my brother."

I chewed my lip a moment, hating myself for possibly misleading her. "Your brother will be fine without you for a little while. Can you still use your magic here?"

"Yes," she whispered, still watching the exit. "But it does nothing against *her*."

"Do you want to use it again where it *will* do something?"

She slowly turned her head to me. That fiery gleam that I remembered from Rome two months ago had returned to her eyes. Like all magi that I'd ever known or heard of, she loved to use her magic. And Helva especially loved to use her magic when it was a righteous cause she believed in.

"Yes," she half-snarled.

37

Having a mission—besides simply surviving the next moment—seemed to have brought Helva back to the woman who had pledged an Oath to William to protect me. She listened as I recounted events from the moment she leaped into the underworld after Silanus, to the attack on our galley, to Terentius, to the burning of Carthage. I hesitated to tell her about my loss of control and use of soul magic, but she'd known my struggles in Rome and had seen firsthand what it did to William. I told her everything.

As I spoke, and her attention focused on my words, the scene around us shifted and blurred. Strangely it didn't bother me. I was so focused on my story that I only noticed the shifting landscape as one would notice the sun moving across the daytime sky. She asked questions here and there and even smiled at some parts.

When I finished my update, we stood in a tent near the seashore. A warm, refreshing breeze moved the tent flaps, blowing through the entrance and out an exit in the back. The ground was covered in patterned rugs, and cushions were arranged in the middle of the tent around a low table. Upon the table sat sweating metal decanters and cups along with the classic Mediterranean fare of grapes, olives, and flatbread.

Helva and I sat down upon the cushions near the table as if we were old friends catching up. I didn't know why cushions and the ground could support my incorporeal form, and yet I could not touch Helva. But support me they did. I don't remember thinking any of it was strange, which that in itself should've been strange. The underworld really messes with your head, even when you're an incorporeal visitor.

"So this Terentius is a god now?" Helva asked. She poured some chilled wine from the decanter—I didn't even wonder how it had been chilled in the desert!—into a cup and took a drink. I wasn't thirsty or hungry, so I didn't try to drink or eat. It would've fallen through my incorporeal mouth anyway.

"Not technically. He's an *aspect* of a god, which means he has a bit of that god's power, although he was certainly acting like one. All of his servants called him *ba'al*, which based on my rusty Punic means something like 'lord'. I still have no idea how he or Rullus became these aspects. All I know now is that Terentius seems bent on remaking the world into something *else*. And the way he plans to do that is to unleash the underworld onto the earth."

That hissing laughter floated upon the sea breezes, and with it came Silanus's anguished screams.

Helva froze, her cup midway to her mouth. She looked outside the tent entrance toward the waves upon the shore. She remained that way for many moments.

"Helva," I said gently.

She blinked several times and then looked at me. She gave a ragged sigh. "If you were not here, I would have gone back to the temple to witness parents' murders and my brother's torture. I cannot stay away from it for very long before she pulls at me again." She took a long drink of wine and then slammed the cup on the table. "We must leave this place." She looked at me with pleading, glistening eyes that almost broke my heart. "*You must help us escape.*"

I wanted to put my hand on hers, but I knew that wouldn't work. Her mind was hanging on by a series of threads that were snapping one by one.

"I swear to you that I will help you and Silanus," I said, "but first we need to find Terentius here in the underworld. I was hoping you could help with that."

She shut her eyes tightly and sagged into her cushions. I thought I'd lost her, for she stayed like that a long time. I couldn't imagine what tortures she'd endured, never mind the strength it had taken to last for what had been years to her.

But she inhaled deeply, released it slowly, and then opened her eyes. Her shoulders straightened and she sat a bit taller in her cushions.

That kind of will can move nations, I marveled as I watched her regain control. For the first time since this all began, I felt like we might all get through this alive.

"It is simple to travel the underworld and find other souls," she said in a flat, emotionless tone. "The hard part is staying in one place. I am constantly pulled back to my brother. You must keep me distracted from that. We will find Terentius, but then what? What can we do to a god's *aspect?*"

"I don't think there's much we can do with our magic. But the aura weapons of Legio III seemed to hurt Terentius and counter his magic. We found some after I..."

I swallowed. Even in this incorporeal form, I could feel shame and guilt twisting my guts. I welcomed it, though. Normal humans felt guilty for their crimes.

"Cana and Paetus gathered some after we escaped Legio III," I finished.

"Then we use these weapons to kill him."

"No. I doubt we can get close enough to use them on him anyway. My idea, though, is if they can counter his magic, then we can use them to block whatever gateway he's opened to Earth. But I need your help to find that gateway on this end."

She leaned forward. "There is a gateway to Earth in the underworld?" she whispered. Hope entered her eyes. Cautious hope, but hope nonetheless.

I nodded. "There has to be if Terentius is using underworld daemons. If we find it, you can escape and then we'll use Rullus's weapons to destroy the gateway. Cana has the knack for picking apart the weaknesses in magic. Between all of us, we'll figure out a way. I know it's a long shot, but it's the only thing I can think of to stop Terentius *and* get you out of here."

She smiled at me and the sun seemed to shine brighter in the tent. But a shadow came over her just as quickly. "I will not leave without Silanus."

"Yeah. I figured that. So I'll help you get him out."

"Really?" She reached out to put her hand on mine and it slipped right through it like mist. She raised an eyebrow at me and said, "What can you do like this?"

I gave her a sideways grin. "Distract you."

She smiled again and the sun came back. "Thank you, Natta Magus. I have not smiled in a long time."

Silanus's screams floated again to us from the sea and the sand dunes. A mad cackle followed. A little reminder that the underworld did not welcome mirth.

Helva's eyes got that thousand-yard stare again. "It will not be easy to break Invidia's hold on him," she murmured. "He will not even acknowledge me anymore."

I stood, and she blinked away the pulling of Silanus's screams. "If his sister's love won't get his attention, then maybe his hatred for *me* will."

I held my hand out to her as if I could really help her up off the cushioned floor. She gave me a sideways grin of her own, the dimple on her right cheek deepening, and stood by herself.

"If that does not work, then nothing will," she said. "He *really* hates you."

"Excellent. Now how to do we get back to him?"

"Stop speaking and I will be pulled back to him."

I closed my mouth and stared at her, waiting for something to happen.

She stood still several moments, looking around the tent as if waiting for it to disappear and turn into a different room. She frowned and then turned her back to me.

"You are watching me with those nice green eyes," she said. "It is too distracting."

Having a beautiful woman say my eyes were "nice" was damned distracting to me, too, but I said nothing.

The tent began to blur like before, and then it swirled into misty colors that resembled the multi-colored aura surrounding Terentius, Rullus, and their weapons.

I had no time to ponder this because the colors coalesced into the same Egyptian temple in which I'd found Helva and Silanus this time around. He sat atop the same throne as before, wearing the blue and gold headdress and holding the scepter and whip of his royalty. His parents stood nearby, looking up at him with pride and love.

But all the kneeling priests were gone. There was only one figure standing before Silanus this time, and it was facing Helva and me.

It was the crone Invidia.

38

The last time I'd seen Invidia was when she was a giant stampeding across the Capitoline with her army of Dea Tacita daemons. This time she was normal human size, but no less terrifying.

A thin, ragged gray stolla covered her lean, wasted body from head to toe. Her neck and back were hunched, and she squinted at us with black eyes that oozed at the corners. Her open mouth showed jagged teeth and spaces where teeth were missing. I couldn't tell if she was snarling or smiling.

She pointed a clawed finger at me, and that hissing laughter seeped from her blue lips. "You would deny me my vengeance, magus? You and your princess whore?" Her voice was like the snapping of bones on a torturer's rack.

Helva stood frozen, her eyes wide. I got the feeling her mind was somewhere else, enduring unimaginable cruelties. Even with my incorporeal form, glimpses of various tortures raced through my mind, physical and mental anguish tailored just for me. This was the revenge goddess, and she knew that one torture would not break everyone. But everyone could be broken with the *right* torture.

I shook my head and tried to think of pleasant things: the sun setting over the sea, holding Vitulus's newborn son, Helva's smile...

I looked back at Invidia. "You cannot keep him here forever," I said, trying to infuse as much boldness into my voice as I could. I'm not sure I could've maintained that boldness had I not been wearing the red cloak. But I was, and there wasn't a damned thing this witch could do to me.

At least that's what I kept telling myself.

She cackled and my mind wanted to shatter with the awfulness of it. "Why not? I am a goddess. He is a mortal, and he presumed to shackle *me* with his magic? Restitution must be made; revenge will be taken."

"Haven't you taken enough revenge?"

That brought huge guffaws of laughter that were as close to actual mirth as an evil revenge goddess could imitate. "'Enough'? Not near enough, little magus. I will break his mind and devour his soul and then vomit him back up to play with him some more. This is my realm. *I* am the queen here. He will *never* leave."

I looked at Helva. She continued to stare straight ahead, frozen in the revenge goddess's presence.

"What about Helva?" I said. "You have no claim on her."

She cackled again, and I wanted to rip my ears off to get away from that sound.

"No, I do not," Invidia said. "She's here because she *wants* to be. Or is under the delusion she can rescue her brother from my claws. She can try, but she will only gain the same madness as her brother for her efforts."

I grimaced. Well that was about what I expected, but confirmation did nothing to help me now. Helva would endure those tortures before she left her brother behind. While I admired her loyalty to her only family, it was damned inconvenient for the rest of the world. All existence, for that matter.

All existence. Everything was threatened by Terentius's plan.

Ah.

I bowed. "You are most generous, my lady. Then I will be taking my leave of you. I have important tasks to perform and must not delay. Even the fate of the underworld is at stake."

Invidia snorted, thick mucus flying out of her nose. "You think highly of yourself, little magus. Perhaps there is a soul on Earth who hates your arrogance...who plots revenge against you. Perhaps you will join your friend in my domain one day."

I shuddered and had to keep reminding myself that I wasn't really here. That I was just a spirit with a body firmly grounded on Earth. But the thought of Invidia getting her claws into me...

"Nah, everyone loves me. But as to my tasks, they are *very* important. There is a man who seeks to merge the earthly and spirit realms. I need Helva's assistance to stop him, but alas, she will not leave her brother here. So I may fail and all of existence will be remade to this man's vision."

Invidia gave a mad cackle at that. "No *man* is that powerful. Not even Jupiter and all his court could do such a thing. You speak fancies to me so that you can trick me into releasing your friend. Do you not think I can see lies in my own realm? It will not work, little magus."

She began to grow taller then, and a black cloud swirled around her feet. Even in my spirit form, I could feel reality closing in around me like a pillow over my head.

"In fact," she said. Her voice grew deeper and vibrated my spirit body to the point that I thought it was going to fly apart. "I take great offense at your presumption that one such as you can trick *me*. Perhaps I will take your princess as compensation."

"No, wait!" I said through gritted teeth. *Damnation, what was I thinking trying to trick a goddess into letting Silanus go.* Even a mad goddess like Invidia would have enough wits in her own realm to see through such a ruse. And now my attempts at trickery might trap Helva in the same insane hell as her brother.

"Wait!" I shouted again. "I speak the truth about this man. He will destroy everything if he's not stopped, including you and your realm."

The feeling that my very atoms were being torn asunder continued to grow and the pain with it. I began to scream. I fell to the ground in spasms, unable to even reach up to my hood and pull it down to escape. What would happen to me if my spirit here were destroyed?

Just as I thought my spirit body would explode, the pain suddenly stopped. There was a scream on my lips as the pain left me, and it too trailed away. I had closed my eyes at some point, so I opened them again.

I was still in the temple, and everyone was still in the same position as before, but now Invidia was normal size again, and she stared down at me with shrewd, assessing eyes. There wasn't a hint of the madness or cruelty that had reeked from her earlier. In fact, those eyes seemed to hold an infinite intelligence that staggered me almost as much as her torture. There was a piece of the Unknowable Will in those eyes.

And I felt like she was a judge about to pass sentence on me.

"I know you speak the truth, magus," she said in a clear *sane* voice. For some reason, that scared me more than the cackle. "I am aware of Terentius and his ilk. All the gods are."

I slowly stood. Helva continued to stare straight ahead. I didn't know if she was truly frozen or even aware of what was happening around her.

"Then why don't you do something?" I asked. "And why the hell did you just torture me?"

She smirked. "I *am* the revenge goddess. You insulted me, ergo, you needed a lesson." Her black eyes flared blue, and in that moment, I felt that same agony again. I flinched, but it was gone by the time my flinch ended. "But do not take my sudden change in demeanor as permission for impudence."

I bowed my head. "No, my lady."

She glared at me down her long, crooked nose, and then said, "Better. As to your first question, we *have* done something. We sent Rullus to kill Terentius. But he failed."

"*The gods* sent Rullus?"

"In a sense. There are rules that even we must follow. We manipulated the portents and auspices that Augustus's flamens read. They told Augustus what they saw, and then Augustus carried out our will."

"So you can't get directly involved? Not even on this side of things?"

Invidia straightened her back and locked her hands behind her back as if she were a commander addressing her troops. "Especially on this side of things."

"But you're gods," I said, growing frustrated. "I thought you could do anything."

"Careful, little magus," Invidia growled. "Your impudence grows…"

I snapped my mouth shut, but my frustration kept me from the bowing and the "so sorry, my lady" thing.

"These rules that govern us were not set up by us," Invidia said. "There is one greater than us who did that."

I stared at her. "The Unknowable Will?"

She smirked. "It has had many different names and will continue to do so as long as humans are around to name it." Then the smirk left her face. "That is, unless Terentius's madness wins."

You know something is bad when even the revenge goddess thinks it's madness.

"So what can we do?"

"'We'?" She snorted. "*You* must remedy this. *I* cannot get involved directly as I've just explained. Nor my brothers and sisters."

Typical… "If that's the case, then what kind of help *can* you give me? I can't do it on my own. That's why I'm here for Helva and Silanus."

She leered at me, a hint of her previous madness contorting her face. "You may have Silanus and thus Helva for this task, but Silanus will return to me afterward. That is the *only* assistance I can give."

I frowned. "What if he doesn't choose to come back? If we survive this task, that is."

She bared her jagged teeth. "The survival of your physical bodies is irrelevant. But you will convince him. Or I will be waiting for all *three* of you at the scales of Ma'at upon your deaths. And my vengeance upon you for breaking this bargain will not be swift. It will last for all eternity."

"My lady," I said hesitantly, "I do not think that is much motivation for Silanus to help us. He is not someone who does something because it is right. He does things for his own benefit. He must have some reward."

She cocked her gruesome head. "His reward will be knowing that his sister will not share his fate. This is my bargain, little magus. Take it or be gone."

She pointed a crooked finger at me. I felt that terrible disintegration begin again, and I knew I only had seconds to accept the bargain or be obliterated.

"Deal," I grunted.

The torture ceased and Invidia smiled at me. I shuddered.

"Excellent," she said. "I look forward to our next meeting, little magus."

And then she disappeared.

When she did, Helva began moving again. She looked around the empty temple and then at me. "This is different from before," she said.

"Helva?" Silanus said from the throne. He was looking at her with wide eyes. He jumped off his throne, threw down the scepter and whip, and ran over to her. "We must leave before the Romans get here. They will kill us!"

He suddenly noticed me, and his face twisted in anger. "Why are you here? We don't need your help."

"Too late," I said. "I just spoke with Invidia, and we came to an understanding. You're free, but you're right, we should leave before she changes her mind."

I didn't want to explain her conditions of freedom because I wasn't sure he'd even want to help.

He narrowed his eyes at me. "Why would she do that?"

"Because she wants to stop Terentius just as much as we do, but she can't do it on her own." I heard several dozen footfalls coming from the dark tunnel behind us. "Can we talk about this later?"

Silanus looked at Helva, and she said, "I will explain it all later, brother."

He sniffed once, and then nodded. Silanus and Helva grasped their hands, and they both took one last look at their parents standing blank-faced near the throne.

The temple room swirled.

39

Helva and Silanus took me to a brick house with a thatch roof. It sat upon a small bluff above a quick flowing, muddy river that gurgled over fallen tree limbs. The soil around the river looked fertile: Wheat stalks grew there in neat rows. Palm trees and green reeds lined the riverbanks. Above the river's floodplains, though, was dry gravel and rocky hills. The house looked well tended and even had purple lotus and white lilies growing around the sides. Three wicker stools stood against the brick wall beneath the shade of the overhanging thatch. The entire scene was idyllic and peaceful.

"What is this place?" I asked them.

Silanus ignored me and strode down a worn path toward the river. Helva stared after her brother a moment, and said, "This is where William taught us magic."

I looked around again. "You mean the *actual* place? We're not in the underworld anymore?"

She nodded wearily. "Invidia allows us to come here when she's not toying with us. We can use our earth magic to heal ourselves and regain our strength." She went to a stool, sat down, and leaned her head against the brick house. "It helps us endure her tortures longer and thus increase her pleasure. We stay here until she pulls us back or if we walk a quarter of a mile in any direction from this house."

I reached a tentative hand to touch Helva's shoulder and my hand passed through her like before. She gave me a sad grin. *Damnation, I'm still in spirt form.* It seemed the cloak worked the same whether I was communicating with someone in the real world or underworld. *Noted.*

I sat down on the stool next to Helva. While I did not feel Helva's physical weariness, I certainly shared her mental fatigue.

"What was the bargain?" she asked, staring after her brother. He had removed his shirt and was bathing in the river.

I bit my lip. She had been here too long. She understood Invidia far better than I did. Helva knew Invidia would never let Silanus go out of the kindness of her heart. If she even had a heart.

But what if the bargain I had struck with Invidia didn't motivate Helva, much less Silanus, to help me stop Terentius?

I sighed. I'd have to tell her sooner or later. She'd figure it out long before we tangled with Terentius. And if she had to figure it out on her own, she'd only be angrier with me.

"Silanus is on parole," I said. "Once we've defeated Terentius, Silanus must return to Invidia."

She nodded, as if expecting that. "And if he doesn't?"

I swallowed. "She will take you and me upon our deaths after we're judged."

She nodded again. It seemed like I was only confirming what she already knew.

"Will Silanus still help us?" I asked.

She watched him dunk his head in the water and begin swimming upriver against the powerful current.

"Silanus is very angry," she said. "Invidia's tortures may have only enraged him further. The only reason, I believe, that he still has his mind is because of me. He may help us or he may not."

"That's not good enough," I said. "His existence is at stake too."

She looked at me. "Which would you prefer: oblivion or Invidia's tortures?"

I clicked my teeth. "Good point. What do we tell him?"

"He already knows he is not truly free. How can he not?"

Silanus swam about fifty paces upriver and then floated on his back downriver toward where he entered. He did it twice more before he stepped out of the river, shook the water from his hair, grabbed his tunica, and strode up the path toward us.

When he arrived, he asked, "What was the bargain for my release, Natta Magus?" He used his tunica to dry off his wet black hair. The guy had spent years—from his perspective—in the underworld and he still had a chest and shoulders like Atlas. *Bastard.* "From your silence, I presume it was not one to my liking."

I glanced at Helva, and she lifted an eyebrow. Like Helva, I knew he'd figure it all out sooner rather than later, so I told him.

He shrugged and said, "I will do this thing."

I stared at him. "Why?"

"Suspicious of my motives, Natta Magus?"

"Well, yeah. You only tried to kill me umpteen times and destroy the city of Rome with revenge daemons. Why *wouldn't* I think you'd rather destroy all of existence than help me?"

He sniffed, draped his tunica over one shoulder, and then aimed his palms toward the earth.

I instinctively tried siphoning my cell magic before realizing it wouldn't work without a body of cells to draw from.

But he didn't attack. His voice took on a reverberating tone as he used his earth magic to infuse his words. "I swear to help my sister Helva and Natta Magus stop Terentius from destroying all of existence."

Then he grabbed his tunica and began drying his hair again.

He'd just sworn an Oath, with a capital "O." I could see the Oath imprint itself onto his aura, which he allowed me to see for the first time. It had a desert tan haze, like Helva's, but with green swirls. He wasn't physically prevented from breaking the Oath, but doing so would diminish his magic. And Silanus was the type of guy who didn't want to give up any more power than he had to.

After his hair was sufficiently dry, he spread his wet tunica on a soft patch of soil in front of the brick house and lay down on it as if he were on vacation. He closed his eyes and soaked up the sun.

"He will help us," Helva said sternly, and I wasn't sure if she was speaking to me or Silanus. "That is all we need to know."

I wanted to know more, but knew I'd have to settle for what I needed.

40

After Silanus finished working on his tan, we prepared ourselves to go find Terentius and his gateway. Preparations for an underworld mission were not like preparations for one in the physical world.

For one, we didn't have to worry about packing enough food and water. Helva and Silanus's physical bodies would be there, but the underworld seemed to alleviate their need for sustenance, unless of course, that was part of Invidia's tortures. And I was here in spirit form. Sometimes I felt my stomach rumble, but that was only because I thought I *should* be hungry after spending over a day without food or drink.

Second, none of us could wield magic there, so we didn't need to prepare any components or meditate to focus our energies. Our wits alone would have to suffice.

No, our preparations involved arguing over chess.

Since Silanus and I never finished the game back in my shop on the Aventine Hill before he tried to kill me, he suggested we do so as a way to mentally prepare for the fight ahead. He had a crude board with hand carved pieces inside the brick house, which somehow had already been set up in the exact position on which we had stopped playing and started fighting. He even offered to move the pieces for me, considering my hand just passed through them.

This time, it only took three moves before we started fighting.

"You always castle before move ten," Silanus growled at me from across the board. "You need to move your king to safety before your opponent's pieces can attack it. It is common sense."

"Then William must've really gone mad by the time he taught you this game," I said, my own voice rising. "Because the William *I* knew taught me that the *board* dictates when you castle. And if the board says don't castle, then by damnation you don't castle."

"*I* make the board *and* my opponent do what I want them to do. Castling early gives me the freedom to attack without worrying about being attacked. That is how I win the game."

"Sometimes you can't force your opponent to do what you want him to do. Sometimes you have to take a few punches to let him think he's winning. Then you strike at him when he thinks he has you trapped. When you castle too early, sometimes you take away the flexibility of that sucker punch."

"You are a fool, Natta Magus," Silanus said.

"That's how this fool beat you on the Capitoline."

Silanus grew very still. I figured his next move would've been to shove the chess pieces down my throat, if he could have. I probably wouldn't have been so brave if I had a corporeal body.

Helva sighed from the table next to us where she was polishing and sharpening a long dagger. "I thought this game was supposed to relax you."

I continued to glare at Silanus. "She's right, this is a waste of time. I don't care about your issues with me. All I care about is whether you're going to keep your promise to help us when the time comes. Will you, Silanus?"

"I have never broken an Oath," he said quietly. "I will help you defeat Terentius. And afterwards, before Invidia takes me back, you and I will finish our...game."

Before I could come up with a badass reply, he stood up and went to a hook on the wall where a sheathed sword hung. He pulled the sword out of the sheath and examined the curved blade. It gleamed and had the same razor edge as Helva's dagger. He glanced at me and then swung it a few times in a masterly fashion. Then he strode out the door and into the sun.

"Show off," I muttered.

"You can trust him," Helva said, standing and sheathing her dagger. "At least as far as his Oath to stop Terentius. We will deal with his promise to *you* later."

"Actually his promise makes me feel a little better. I figured he'd choose killing me and suffering Invidia's eternal tortures over entering oblivion knowing I bested him. So this chess game *was* a good idea. It reminded him of that."

Helva sighed again and left the house. I followed.

The three of us stood outside the brick hut for a moment, reveling in the tranquility of the scene. Helva and Silanus nostalgically scanned the house, the river, and the rows of crops growing in the floodplains. I just lifted my head and faced the sun, soaking it in like Silanus had done before. Despite the apparent location of our refuge somewhere in Lower Egypt, the sun was not harsh like it would have been on my physical body; on my spirit body, it was warm and nourishing.

In the coming years, I would think often on that last moment of peace.

I looked at both Helva and Silanus. "So you're sure you can get us near Terentius but not, like, *right* in front of him?"

"We have done this before, Natta Magus," Silanus said in a suffering tone. He held his hand out to Helva, and she took it.

"Because that would be awkward," I said, "not to mention deadly."

"We know his full name and nature," Helva said. "We can find him and get as close or far as we wish. Are *you* sure your cloak will enable you to follow us?"

I shrugged. "I hope so."

"Then we go," Silanus grumbled. "At the very worst we will be rid of you..."

The scenery around us swirled again, yet Silanus and Helva remained solid in my view. The swirling colors gave my incorporeal stomach momentary queasiness. The sounds of the river and birds muffled and then turned to a low buzzing sound in my head as if my ears were recovering after a large cannon blast had gone off next to my head.

The eyes of Helva and Silanus were distant but moved rapidly. Their brows were furrowed like they were scanning the horizon.

"I have him," Silanus murmured. His voice was muffled and had that same buzzing quality that surrounded us.

"I see him, too," Helva said, "but..."

Then she gasped.

The colors around us darkened from a bright mishmash to grays and then to oranges, reds, and black. The sounds changed from the neutral buzzing to shouts and screams.

That was not good.

I was suddenly falling backward, gaining speed with each moment, the wind blasting past my ears. I don't know how long or far I fell, but I landed in a soft patch of sand with a thud that knocked the wind from my lungs. I heard two other thumps and grunts nearby. I took a couple of seconds to gasp for breath before looking around me.

I was indeed on a sandy ground, but the sand was completely black and fine, more like powder than sand grains. Next to me lay Silanus and Helva, both of them groaning and breathing heavily from the fall.

I looked around me and felt the breath once again leave my lungs.

The three of us lay in the middle of an arena. And when I say arena, I'm not talking about the great arenas of Rome that could hold over 100,000 spectators. Those were quaint compared to this one.

My mind could barely comprehend its size. The bowl around which we were surrounded was filled with bleachers that rose up and up and...well, I couldn't even see the top of the bleachers. They were covered in a smoky mist beneath a black and orange sky. Red lightning flashed and forked here and there throughout the dark clouds, but there was no thunder.

I doubted I would've heard it anyway.

Sitting in the bleachers were...things. A multitude. A horde. Damnation, it could've been an infinite number, for all I knew, since I couldn't even see the top of the damned arena. And no two seemed alike. They were all slimy limbs, chitinous skin, and drooling mouths filled with savage teeth. They were all shrieking and waving their grotesque arms/tentacles at us as if we were the star attractions in whatever contest the arena had been built for.

The three of us stood. Silanus drew his sword and Helva her dagger. I had my gladius with me, but didn't think a spirit gladius would do much good against these creatures.

Hell, nothing would against these numbers.

"I'm so happy you finally joined us," boomed a voice. It echoed throughout the arena, and the creatures abruptly silenced as if their voices had been turned off.

I scanned the bleachers, looking for the source of the voice. About fifty paces away was a large viewing box—beginning in the front row and taking up ten rows above it—that looked similar to the one in the Circus Maximus where Augustus and his retinue would watch the races. It was draped in blue flags and pennants in stark contrast to the black and gray monstrosities surrounding it. A dozen or so men, wearing blue tunicas with gold trim, sat in the box. Their hair and beards were trimmed, and each one had a beautiful woman at his side who whispered seductively in his ears or coyly stroked his arms or legs. Unsurprisingly, each "woman" had eyes that reflected red like a predator at night caught in lantern light. None of the men seemed to care, though, as they smiled and groped at their dates.

One man, adorned in a blue toga with gold trim, stood. Terentius. I noticed Himilco sitting at Terentius's right hand, his dark eyes staring directly at me, his head firmly attached to his neck.

"I was beginning to wonder if you'd forgotten about me, Natta Magus," Terentius said. "That would've been rather damaging to my fragile ego."

As if Terentius had just uttered the greatest joke in history, the things in the bleachers roared what apparently passed for laughter in the underworld.

"This should not be possible," Helva said next to me over the roaring monsters. "Only the lord of the underworld could gather so many minions in one place. I thought you said he was only an *aspect* of Pluto?"

"He is," I said. "Or...at least that's what Rullus said."

Silanus leaned toward us to be heard. "Your friend was grossly mistaken, Natta Magus," he yelled. "Behold, he wears Pluto's blue toga and adornment. What doom have you brought us to?"

"Me? You were supposed to drop us off in a safe spot away from—"

Terentius waved a hand and the creatures abruptly silenced.

"You did surprise me, though," Terentius boomed, "as I thought you'd come to me from more earthly means." He shrugged. "No matter. Either way I give you the same choice I gave you in my camp—join me and together we can remake the world so that *all* humans have magic."

A growl arose from Silanus. "Enough of this. If we die here, then we will die while striking at this arrogant fool." He began striding toward Terentius.

I heroically suppressed a grunt over him calling someone arrogant and stepped in front of him before he could stride by me. I knew he'd pass through me like I was mist but—

His shoulder rammed into mine and knocked me to the side. He took two more steps, stopped, and then turned back to me in shock.

My face probably matched his.

"Your body is here," Helva said. She grabbed my forearm. Her fingers dug into my muscles in a tight grip. "How?"

I just shook my head. Silanus came over and helpfully punched me in the shoulder. Hard.

"He *is* real," Silanus said.

"I think we've already established that," I yelled, rubbing my shoulder.

"I see you are wearing the cloak," Terentius said. "You may be disoriented. I shall clear it up for you." He held his hands out. "Welcome to Carthage. Or as I call it now, Carthago Terentius."

41

I was somehow back on Earth. I reached for my cell magic and felt its reassuring warmth spread across my skin.

Next question: How did Helva and Silanus get here? I had assumed they'd only be allowed to traverse the underworld. I guess Invidia was patient. She'd get Silanus back sooner or later, no matter where he died.

Last question: How in damnation did Terentius build this impossibly large arena? And populate it with so many monsters from Pluto's own nightmares? In the ruins of Carthage?

Both Helva and Silanus pointed their palms to the ground. I sensed tremendous magic flowing into them and saw the air shimmer around their hands. Both reveled in their earth magic a moment, their eyes glassy with pleasure. Then they focused with grim determination on Terentius.

"Your magicks are with you," Terentius said with his magically enhanced voice from his imperial box in the bleachers. "That will make this more entertaining. I'm waiting for your answer, Natta Magus. Will you help me bring equality to the world?"

"You make it sound so noble," I yelled to him. The monsters had ceased their shrieking and cawing, but the windstorm created by the fires surrounding the arena threatened to drown my words. "But your way would destroy a world not yet ready for that power. Unless that is your plan?"

He shrugged his blue clad shoulders. "The old world must be wiped clean before the new can begin. It is the nature of things. And when it does, the common people will look to you and me as the world's saviors."

"We can take him," Silanus murmured beside me. "He loves to talk."

"Quiet!" I hissed.

"There is even a place for your friends in the new world," Terentius said. "Your friends here and even your student and biographer. In fact, you may save anyone you wish, Natta Magus. I am merciful." He glanced around at the wind whipping through the arena, gave an annoyed scowl, and then jerked his right hand once in a horizontal slashing motion.

The wind stopped and the arena was eerily quiet. It was creepier than when the monsters were screaming.

"Now we may speak as civilized men," Terentius said from his box. "Bear in mind my offer comes with an expiration. No more questions, no more comments. You've had plenty of time to think about this since I told you in my camp. You must give me an answer now with your next words."

So. Join Terentius, possibly save the people I cared about—Silanus, too, I guess—and then watch the rest of the world burn. That is, if Terentius kept his word, which I had no reason to believe he would. Burning a city and populating it with daemons tends to make one untrustworthy. But even if I took him at his word, there would come a point where I'd have to decide whether or not to go along with his plans. Could I destroy the world and all of future history just to save my friends?

It was either that or tell Terentius to shove it and be torn to pieces by a sea of monsters out of Invidia's torture fantasies.

I looked at Silanus and Helva. He stared at Terentius like an alpha wolf figuring out the best way to another alpha's throat. She looked at me, all resolve and bravery.

Damnation, I wish I could emulate either one right now. It was all I could do to keep my quivering knees from buckling.

I turned to Terentius. "My answer is the same as it was in the camp: I will never help you do this thing. *Never.*"

Then I sighed, feeling strangely peaceful that I'd made a decision. My fate was now up to the Unknowable Will.

Terentius glared at me, his eyes smoldering with the same fire that raged around the arena and blackened its skies. I siphoned my cell magic and prepared to defend myself...for a few moments at least. All I could do was wait for a quick death.

Then he said, "That is disappointing. I thought as much, but I had to try. Very well then, you may go."

I stared at him, waiting for the punch line.

He pointed to my left. "The door is that way."

I glanced to the left and saw thick wooden doors over a hundred paces away slowly opening on their own. Beyond the doors was a dark, smoky street.

I looked back at Terentius. He made a shooing motion with his hands. Himilco continued staring at me with dark eyes that revealed nothing of his thoughts. The men and "women" in Terentius's box seemed more focused on pawing at each other than on me.

"Let's go," I said to Helva and Silanus.

Helva continued to keep her hands pointed to the ground, but she nodded. Silanus looked disappointed, and for a moment I thought he would attack Terentius anyway. If he did, he'd be on his own. I'd be running for my life toward the open doors.

But Silanus ground his teeth and began walking with Helva and me. "This is a trick," he growled.

"Your *caccing* right it's a trick," I said. "But who cares? You think we can take all these monsters? That we can take Terentius when he can build something like this arena within days? This is our best chance to get out and fight another day."

"If we make it through the city," Helva said. "Perhaps the smoke and fire will kill us anyway."

"That's the spirit," I said.

As we walked across the black sand arena, the monsters were inhumanly quiet. I could feel their eyes—at least from the creatures that had eyes—upon me the whole time. It took all my strength not to begin sprinting for those doors. It was so quiet that I could hear my feet shuffling in the sand, Helva's breathing, and Silanus's grinding teeth. I didn't even want to hazard a look over my shoulder at Terentius for fear it would cause him to say "Just kidding" and then release his horde upon us.

It was the longest, most agonizing one hundred paces that I'd ever walked in my life.

But we got to the doors without being attacked. Like the arena, the doors were much larger than anything I'd ever seen even in the twenty-first century. At least three stories tall and wide. I saw no machinery that could've operated them, so they must've been under Terentius's magical command. Why not?

We walked through a long stone corridor that was almost as long as the walk we'd taken across the arena and then stepped out into the hell that was once Carthage.

I didn't see a building left standing. If a structure wasn't on fire, then it was a pile of charred rubble. Smoke billowed from burning fires here and there, which choked the air around us, made my eyes water, and burned my throat.

It felt like heat from all the infernos was blistering my skin. I began coughing immediately and considered moving back into the corridor we had just left.

But when I turned around the corridor was gone.

In fact, so was the arena. All I saw was more rubble and burning buildings, and that was only when I could see through the black smoke.

"No wonder he let us go," I managed to say through my coughing. "There's nowhere *for* us to go!"

Silanus shook his head. "I do not know how you have survived this long, Natta Magus."

He pointed his palms toward the ground, muttered something under his breath, and then a burst of earth magic exploded from him. I felt it more than I saw it since my cell magic prevented me from really experiencing his earth magic. It rolled past me like a burst of warm, refreshing desert air. The smoke around us was blown away in that wind, and even the heat dissipated dramatically. The smoke stopped just outside a tall column of fresh air that had formed around Silanus in a twenty-foot radius. The top of that column reached upward hundreds of paces and punched through the top smoke layer so that I could actually see blue sky. It was like we were in the eye of a fiery, smoky hurricane.

Silanus barely looked like he was expending any effort at all. He gave me a level stare with a raised eyebrow.

I shrugged. "I guess that'll work."

I noticed Helva staring up at the blue sky. Despite the hellish landscape surrounding us, the serenity in her smile and glistening eyes at that moment could've brought peace to a gladiatorial match. She turned to me with those deep, gleaming eyes.

"We are free," she said.

Then she was suddenly in my arms, her own arms wrapped tightly around my neck, her warm body pressed firmly against mine. I returned her embrace. I hadn't held a woman like this since Brianna. Nor felt how I did at that moment.

Which brought a whole other level of confusing emotions.

"I knew you would come back for us," she said looking up at me. "All the time we were there, I had faith in you."

"I barely did anything," I said modestly.

She gave a small, endearing giggle; more so endearing because she never "giggled." Snorted, yes. Grunted, sure. She'd sneered at me a many of times. But giggle was not something a warrior princess like her did.

What did that mean?

"Of course not," she said with a coy smile. "You never do anything."

As I held Helva, I glanced at Silanus. He stared at me with a blank face, but his left eye twitched. It was that blank face that froze my limbs despite Helva's warm body against mine.

If he'd made a sarcastic comment or an angry outburst, I would've shrugged it off.

But there was murder in that blank face.

I broke my embrace with Helva. "Right. Now we need to get out of these ruins."

Helva looked surprised for an instant at my sudden retreat, but she soon turned all business again.

I already missed her coy smile.

"Silanus, will this column you built follow you, or is it stationary?"

He continued staring at me with that cold, blank face. After several moments, he said in a neutral tone, "It will follow me."

"Good," I said, acting as if I didn't notice his stare. "At least we won't choke to death while walking out of the city."

"I cannot see the sun above us," Helva said, looking up at the blue hole that the column made. "How will we know which way to go?"

I grinned at Helva. "I'm a Finder, remember."

I only hoped Cana and Paetus still wore their braid bindings.

I siphoned my cell magic, felt its comforting warmth spread across my skin. I concentrated on Cana's braid and then felt my feet want to walk in a direction directly behind me. One question answered.

I looked at Silanus and pointed. "That way, big guy."

He nodded once and then strode in the direction in which I pointed. Helva glanced from him to me and sighed through her nose. She murmured something in Coptic beneath her breath and then followed Silanus.

As did I, for I sure wasn't going to show him my back.

42

My feet told me the direction and general distance to where Cana was, but unfortunately not the best route to get to her. We often found ourselves blocked by a burning building or a dead end alley, and then we were forced to retrace our steps to find a route around the obstacles. We had walked for hours and seemed no closer to getting out of the city than when we first started.

Bodies lay everywhere among the ruins. Men, women, children. Also animals of every species: horses, goats, sheep, dogs. Some were burned beyond recognition some looked to have died by smoke inhalation. And some had been partially eaten alive or torn to pieces. I didn't have to imagine what kind of creatures could've done that, for I had seen them in Terentius's magical arena.

Silanus's column of fresh air kept the smoke and fires at bay, but it did nothing to ease our growing thirst and fatigue. Even Silanus was beginning to look after maintaining an industrial strength spell.

At least his murderous eyes weren't aimed at me.

"Why did he let us go?" Helva said as we sat down to rest for a few minutes. "He could have killed us at any time."

"I've been thinking about that ever since he told us to leave," I said. I used the fine material on the red cloak to wipe the sweat off my forehead. My ball cap was drenched and smelled like a hockey locker room.

"He's following us," Silanus said, his voice distant with concentration on his spell.

I looked at him, surprised. It was the first time he'd said more than two words since the arena.

"I can imagine a dozen different reasons," I said, "and, yeah, that's one of them. He let us go because he still needs me alive. He told me once that he wanted me to help him of my own free will so that he didn't have to worry about me undermining him. I guess he still thinks he can persuade me somehow."

"Mm," Silanus rumbled, "for you are always so important to the world, Natta Magus."

"I don't like it any more than you."

"Then why not cast yourself off a cliff or fall on your sword? Those are sure ways to freedom."

"Brother," Helva said in a warning tone.

I smiled at Silanus. "You'd love that, wouldn't you? And if I did that, what then? You'd still be a lousy chess player."

"Natta," Helva said in the same tone she'd used with Silanus.

Silanus returned my smile and stood, facing me. He was a few inches shorter than me, but his broad chest made him seem a foot taller. He began walking again, the column of fresh air following him. Helva and I were forced to go with him or be left behind in the smoke.

"You should not taunt him," she whispered to me.

"So it's okay for him to taunt me?" I replied in an angry whisper.

"No. But madness does not stalk you like it does him, awaiting a small provocation to take over."

I wanted to tell her that might be the one thing Silanus and I had in common, but I kept quiet.

The sky in that clear hole above us had turned orange by the time we finally reached the edge of Carthage. The city had not been rebuilt with high walls, so we didn't have to traverse through any gates. I got the feeling the gates would've been demolished anyway, just like all the other structures in this city. Terentius had been quite thorough in his devastation. If he had his way, the whole world would look like "Carthago Terentius."

Once we left the city, the heat dissipated to a tolerable level, and the smoke took a westerly track behind us. Silanus finally released his "Clarity Column," as I had dubbed it. He tried to act strong, but his mouth was open, his chin was lower, and his shoulders were slumped. The man was exhausted. I couldn't imagine maintaining a spell that strong for a few minutes, much less the hours that Silanus had done. I didn't want to tangle with this guy again.

My feet took us west, which was pretty much the direction of Danel's farm. The roads out of the city were littered with debris: broken carts, abandoned luggage, valuables of every shape, size, and color. It seemed that people started out carrying their valuables and then began dropping whatever impeded their ability to run for their lives. We searched the debris for food and water, but didn't find a crumb or drop.

We did find a lot of human bodies. As the sun descended into the west, I watched the bodies warily, remembering the undead attack at Danel's walls.

Once Helva seemed reasonably sure Silanus and I wouldn't murder each other, she strode ahead of us to scout each hill we ascended and each building we approached. I got the feeling she was more interested in avoiding me than worried about something sneaking up on us. After the hug we shared, she seemed to avert her eyes whenever I looked at her. Silanus didn't approve, so I figured she didn't want to give him any more reason to strangle me than he already had.

"You would woo my sister, Natta Magus?" Silanus asked beside me.

He startled me out of my thoughts. "Woo? What? That's silly. I mean, I care about her, yes. But woo? No. Hah, what gave you that idea?"

I kept my eyes on the road ahead, but I felt him staring at me.

"You are not good enough for her," he said quietly. "She is royalty. You are...common."

I shifted my eyes to him. "I'm aware of that."

"You could never give her the life she deserves."

"I'm aware of that, too," I said. "But maybe she should decide for herself."

"And you are dangerous. You know of what I speak."

That one hit home. Yes, I was dangerous. The soul magic could explode from me unless I concentrated on keeping it at bay. But I couldn't always control it, and I knew that someday I would release it again. And each time I did, it would become that much harder for me to keep control over it in the future. The day would come when I gave into it permanently, eventually going mad and killing all the people around me that I loved.

Silanus was right. I wasn't good enough for Helva. I couldn't give her the life she deserved. And I was too dangerous to be around her.

"If you do care for her," he said in a flat tone, "you will not encourage her infatuation with you. We will finish this task because she wants it so. But when it is done, we will leave. And you will never see us again. If you do anything to prevent that, then I will kill you."

I returned his flat stare. "Deal."

At that moment, Helva came jogging back from down the hill ahead of us. She glanced from me to Silanus with a raised eyebrow, and then said, "I believe I see your friend's villa about a mile distant. It is the only one that looks occupied. But you should see something, Natta Magus."

"What?"

"You must see it for yourself," she said, and then jogged to the top of the hill.

"Why can't you just tell—?" I called after her. I grumbled something else and then jogged after her with Silanus.

At the top of the hill, I looked down into the valley where Danel's farmlands lay. The sun had half set below the mountains to the west. My first thought at spying the dark figures surrounding Danel's walls was that Terentius had unleashed his hordes and they were already attacking. But I looked closer and saw that the dark shapes were hundreds of refugees gathered in haphazard groups around the walls.

And nearby were hundreds of Roman legionaries camped in straight-rowed tents beside the refugees.

My feet wanted to take me directly to the farm, so Cana was still there. I'd just need to walk through a Roman legion to get to her.

And to top it off, we had been spotted. Four Roman cavalrymen were riding up the hill toward us at a gallop.

43

I stared closely at the Romans galloping up to us. None of them carried the multi-colored batons that Seius's Legio III had wielded. All four were armed like regular Roman cavalrymen.

I also scanned the Roman camp, looking for banners. I finally found one fluttering near the front of the camp's outer tents. It had a boar's head emblazoned in gold upon a field of red. I wasn't sure what legion that signified, but it wasn't the plain old "III" on Seius's banners.

Silanus aimed his hands to the ground, and I felt his earth magic surge into him. Helva did the same.

"Wait!" I said. "Let me talk to them first!"

"If we wait," Silanus growled, "we give them a chance to attack."

"If you attack, we won't get to my friends! They have the artifacts we need to stop Terentius."

"Not if we kill all four of them," Silanus said coldly.

"There are innocent people down there," I cried.

I saw doubt cross Helva's face as her eyes took in the refugees. She released her earth magic and said, "Brother, he is right. We are here to help these people, not fight them."

"I will not be taken prisoner," Silanus said. His eyes smoldered as he watched the Romans get closer.

"They won't know you," I said. "I'll just tell them you're refugees that I found in Carthage. Stand down, they're almost here!"

For a long moment I thought Silanus was going to wipe out the cavalrymen with a wave of his hand and then proceed to take out the legionaries beyond. And there wouldn't be a damned thing I could do to stop him...outside of soul magic.

But he released his earth magic with a savage grunt. He took a deep breath, released it, and then his face was calm as though he were about to greet old friends instead of Roman cavalrymen.

"Their lives depend on your silver tongue, Natta Magus," he murmured.

I took a dry swallow. I wished I could look as calm and confident as Silanus.

The four riders pulled up their reigns in front of us. One of the armored men, a centurion by the transverse crest of red horsehair across his helm, stared at me and my battered Wolverines ball cap.

"You are the one called Natta Magus," he said. It was more a statement than a question, and he said it with a surprised tone. I was expecting more of an "I'm-gonna-run-you-through-if-you-don't-follow-me" tone.

"I am," I said cautiously.

"I fought with you on the Capitoline," he said, wonder in his eyes. "The gods were literally with you that day, sir." His eyes shifted to Helva and widened even more. "You were there too, my lady. Your powers overwhelmed the crone Invidia! I'm honored to meet you."

Helva gave him a jerky nod in thanks.

Then he looked at Silanus.

Aw, damnation. Out of 120,000 men in the empire's legions, we had to meet one of the couple hundred who was on the Capitoline the day.

"I do not recognize you, sir," the centurion said. "Are you also among Natta Magus's cohort?"

"Me?" Silanus laughed. "No, sir. I am merely a refugee whom these two fine heroes rescued from the city."

The man stared at Silanus a moment longer, his eyes narrowed. *If he recognizes Silanus...*

But the man's eyes shifted back to me, and his body language didn't indicate he knew Silanus. "The general will be most pleased to see you, sir."

I exhaled slowly. Silanus had been clean-shaven during his attack on Rome, whereas he currently had a full black beard. I hazarded a glance at Silanus. His palms were casually pointed toward the ground, but once the centurion's attention was back on me, he clenched his fists behind his back.

"General Seius?" I asked the centurion warily.

"From Legio III? No, sir, we've had no contact with Seius. We are a Praetorian legion from Rome. We arrived two days ago to find..." He nodded in the direction of the still burning Carthage.

"Praetorian?" I breathed. "Who's your general?"

In the courtyard of Danel's complex, I greeted my old friend Marcus Aurelius Vitulus with a manly, backslapping, celebratory hug. It had only been two months since I last saw him, but you'd think our team had just won the World Series. He was decked out in chain mail and banded chest armor, so I felt like I was hugging a steel golem from a Detroit manufactory.

"*General* Vitulus?" I said. "Whose wine did you piss in to get this assignment?"

"I serve the State and the gods, my friend," he said, grinning. "*I'm* the one who gets pissed on."

"And a beard?" I said, studying the ruddy brown growth around his face and neck. "Since when do proper Romans wear facial hair?"

His grin melted. "Since they are ordered to guard a certain magus on his travels throughout the Republic."

My own smile disappeared. "Augustus ordered you to follow me?"

Vitulus shifted his jaw, which is what he always did when he didn't want to give me an answer he knew I'd hate. "The Princeps wants to ensure you're not a danger to yourself or to other citizens. I volunteered for the command to ensure you were treated fairly."

Damnation, I should've expected that. There was no way Augustus would just let me be free. He never would. I'd be looking over my shoulder for the rest of my life.

And I couldn't help but feel a twinge of betrayal that Vitulus had actually volunteered for this assignment. It didn't take long, though, for me to realize how ridiculous that was. Vitulus hadn't betrayed me; he was protecting me from an overzealous commander who probably would've zapped the *cac* out of me with one of those magical batons by now.

Vitulus's eyes shifted to Helva behind me, and he nodded a greeting to her.

When his gaze found Silanus, his whole body froze. Silanus returned the gaze with a nonplussed one of his own.

"It's alright," I said quickly under my breath. "He's not a threat." *I wish I could believe that myself...*

"Really," Vitulus said with preternatural calm. "And why should I believe that?" The Praetorian soldiers milling about in the courtyard did not seem to pick up on their general's sudden wariness. I did because I'd spent virtually every day with the man for almost two years, including some pretty scary battles with daemons and patricians.

"Because he's sworn an Oath," I muttered. "An Oath with a capital 'O.'"

He glanced once at me and returned to glaring at Silanus. Vitulus new about the Oaths and how binding they were. "As I understand it," he said, "*Oaths* can be broken by those with no honor. Seems to me that a murderer and a thief has no honor."

Silanus snorted. "Like your First Citizen, Praetorian?"

"Buddy," I said to Vitulus, "I don't trust him either. But I need you to trust me. Right now he is not our enemy. We have much bigger problems. We just came from Carthage and Terentius has an army of monsters that will pour out of the city like fire ants."

Vitulus pulled his eyes from Silanus and looked at me. "I trust your heart, my friend. I always will. But sometimes I fear what you might *unintentionally* do."

He gave me a meaningful stare. Which told me he either knew what I did to Seius's legion or he was referring to my struggles with the soul magic, about which he'd known since Aventicum.

Before I could respond, he said, "Come. Your friends are waiting inside, and we have much to discuss. Your...colleagues are also welcome."

He turned and strode toward Danel's main house. Helva, who'd been grasping Silanus's arm with a stony face, released her hold. Silanus strode past me and smirked. "This is going to be fun," he said. He looked genuinely amused.

When he walked past me out of earshot, I said to Helva, "Is this going to be a problem?"

She sighed. "He will taunt and needle, yes. But he will behave himself. Unless, of course, he is attacked. Will your Roman friend behave?"

"He trusts me," I said, watching Vitulus disappear into the house. "He won't do anything while Terentius is out there. After this is over, though...there could be trouble."

Helva nodded sadly. "After this is over, it won't matter. Silanus will return to Invidia. The Romans can do nothing to him that will compare to Invidia's punishments."

She slipped her warm hand into mine and laced her fingers. "I look forward to fighting beside you again, Natta Magus." She gave me a coy smile that got my heart racing. "Perhaps we will find some quiet moments together," she said, almost shyly.

And by all the gods, there was nothing I wanted more at that moment.

But Silanus's warning came back to me: *You are not good enough for her. You do not deserve her.*

You are dangerous.

I pulled my hand from hers and said, "I don't think Silanus and Vitulus should be in the same room together without us. Let's go."

My voice was gruffer than I'd intended. Helva's brown eyes went from playful to hard in an instant, and that dimpled smile that sent jolts of electricity across my skin transformed into the straight-lipped scowl that had greeted me when we first met in the Circus Maximus.

"Very well," she said, all business, and then strode toward the house.

Leaving me to wonder if I'd just made a mistake or if I'd just saved her life.

Inside Danel's house, I found Paetus and Cana standing against one wall in the atrium staring wide-eyed at Silanus like mice corned by a tomcat. Silanus wasn't helping anything by studying them with a predatory expression, his massive forearms folded across his chest.

When Paetus and Cana saw me, they practically scraped their backs against the wall to stay as far from Silanus as possible and then hurried over to me.

"What happened to—?"

"Where did you—?"

"You disappeared into—!"

"One moment you were—!"

Their words flooded over each other, and I couldn't follow a single sentence. But I got the gist.

"Guys," I said, holding up my hands, "I'm fine. Things got weird, even for us." I glanced at Helva, who stood nearby, unsure of whether she was welcome in our little cohort.

Once Cana ensured I was okay—and that Silanus wasn't going to unleash Dea Tacita daemons on them—she rushed over to Helva and gave her a big hug. Helva smiled and returned it. "It is good to see you, too, Cana. Natta Magus has not corrupted your talent too much, has he?"

"He is the worst teacher. He will not let me do anything fun. Just practice 'mindfulness', whatever that is. And he tries constantly to save the world."

I rolled my eyes and asked, "Where did Vitulus go?"

"He's talking to Danel," Paetus said as Cana and Helva continued to speak, "in the kitchen." Now that I was in the same room with him, he glared at Silanus, who was studying the painted frescoes upon Danel's walls. "So," he murmured to me. "You got him out, too."

"It was a package deal," I said. "Helva wouldn't come without him."

"Is he dangerous?"

"Yes. But he swore an Oath to help us. Once that's fulfilled, Invidia gets him back."

"Good," Paetus said.

Not only did Paetus hate and fear Silanus for what he did in Rome, but Silanus had trapped Paetus in his own house with a Dea Tacita daemon. Paetus spent a night and a day stuck in a small magical circle with the monstrous daemon sitting there, watching him with slavering teeth and sharp claws. Waiting for Paetus to fall asleep and maybe fall outside the circle.

Paetus wasn't about to forget that humiliation and terror.

Vitulus entered the atrium with Danel at his side. Two Roman officers followed whom I didn't recognize. They were both older than Vitulus and had the grizzled faces of longtime veterans.

"Natta Magus," Vitulus said, "tell us of this army you saw in Carthage. How large is it?"

I gave him a grim chuckle. "How many stars are in the sky? How many grains of sand are there on the beach? It was huge, buddy. Rome couldn't possibly muster enough legions to stop it."

Vitulus glanced at Danel and his officers. The three of them looked back at him with faces that could've been chiseled in marble. Some sort of confirmation passed wordlessly between them.

He looked back at me. "Is this army on the move?"

"They were sitting in an arena last I saw them. And then the arena disappeared when we left it."

"Disappeared?"

"Yeah. As soon as we walked out, the arena disappeared."

"Huh," Paetus said next to me.

I turned to him with raised eyebrows.

"Well," he said, "that might mean he hasn't established a foothold in this world yet. The arena you describe could not have been built in the physical world within a day or two. The underworld, however, is less constrained."

"But I could siphon my cell magic," I said. I waved a hand at Helva and Silanus. "They could tap their earth magic. We couldn't do that in the underworld."

"Perhaps the arena was located in a...bridge world, if you will. A place that is of both worlds, but not."

"This is all very interesting," Silanus said in a tone that indicated it was *not* interesting to him, "but am I the only one here who thinks we should focus on *why* this man Terentius is doing these things rather than *how?*"

When everyone looked at him with less than friendly eyes, he smirked. "I know I am the villain in the room, so you will likely ignore my words. But I will say this anyway: Terentius did not kill us. Why? He let us leave the arena. Why? He let us roam the streets of Carthage without sending his creatures to bother us. Why?"

Silanus looked directly at me. "He let us come here." A pause, and then, "Why?"

"He still needs me for something," I said.

Through clenched teeth, Silanus asked, "Why?"

"You heard him," I said, growing impatient. "He needs me to help him give magic to everyone in the world."

"He can do that?" Vitulus asked.

I paused. "I don't know. Maybe. If he can, though, it would be very bad. This world isn't ready for magic and would have no idea how to use it."

"Maybe," Cana said quietly, "he needs your soul magic."

I gave her a sharp look, but she didn't flinch away.

"Soul magic is too simple," Helva said. "From what you told me, Natta Magus, you only need to get angry and lose control for it to emerge. He could have done that in the arena by attacking us."

My mind was whirling now. "Maybe he needs my magic under certain conditions. Maybe at a certain time or place or…"

Oh, damnation.

"Or with certain artifacts," I breathed.

So I had *done exactly what he wanted. I led him here.* Terentius had lost the artifacts when Himilco had rescued him back at his camp. And Himilco had returned to the camp to steal the artifacts, but Rullus and I had stopped him. When Himilco failed, Terentius lost track of the artifacts after my battle with Seius's legion…which forced him to wait for *me* to use them.

Particularly the cloak. He knew I'd use it to find Helva, and when I did, I would also try to find him. So he waited.

I still didn't understand the arena or how he had pulled me back to Earth from the underworld. Or even how the arena had existed in Carthage, yet not.

I'd figure that out later. I turned to Cana and Paetus. "Where are the artifacts?"

"Locked in the wine cellar," Cana said.

"Show me."

They led us all out to the wine cellar door in the courtyard. Sure enough, there was a padlock on the door and it was secure. Danel opened the lock and pulled open the door.

I hurried down the rough-hewn steps, casting a spark globe along the way to illuminate the dark cellar. I found the leather pack where we'd stored the artifacts: the evergreen glove, the teddy bear, and the two torches. I was still wearing the red cloak. I picked up the pack and opened it.

I took a deep breath and tried to calm my thumping heart. "They're still here," I called out to everyone standing in the sunlight above.

"Excellent," came Silanus's sarcastic voice. "Now we know where Terentius will strike next."

I shook my head, wondering how I *had* survived in ancient Rome so long because I was probably the stupidest man in the world. It hadn't even crossed my mind back in Carthage that Terentius might be after the artifacts. I mean, he only had the artifacts in his possession back at his camp. Why *wouldn't* he try everything in his power to get them back? And here, in Danel's farm, he had the artifacts and me in one place. And no Rullus with an anti-magic legion in his way.

I knew why it hadn't crossed my mind. I had been so happy to see Helva that everything else had been pushed to the back of my mind. To see that smile directed at me, all the more special because it was so rare. To feel her hugging me tight, her body pressed against mine...

And Silanus's death threats hadn't helped my concentration either.

I'm not saying it was Helva's fault or even Silanus's. I should've thought of it, so it was all on me. But at that moment, I knew that any fantasy I had of a relationship with Helva would have to remain a fantasy. I *was* too dangerous for her. I had a destiny to fulfill, and happiness for me of any sort *was* a distraction.

Once again I had royally screwed up, and I had to do everything I could to fix this.

As I thought about all this, Cana, Paetus, and Helva came down the cellar steps. Vitulus followed them, and Silanus stood behind Vitulus with his arms folded. They all had the same *what do we do now?* question etched on their faces. Except for Silanus, whose smirk made him look like he was having the time of his life.

I held up the pack. "We need to figure out what these things can do before Terentius arrives. Hey *leerling*, want to learn how to Scan artifacts?"

44

"We don't have much time," I told Cana, "so this is going to be a quick lesson."

I had asked Danel to move some of the wine barrels out to make some room for us. Danel helped his slaves carry six of the heavy barrels out, so we had the room I needed within minutes. I took each artifact out of the pack—and pulled the cloak off my shoulders—and placed them on the cellar floor, side by side.

Cana, Helva, and Silanus stood next to me. I told Paetus, Vitulus, and everyone else to wait outside the cellar door. Yeah, if things went bad here, it was unlikely the wooden door or five feet of desert soil would protect them from an artifact meltdown. But it was better than nothing.

"Silanus, can your column thingy contain magic?"

"'Column thingy'?"

"You know what I mean."

He smirked. "Yes, it can contain magic. Although directed magic will eventually find a way through it."

"What is directed magic?" Cana asked.

"Magic with a mind," Silanus and I said at the exact same time. We looked at each other, surprised. But then again, we'd been students of William Pingree Ford. That was one of *his* terms.

"It's magic," I said to Cana, "that's directed either by the will of a magus or by some other intelligence. Wild magic is mindless, without thought or purpose. It's the difference between fighting a golem and a magus."

"My thingy," Silanus said, "will be sufficient for wild magic. If those artifacts, however, have magical intelligence and can direct their magic to attack my thingy, then my thingy will fall." Silanus looked at me. "What will your Scan thingy do?"

I glared at him. "Stop saying 'thingy' now."

Helva interrupted Silanus before he could speak again. "I will combine my magic with Silanus's to strengthen the column. It will hold."

"Good. Be ready with that column just in case things go badly. Most artifacts ignore Scans, but some don't like it all that much."

I thought about the Ring of Saturn, the artifact that brought me to ancient Rome. *No, not much at all.*

"We're going to start with the stuffed bear."

"Why that one?" Cana asked. "Don't we already know what it can do?"

"We know some, but we don't know if that's *all* it can do."

I quickly explained to her the basics and magical theory behind First, Second, and Third Scans—how First was the least invasive, with Second and Third becoming progressively more invasive. And those were just the Scans I knew how to do. The Scanning arcanum in my time went up to Six. I think I did a pretty good job of distilling my three years of university study on the topic into a five-minute lecture, for she claimed she understood everything and looked eager to proceed. I wasn't whether she *really* understood or was just excited to get on with new magic.

"Ready?"

She nodded, her eyes bright and her lips parted.

I looked at Helva and Silanus. "Ready?"

Helva nodded, tight lipped.

Silanus said solemnly, "My thingy will not fail."

My soul magic lurched. I thought that burning a bit of my soul would've been so worth it to knock Silanus into next week.

I took a deep breath, stamped down the soul magic, and calmed my mind. Once I was as calm as I could get with the limited time I had—and the distractions in the room—I nodded to Cana.

"Let's do it."

We both walked around the stuffed bear twice. I opened my magical senses to take in a general sense of the artifact's power. It pretty much confirmed what I'd already figured out about the bear. It was made of cell magic, albeit a very powerful and ancient cell magic. It gave me the same sense of majesty and infinity that I felt the first time I saw the Milky Way galaxy spread across the sky outside the city lights of Detroit.

"What do you see?" I asked Cana. I had to shake off the powerful sense of déjà vu, for William had asked me the same thing back in our Detroit lab just before the Ring of Saturn kidnapped me.

Cana stared at the bear with distant eyes. "Peace," she said. "Comfort. Vastness." She sighed contentedly as if the artifact's power was activated.

"Good," I said. "Start Second Scan."

We walked around the bear twice, but in the opposite direction as First Scan. I tried to ignore the amused way Silanus watched our cell magic rituals. Maybe earth mages Scan artifacts by blowing them up and then sifting through the pieces.

Focus.

Cana and I raised our hands and placed them gently on the bear. Its manufactured fur was soft beneath my fingers.

I used my cell magic to direct a question into the bear: *Who made you?*

Second Scan didn't take long to show me.

I stood on a factory floor. It was well lit by the bronze sunlight flooding through the windows that lined the walls near the girder ceiling. All around me were mechanical golems working on an assembly line filled with the same bears. Each golem operated a specific machine that would stuff the bears with cotton, stamp the green glassy eyes into the bears' light brown heads, and stitch up the limbs. The golems moved with mechanical, programmed efficiency. They must've been making hundreds of the bears per day. I could smell the oiled machinery and taste the cottony dust floating in the air. The whirring and hissing of the steam-powered machines would've made it impossible to talk to or hear anyone on the floor.

Were *all* the bears artifacts? I saw no magi casting spells upon the bears once they were finished, nor did my magical senses pick up enchantments on the materials used to make the bears. The assembly line looked like any toy factory from my time.

Except...

The sunlight streaming through the windows began to shift and dim rapidly as if the sunset were sped up. But the golems weren't going any faster. Only the sun was moving.

The golems continued their work at the same pace even as the sun went down and the sky outside turned dark. Spark globes among the girders illuminated. It remained this way for several minutes. Then the sky began to brighten as morning broke and sunlight flooded through the upper windows. The spark globes extinguished and the factory floor took on the same bronze tint as when I arrived.

My eyes were suddenly drawn to a bear on the assembly line conveyor. There was nothing particularly different about it other than my Second Scan spell telling me this was the one I was looking for. The bear moved along, was given its glassy eyes and limbs like all the others, and then dumped into a large bin filled with bears at the end of the conveyor. A golem operating a forklift picked up the bin and carried it to an open garage door that emptied out onto a loading dock.

My body floated along the dusty floor after the bin. When I looked outside, I saw why the sun was acting weird.

The entire factory and loading dock were encased in a bronze tinted dome. An imprint of the sun travelled from one side of the dome to the other. Where the sun sank below the horizon of one side, an imprint of the moon arose on the opposite side, giving the illusion of a rapidly moving day-night cycle.

Outside the dome, though, was a hellish landscape of blackened hills, bright orange lava rivers, and tortured skies filled with smoke and ash.

Where in damnation were we?

The bin of bears was loaded onto a wagon that was pulled by—

I would've rubbed my eyes if I could.

Three white-winged horses were tethered to the wagon, each one stamping its hooves and shaking its head as if impatient to get moving. Once the golems secured the bin onto the wagon, the winged horses instantly galloped forward a couple dozen paces before taking off into the sky. The horses circled the factory once and then shot toward the side of the dome where the moon was just beginning to rise. They sped toward the moon, leaving a streak of golden sparks like an aero-plane's exhaust. They timed it perfectly: Just as the moon rose to a spot above the horizon, the horses flew into it and vanished.

I didn't have time to wonder where they had gone, for my body was yanked back into Danel's cellar. I gasped, as the return was jarring to say the least.

Cana was not as experienced as me. She gasped, stumbled, and would've fallen if Helva hadn't caught her and steadied her.

Cana looked at me with wide eyes. "What was that place?"

I shook my head. "It looked like a factory from my century, but that landscape outside the dome definitely wasn't Detroit."

I quickly described to Helva and Silanus what we'd seen. When I mentioned the dome and the hell beyond, Helva gave Silanus a sharp look. Silanus's eyes narrowed, but he said nothing.

"What?" I asked them.

"I think we have seen this place," Helva said. "It was in the underworld."

"You're telling me there's a teddy bear factory...in the underworld?"

"It sounds foolish," Helva said, "but we did see a domed village surrounded by the blackened earth and volcanoes you described. It was one of the lands we fled to while running from Invidia. It was very strange, with buildings and machinery that we did not understand. We, too, saw the winged horses."

"I don't understand any of this," I said, shaking my head.

Of course nothing about artifacts ever made sense to me, and I had studied a few with twenty-first century magical wisdom. Theories abounded in my time that they were from a forgotten past or—even more mind-bendy—from a distant future where infinity and time looped around to our present again.

But if it were true that some of them were made in the underworld, then I supposed that would explain their strangeness. An underworld origin meant they could be transported to any point in time, which would explain how an obviously manufactured children's toy ended up in an underground temple tens of thousands of years old.

"Should we do a Third Scan, *leraar*?" Cana asked. She had regained her equilibrium and stood ready to go, resolve on her pale Gallic face.

I glanced at the other artifacts lying beside the bear. Third Scan was pretty invasive, for it involved the Scanner siphoning a bit of the artifact's magic into a receptacle for further study. I had enchanted one of Danel's empty wine barrels for that purpose, but I didn't want to use it unless absolutely necessary. I certainly didn't have the same confidence in it as I did in the sturdy receptacles of my twenty-first century labs.

I shook my head. "Let's do First and Second on the rest of these. I want to see where they were made, too."

We started with the evergreen glove. Our First Scan revealed pretty much what I already knew: The glove was not Dark, but it did give off waves of military purpose. I felt discipline, the urge to obey, and a surge of adrenaline. I also felt anger, but not the destructive or wild anger that triggers the soul magic. This was the anger you feel when you see a terrible injustice and choose to fight for a noble cause. I felt resolve strengthen my muscles and my chin lift a little higher. It was how I felt when I stopped Silanus and how I felt now about stopping Terentius. They had both decided to kill *a lot* of innocent people, and there was no way I would stand by and let them.

I glanced at Cana. Her jaw was clenched, her nostrils flared. She was ready to go to war on the side of the angels.

"Start Second Scan," I said to her, mostly to break her out of the same heart thumping desire for righteous battle that was burning through me. She blinked, took several deep breaths, and then refocused her cell magic on the Second Scan.

When we proceeded to Second Scan, my suspicions were confirmed. I landed in another golem-run factory where the gloves were being made *en masse*. Everything about the factory, the dome in which it sat, and the hellish landscape beyond were the same. Even the same winged horses carried a bin of gloves into the moon as it rose across the dome.

My Scans on the red cloak surprised me. I had assumed it was a communications device, but it actually turned out to be an artifact for instant travel. My First Scan made me feel like I was flying in an aero-plane or on one of the many auto-car trips my family took to northern Michigan when I was a kid. With the cloak, I could travel instantly to anyone I imagined in the physical world. Maybe I was incorporeal in the underworld only because I did not belong there...yet.

And Second Scan gave me the same factory with golems stitching the cloaks, dumping them into bins, and winged horses delivering them through the moon.

The two torches were last, and the only artifacts that I hadn't messed with yet. Based on my experiences with the other artifacts, I had an expectation of where these originated, but I tried to keep an open mind.

First Scan made me feel as if I were standing at a crossroads. I heard what sounded like barking dogs in the distance, just below my hearing. I felt like I knew what lay in both directions, but I couldn't make up my mind which way to go. If only I could hold the torches up to either path, then they'd illuminate the road that I was meant to take.

We proceeded to Second Scan.

Rather than a factory floor, I found myself standing at a *real* crossroads. It was night in a deep forest, but I could see the moon and stars above. A cool breeze fluttered behind me and with it came the scents of evergreens and damp, decaying leaves. Ahead of me lay three paths: one directly ahead, one to the right, and one to the left. I felt no danger here, but that same sense of decision lay upon me like a heavy blanket.

I heard a cracking and ripping come from the dark forest on the path directly ahead. It startled me, and I suppressed the urge to run in the opposite direction. But I felt no fear or terror coming from the sounds, not like the incomprehensible fear daemon that manifested in Terentius's camp.

A figure walked toward me from the path ahead. I could only see its dark outline, but I noticed it was holding what looked like clubs in each. When it got within a few paces from me, the tops of the clubs flared into white ethereal fire like spark globes. They were the bronze torch artifacts.

And I finally got a look at the figure's face.
"Hi, Remi," Brianna said.

45

I stared at Brianna for I don't know how long, unable to form words, breathe, or even think much.

"It can't be," I finally managed. "It's not you. Is it?"

Brianna smiled. She looked just like the last time I had seen her in Detroit. Her dark brown hair was tied back in a ponytail, wire-rimmed spectacles near the tip of her nose. She wore a red and white Detroit Cougars hockey sweater. She even wore the engagement ring that I had given her just two weeks before William sent me to ancient Rome.

But I knew before she spoke that it wasn't her.

"No," she said with Brianna's voice. "I thought this form would please you more than my true form."

A jolt of disappointment made my shoulders slump. "It does not please me," I growled. "It actually hurts me."

Brianna cocked her head in a very un-Brianna like manner, which suddenly made this all the more infuriating. "You loved this woman and yet you chose a different path that took you away from her love. Would you not want choose a path back to her if you could?"

I stared at this...image. "Who are you?"

"I have many names. The Greeks call me Hecate. The Romans call me Trivia. I am Isis to the Egyptians, and the Indians honor my spirit by calling me Dhatri. You have called for my wisdom. What path do you seek?"

Damnation. My Second Scan would only show me how the torches were made. Instead, I'd activated the artifact. That was the only way I could be carrying on a conversation with...whatever spirit inhabited the artifact.

"I seek the origins of the two torches," I said quickly.

"Brianna" cocked her head in a different direction. "That is not the path you seek."

"Actually it is. I really want to know where these—"

"There are bigger questions in your mind, Remi. I see them. That is how I can project this woman's body to you. None of the paths before you lead to the 'origins of the two torches.' What path do you seek?"

I exhaled in frustration. The artifact could see into my mind, so it likely noticed how exasperated I was getting with it.

"You may leave this crossroads at any time," the artifact said. "Simply turn around and you will go back to the cellar." She gave me a knowing smile. "But I don't think you want to do that."

Okay, think bigger. "I want to defeat Terentius. Which of these paths will show me how to do that?"

The artifact stepped aside and waved its two torches toward two of the paths, the left and the right.

"Two choices, two paths," it said. "Either will lead to the outcome you desire."

"What about the center?"

"The center is always reserved for the one option you have no matter what decision you struggle to make."

"And that is?"

The artifact cocked her head again. "To do nothing."

I glanced at all three paths. "Do I get a sneak peek, or do I have to guess?"

The artifact laughed, which sounded like Brianna's laugh, but wasn't. Nonetheless, my heart, which was already scarred from losing her once, began to crack again. It brought memories of happiness and soft skin and optimism for the future.

"You may 'peek' at any path you desire," she said. "I only *show* you the paths. You must decide for yourself—later, in your reality—which is the wisest."

I glanced at the paths with pursed lips. All three were equally dark and misty and right out of a twenty-first century suspense drama. I had Scanned the artifact to find its origins, but now it appeared that it would give me far more important information.

But would it be true? How could I trust anything this artifact showed me? My magical senses, again, detected no Darkness or deceit. That didn't mean it wasn't well hidden. That had happened to me before. Besides the fact it tried to pretend it was Brianna, my magical senses, honed from a lifetime of use, only detected honesty. So my first decision was to decide whether or not to trust the artifact.

Well I didn't need to trust it in order to listen to what it had to say. I could see these paths and then decide for myself.

"Let's try the 'do nothing' path first," I said. "What do I do?"

The artifact pointed the two torches toward the center path like a groundsman waving in a docking aero-craft. "Start walking."

I started walking. When I passed "Brianna," it took all my will to keep from taking her in my arms and never letting her go. I even caught a whiff of her flowery shampoo.

Damnation, this is killing me.

But I made it past her without breaking down and proceeded up the center path.

I only walked two paces upon the misty path, and then I was standing upon the walls of Danel's home. Just outside the walls stood a thousand Roman legionaries in their classical block maniple formations. Vitulus sat atop a horse in the exact center of his army. I don't know how I picked him out, for he had no standard bearer nor wore armor and helm that was different from the other officers. But I knew it was him.

Beyond the legion was a white-tinted dome covering all of Danel's home and the entire legion. It was transparent, but slightly distorted, like looking through a white stained glass window.

When I saw what was on the other side of the dome, I wished it was opaque.

Outside the dome was a vast ocean of madness beneath a red and black sky. It seemed that all the creatures that I had seen within the arena surrounded us from all directions. They screamed and writhed, cracked their bones, and squirted acid and other disgusting fluids. They crawled over each other like swarming millipedes. There was no order to their ranks, just chaos. Only the dome was holding them back.

I turned around, knowing before I saw them that Helva and Silanus were powering that dome. They stood in the center of the farm's courtyard, their palms pointed toward the earth, both of them sweating and stone-faced with concentration. A column of white-tinted light rose from each of them, intertwined like a braid, and rose a hundred feet into the air. The braid of lights connected with the dome, powering it.

Surrounding Helva and Silanus were hundreds of Carthaginian refugees who had been camped outside the walls when we arrived. They had given Helva and Silanus as much room as they could, but the courtyard was almost standing room only. Men and women, children and elderly, wounded and sickened. They all looked dirty, exhausted, and out-of-their-minds terrified.

Cana stood on my right and Paetus on my left.

Paetus wore a legionary helmet, a chain mail shirt, and held a bow with an arrow nocked. He looked more ridiculous than intimidating, but he wore the determined expression of a man who knew he was in a hopeless battle, but would fight nonetheless.

Cana wasn't wearing any armor, but she did wear the evergreen glove artifact. She held a gladius in the gloved hand and had the same expression as Paetus. She turned to me and glanced up at my head.

"Should you not turn your cap around, *leraar*?"

I raised my eyes and noticed the bill of my Wolverines baseball cap was pointed forward. "Right," I said, turning the bill around so that it faced backward.

I said and did this, and yet it wasn't *me* controlling my own mouth or my hands. I was standing in my own body, yet I was simply a spectator to what it was doing. I could feel the emotions running through it—fear, resolve, anger, despair—but I couldn't read its thoughts. It was strange, but I went with it.

Which goes to show how many strange things I'd gotten used to in ancient Rome.

Terentius's voice boomed from directly in front of me, just outside the dome.

"I do not want to kill you, Natta Magus," he said.

I looked closely at the lines of slathering monsters and picked out Terentius from among them. It wasn't hard: He was the guy wearing the same bright blue toga that he'd been wearing in the arena. Himilco and a couple dozen other men stood next to him, wearing bright blue turbans and holding curved swords. The men looked the same as they had back in Terentius's camp, except for the blue fire that flickered in their eyes.

It surprised *me*, but it didn't seem to surprise my *body*.

"We should be working together," he said. "You and I can remake this world into one that—"

"Shut him up," my throat growled.

Cana raised her evergreen-gloved hand. It flared and then a bright green flame shot into the air like fireworks on Union Day in Detroit. The green burst flew right into the dome above us, blended into it, and turned the dome into an iridescent green.

Behind me, Helva and Silanus yelled out something in Coptic. I felt the pressure of their earth magic compress my chest and make my ears pop.

The dome surrounding us surged outward and slammed into the hordes of dark creatures. The monsters within the first dozen paces of the dome screamed in pain and terror and then disintegrated into daemon pus that sizzled and evaporated. The daemons behind them tried pushing backward, but the push forward from all the daemons in the horde behind them prevented their escape. The dome surged forward at the speed of a sprinting human. There was nowhere for the daemons to run. The dome took out hundreds of them before its surge slowed and stopped about fifty paces from where it started.

I wondered why the artifact considered this the "do nothing" path. It sure seemed like my friends and I were doing something here.

Well, I wondered that until I noticed Terentius. Whereas the dome surged uniformly outward toward the monsters, it flowed *around* Terentius and his cohort of men, encasing them in an iridescent bulge in the dome's perfect circle.

"The dome isn't working on Terentius," my mouth yelled to Helva and Silanus.

Helva and Silanus clenched their teeth and bore down on their earth magic. All of that earth magic made the chaotic noise around us feel like it was burying me.

I turned back to see Terentius and his men pushing, as if walking into a gale wind, toward Vitulus's Praetorian legion. The dome was slowing them, but it wasn't stopping them.

Helva screamed and Silanus issued a growling cry. I watched them both collapse at the same time and lay on the ground, unmoving. Some of the refugees surrounding them leaned over the siblings, but their eyes were closed and they didn't move.

On the battlefield, the dome flickered and then burst into tiny grains of radiant sand that floated to the ground and dissipated.

The world seemed to pause for a second.

I felt the terrible soul magic rise up from my body, but I pushed it down just like I always did. And I knew why: *Better to die with a soul and exist, than to enter oblivion.*

The black wave of monsters shrieked in victory and surged forward.

Vitulus and his legion were the first to be consumed. The monsters slammed into the legionary shields, and the Roman lines disintegrated. Monsters leaped over and into the Roman ranks, instantly decapitating, goring, and ripping men limb from limb. The black tide rolled through the legions and finally reached Vitulus's position. He raised his sword and spurred his horse forward...only to disappear beneath spear-like claws, choking tentacles, and bloody teeth.

Terentius was jogging forward now and had used his magic to form a multi-colored wedge that cut through the legions in front of him like a molten sword through limbs. All arrows and javelins that touched the wedge burst into flame and floated to the ground as ash. Any soldier that attacked him disintegrated like the daemons that had touched the dome. Even brushing past the wedge meant the loss of a limb. The wedge left a wake of men screaming at the sudden loss of an arm or leg, only for their screams to be silenced by the wave of daemons that followed Terentius.

When the daemons got past the legions, they attacked Danel's meager walls. Most of monsters didn't even attempt to climb the wall; they just jumped.

Paetus shouted a war cry, swung his sword at a spindly daemon that looked like a gnarled gray branch with spearheads for limbs. The daemon took Paetus's swing on the arm with a wooden *thunk* then thrust one of its other spear-like limbs into Paetus's throat. My friend just gurgled on the blood spurting from his mouth, his eyes rolled up into his head, and he died mercifully quick.

Cana, wearing the evergreen glove, managed to hack to pieces several centipede daemons that had skittered over the top of the wall with stabs and swings that seemed too fast for my eyes to follow. But even with the glove's magical foresight, the daemon onslaught was too much. A daemon with long tentacles at the base of the wall wrapped one around her ankles and yanked her off her feet. My body leaped to grab at her outstretched hands but missed them by mere inches. Our eyes met for an instant, hers wide and terrified, and then she was gone. She never screamed.

The daemons took out the other men and women who stood upon the walls as easily as they had taken out the legions. More daemons leaped over the ones attacking the walls and into the midst of the defenseless refugees. It was a slaughter. I saw Danel swinging his curved sword at any daemon that came near him, but he was soon overwhelmed. Elissa came from out of nowhere with her own sword, screaming her rage when she saw her uncle go down, but she died within seconds of her uncle. I had no idea where Alishat was, but I had the presence of mind to pray that she was hiding somewhere.

My body took this all in with utter despair. I'd never felt so low and without hope, not even when I'd learned in the Ring of Saturn that I'd have to give up a life with Brianna and stay in ancient Rome. My friends were dead. The innocent people I tried to protect would all soon die. Then it would be my turn.

All because I didn't want to use my soul magic to save them. When it came down to it, I wasn't the self-sacrificing man I wanted to be. I was just selfish.

I blinked and then I was back on the dark, misty crossroads with the artifact. Brianna's face watched me expectantly.

"What happens?" I gasped. "Where did Terentius go? Does he—?"

"The answers to those questions are beyond my abilities," the artifact said. "I can only show you the immediate consequences of each choice."

"Well that's *beyond* useless!" I snarled. "How can I make a decision if I don't know how everything will end up?"

The artifact once again cocked its head in that non-Brianna way. "Not even the gods can see how all paths 'end up.'"

Its answer and the way it tried to be Brianna just infuriated me even more. "You are not Brianna! Why did you have to pick the love of my life? The one person that I can never see again?"

"You would prefer my true form, then?"

I paused. "Um—"

"So be it," she said.

Brianna split in two. Well not exactly, more like her body began to form a second body that tried pulling out of the first one, but then got stuck. For a moment they looked like conjoined twins, with the backs of their heads and shoulders still connected. Then the duplicate began creating a third version of Brianna, which merged into the first, forming a triangle with their connected heads and shoulders.

Then the forms of Brianna blurred and grew. When they stopped changing, the three-bodied Trivia looked like beautiful Roman women with black braided hair beneath elegant palla shawls and styled stola dresses. Who happened to be connected at the heads and shoulders.

The woman facing me held a set of keys, while the two women on the left and right each held one of the artifact torches.

"Do you prefer this form?" the woman facing me asked.

I stared at the three of them and then said, "Yes, actually. What about the two other paths?"

The woman on the right said, "Two paths that will achieve your goal."

The woman on the left said, "One leads to your ruin."

The woman in the front said, "One leads to the ruin of the world."

"So...both paths lead to me defeating Terentius?"

"Yes," all three said at the same time.

"But one 'leads to *my* ruin' and the other 'leads to the *world's* ruin.'"

"Yes," they said.

"Can we save some time and you just tell me which is which?"

The center woman gave me a blank face. The two others stared straight ahead with the same expressions.

I hated artifacts.

"Right hand rule," I muttered, and then walked up the right path.

46

For a second, I thought I'd mistakenly gone down the first path again.

I stood upon the walls of Danel's home. Just outside the walls stood a thousand Roman legionaries in their classical block maniple formations. Vitulus sat atop a horse in the exact center of his army. I don't know how I picked him out, for he had no standard bearer nor wore armor and helm that was different from the other officers. But I knew it was him.

Beyond the legion was a white-tinted, transparent dome covering the entire complex and about a hundred paces beyond it in all directions.

And outside the dome was a vast ocean of madness beneath a red and black sky.

My body didn't blink, but the part that was *me* did. This *was* the exact same view that I'd seen in the middle path.

Paetus once again stood to my left and Cana on my right, both wearing the same armor and evergreen glove, respectively. I turned around to see Helva and Silanus struggling to maintain the dome. Hundreds of refugees were crammed around them in the supposed protection of Danel's walls.

Cana glanced up at my head and said, "Should you not turn your cap around, *leraar?*"

"Right," my body said, and then reached up and fixed it.

Just in time for Terentius's voice to boom, "I do not want to kill you, Natta Magus."

I looked out onto the battlefield and saw him standing among the monsters and his blue turbaned men just like in the first vision. "We should be working together. You and I can remake this world into one that—"

"Shut him up," my throat growled.

And like last time, Cana raised her evergreen hand and shot some kind of green fireworks into the sky that merged into the dome and turned it an iridescent green. Then Helva and Silanus yelled out their Coptic words, and the dome surged forward. It obliterated that first line of monsters...but again, Terentius and his men stood firm against it and began pushing their way forward.

Helva and Silanus screamed. The dome burst into green, shimmering grains of sand.

And everything paused for a second.

During that second, my soul magic surged within me, wanting to unleash itself onto the oncoming hordes like it had on the first path.

But this time my body did not try to push down the soul magic like I'd always done.

Instead my body welcomed it.

I held up my hands, cried out nonsensical words, and then thrust my hands outward as if I were pushing someone away from me. Blue white fire shot from my palms in tight beams brighter than the noonday sun. I could look on the beams without hurting my eyes, but I was aware of everyone around me either shutting their eyes or turning away.

I didn't care. All I felt was anger and annoyance directed at Terentius. Even if I could've read my body's thoughts at that moment, it wouldn't have been necessary to know what it was thinking. Its emotions told me everything: *That primitive fool thinks he can play god, eh? He has no idea what gods can do. I'll show him.*

The blue-white beams hit Terentius and his crew of daemon men, disintegrating them all with barely a scream, and then proceeded past them into the monstrous hordes. The beams cut a swath several paces wide right down the middle of the monsters and then continued on over the horizon. I slowly spread my hands apart. The beams followed, their widening arc destroying even more monsters until there was a forty-five degree cone of empty, blackened landscape where the monsters had once been charging.

I turned in a full circle. From my spot on the walls, the tallest part of Danel's villa, I could sweep the beams of soul magic across the entire valley. And where they swept, monsters died in bursts of sizzling pus.

The power of this moment was indescribable. It was all consuming. There was nothing else in the world except that power; all I wanted to do was keep using it.

My body didn't care that it was moments away from burning away my entire soul. In fact, it seemed to want to hurry the process along. It didn't care that once my soul was gone, my body would die in a cataclysmic explosion that would kill all my friends and the people I was trying to protect.

But at least I had defeated Terentius. The intense satisfaction of it was infectious, and I found myself thinking, *Who's the god now, you Roman piece of—?*

I blinked. I was back on the dark, misty crossroads. Trivia's creepy three-bodied body still stood in the center of the crossroads. The woman in the center with the keys stared at me expectantly.

I took several deep breaths and put my hands on my knees. The horror of watching my body destroy itself—paired with my overwhelming desire to do that for real—took its toll. This was all happening in my mind, but damnation, my body felt like I'd just drained all its magic.

"I don't suppose," I said, my hands on my knees, "you're going to tell me what I did with all that soul magic after I killed Terentius?"

All three faces could've been fashion golems for all the expression they showed.

"That's what I thought," I said. I straightened my back, took a few more breaths, and then walked toward the final path on the left.

47

Final path, same setup. I was noticing a pattern here.

I stood upon the walls of Danel's complex looking down on a Roman legion, a white-tinted dome, and a vast ocean of darkness and madness outside it.

"Should you not turn your cap around, *leraar?*" Cana asked on my right. She wore the evergreen glove. I noticed pin pricks of blood around her arm where the glove's needles dug into her skin

"Right," my body said, and then reached up and turned it around.

I didn't have to turn to my left to know Paetus was there, all armored and ready to fight despite not knowing a thing about fighting. Brave, glorious Paetus.

"I do not want to kill you, Natta Magus." Terentius's voice sounded exactly the same as the other two paths.

Here we go again, I thought.

"Shut him up," my voice growled.

Cana raised her gloved hand. The blast of cell magic that she sent into the glove raised the hairs on my entire body. A burst of green fireworks shot up into the dome above us. With a green flash, the dome surged into the monsters.

As before, every daemon in the first hundred paces of the dome's path disintegrated into pus that sizzled and evaporated before hitting the ground. But as before, the daemons filled the entire valley. There were a million more replacements.

Terentius and his cronies were still immune to the dome's power. They stood against it for a moment and then pushed their way forward to Vitulus's Praetorian legion. The dome struggled against them, Helva and Silanus behind me groaning with the effort to push back against Terentius's own multi-colored shield.

But again, their dome failed. Helva and Silanus collapsed to the ground, their eyes closed and their bodies still. I suppressed a groan at seeing Helva look so lifeless.

And then that same pause from the other two paths came to the battlefield. My body knew exactly what to do.

I reached for the pack at my feet, pulled out the red cloak, and draped it over my shoulders. At the same moment, Cana yanked the evergreen glove off her hand with a pained grunt and thrust it into my hands. The needles pricked my palms, but I ignored the pain and shoved the glove into the pack from which I'd retrieved the cloak. The teddy bear and torches were in the pack, too.

I pulled the hood of the cloak over my head. The last thing I saw before disappearing was Paetus and Cana wishing me Fortuna's grace with their desperate eyes.

I was suddenly standing upon a mesa in what looked like the deserts of the American southwest. The air was still and cold, and I could see my breath. The sky was hazy with a pink and brown taint as if a sandstorm had just rolled through at dusk. The mesa itself was about a hundred paces in diameter, and I could see other mesas miles away rising out of a black mist. I caught flashes of multi-colored light and serpentine movements within that mist.

On my mesa, I was encircled by black, red-veined marble columns that rose all the way into the hazy sky, seemingly to infinity. Lit braziers stood next to each column casting the area in an orange, flickering glow.

A circular, black marble dais arose from the gravelly mesa in the middle of the column circle. The wicker basket artifact sat at the top.

My legs jumped the three wide steps to the top of the dais, and then I opened my pack. I dumped the teddy bear, the glove, and the two torches into the empty basket. Then I took off the cloak and shoved that into the basket, too.

I took out the last item in my pack—a clay vial with a wax stopper. I pulled off the wax, held the vial over the basket...and hesitated. It was as if I was unsure of what to do next. Or perhaps afraid to do what I knew I had to do. I had no idea what the problem was, because I couldn't read my body's thoughts.

I heard scratching and clawing coming from the edges of the mesa all around me. I looked up to see Himilco and his blue turbaned men leap from out of the black mist surrounding the mesa and charge toward me.

That made up my mind. Everything seemed to happen within a couple of seconds. Himilco and his men passed the black columns, converging toward the dais. I poured the contents of the vial, which looked like blood, into the basket, threw the vial away, and placed my hands over the basket. I took a deep breath, and then I opened up my cell magic and poured it into the basket.

And it wasn't just a jolt of magic. With growing alarm, I felt my body draw in as much cell magic as it could and send it into that basket artifact. The basket flared with the colors of my aura, a swirling red mist with blue sparks. My voice screamed with the effort and pain of channeling so much magic. But my body didn't ease up. It just kept pouring more into the basket.

Damnation, I thought, *I'm draining myself.*

What was I hoping to accomplish? One of the biggest lessons we learned in the twenty-first century, since before we could cast our first spark globe, was to never drain all of our magic from our bodies. The results of doing so were different for every magus: One might go nova like a mad soul magus, or one might simply drop dead without a sound. Some might lose all ability to siphon their magic again. I'd almost done that two years ago in Aventicum and had temporarily lost the ability to wield my magic for months afterward. I eventually got it back after realizing that I had to "re-learn" a new way to siphon it again. Was I hoping this would happen again?

And, again, why was I doing this at all?

My body didn't seem to care about the consequences.

And then I was done. I had emptied my cells of magic. At the same moment, the basket flared in a brilliant blue and red light, and an explosion of air flung me from the dais and onto the mesa's rocky surface. I slid a dozen paces, scraping the hell out of my face and arms, and came to a stop lying on my stomach.

I was thankful that I was still in Observer mode. That had looked painful.

My body groaned, turned over, and looked toward the dais. Only charred bits of wicker and a pile of ash remained of the basket. The light had reduced to a viewable level, but blue swirls and red sparks still floated above the artifact's remains.

I heard Himilco to my left snarl something in Punic. He and his men had also been knocked down by the basket's destruction, but they were all rising slowly. Himilco stared at the basket for several seconds and then turned his enraged eyes on me. He lifted his curved sword and strode toward me with killing purpose.

And that's when I returned to the misty crossroads with Trivia.

I clenched my teeth. I knew I would be disappointed with the answer to the question I was about to ask, but I had to ask anyway.

"What. Happened."

The woman with the keys said, "You defeated Terentius."

"But what did I do?"

The woman on the left, her eyes still on the left path, said, "You saw—"

"I know what I saw!" I yelled at the goddess. Part of me said it probably wasn't wise to scream at a goddess, but damnation, I just watched my body drain itself of magic for a ritual I couldn't explain. "Why did I do what I did? What did I do to Terentius? He wasn't even there!"

The woman on the right, watching the right path, said, "You defeated him."

The very definition of "frustration" is any communication with ghosts, gods, or artifacts.

I sighed heavily, took off my ball cap, and scratched my head. I set my cap firmly back on my head and said, "Okay. You've showed me two ways to defeat Terentius and one way to lose horribly. Although that second way was technically a win, I'd say it's a loss in the long run. So that leaves the final way. How can I learn what the goal of that ritual was?"

As I expected, the woman with the keys said, "The answers to those questions are beyond my—"

"Abilities, right," I said, rubbing my eyes more out of annoyance than any attempt to clear them. "So what happens now?"

The woman with the keys said, "You return to your body and make a choice. You may never again use these torches to communicate with me."

"What? Why?" I'd never heard of an artifact that had an expiration date or a usage allotment. "You mean nobody can use them or just me?"

"Only another magus," said the woman on the right.

"One who is not you," said the woman on the left.

"The maker of these torches felt it was safer that way," said the woman in the middle.

I sighed and then nodded. Mucking around with time tended to have dangerous side effects. And that's speaking from personal experience.

"Fine. How do I go back to my body?"

All three bodies of Trivia said, "Turn around, Natta Magus."

So I did.

I blinked and was back in Danel's wine cellar still holding my hands over the torches for Second Scan. Cana stood facing me in the same way. Our eyes met.

"Trivia," I said.

She nodded slowly. "I saw how to defeat Terentius." She paused. "And how we could lose."

"You saw the *future*?" Helva asked, looking from me to Cana impatiently. "I thought your Scan would only show you the artifact's origins."

"Their Scan activated the artifact," Silanus said in a bored, condescending tone. "Fortunately it only muddled *their* minds and not ours, sister."

"My mind is not muddled," I said. "But I know what we need to do."

"And what not to do," Cana said with a haunted expression.

"Yeah," I said. "We have some decisions to make."

48

We all reconvened in Danel's library. It was tight, for the "library" was a ten-foot by fifteen-foot room with shelves on opposite ends filled with scrolls, leather-bound books, and clay tablets held together with wire rings. A desk was arranged at one end of the room between the shelves, where a half-burned candle sat in a holder overflowing with solid wax dribbles.

While it was about the same size as the wine cellar, it had the psychological bonus of not being closer to the underworld. And with the entire farm complex filled with scared refugees and soldiers running errands, the library was about the quietest place we could gather.

Cana and I described each path vision in turn. Her first two paths matched mine exactly. She remembered doing everything I saw her do in my visions, from our encounter with the three-bodied Trivia to the battles. Apparently she was only given two paths to choose from: either follow my lead in using our cell magic to fight Terentius or allow me to wield my soul magic without shouting "warm milk" to knock me out.

Vitulus and his two officers absorbed our stories with grim faces: especially when I described how Terentius and his horde rolled over the Praetorian legion each time as if it weren't there.

One of Vitulus's officers rubbed his chin. "Filled the valley, you say?" He shrugged. "I'd put them around a hundred thousand, give or take a century."

Vitulus said nothing.

After I described my third vision, including my confusing encounters on the mesa with the basket and Himilco, I listened intently to Cana's version. To my disappointment, she described the battle exactly how I remembered it. She, too, couldn't read the thoughts of her body, so she had no idea what our plan was.

"Then you disappeared," she said.

"What about after I disappeared? Did you see what happened to Terentius or his army?"

She hesitated and then looked at Paetus. "You said something curious after he left: 'I hope he gave enough blood for this.'"

Paetus raised his eyebrows. I felt mine go up, too.

Silanus chuckled darkly. "So you must give up your own blood for this spell? May I be the one who takes it, Natta Magus?"

"Brother," Helva said in a suffering tone.

I ignored him and asked Cana, "What else?"

Cana fidgeted with her long braid. "Terentius screamed something. There was a flash of light, like what you described in the temple...and then he died. The vision ends after that."

"What did he scream?" I pressed. "How did he die?"

She shrugged. "He screamed 'not him.' I do not know what that means. Then came the flash, and he was gone."

"What do mean gone? Did he disintegrate? Was he a pile of ash? Did he—?"

"He was just gone!" she snapped, tugging on her braid. "After that, the vision ended." She sighed. "I am sorry. I cannot remember more. Speaking to a goddess was a very disturbing experience."

I'd been thrown into alternate dimensions and talked with godlike beings many times since I arrived in ancient Rome, so I forgot how disconcerting the whole thing could be to someone who'd never done it before. Especially for someone who grew up knowing of those godlike beings as articles of faith rather than mythology.

I put a reassuring hand on her shoulder. "It's okay. You did well, *leerling.*"

She nodded absently, still tugging her braid.

Silanus sniffed and then grinned. "This a wonderful tale. Adventure and heroism that rivals the exploits of Heracles. Makes me shudder with excitement." His grin melted. "How do we know what you say is not a myth as well?"

Vitulus shifted his stance. I recognized the threat that implied even though I doubted Silanus noticed or even cared.

Before I could respond, Cana took a step toward him. "Why would we create a fiction like this? We saw the same things! Does that not prove our words are true?"

"No, it does not," he said mildly. "Natta Magus gave his story and then you nodded obediently like a good *leerling.* 'Yes, dominus, quite right, dominus. I saw it too, dominus. May I fetch your sandals, dominus?'"

I spread out my hands and said, "I don't know what to tell you, Silanus. We can't prove to you what we saw. Either you help us or you don't. Which is it?"

"Let me use the torches to verify your story," he said.

"No!" Cana and I said at the same time. We shot a glance at each other, then returned our glares to Silanus.

"Not gonna happen," I said to him. "You'd just use the torches to weasel a way out of your Oaths. No way. Again, are you going to help us or not?"

His smile chilled me. "I am not going anywhere."

With that settled—for the moment—I tried to think furiously. Terentius had sacrificed two Roman legionaries to activate the basket back at his camp, so the basket required a blood offering to work. Why would I need to use *my* blood? Was it because it required the blood of the one who would use it to stop Terentius?

And just what had my blood done?

Paetus suddenly turned to Danel and asked, "Do you have *In Medio Mundi* by Sallustius?"

Danel, silent until now, unfolded his large arms, his eyes suddenly bright. "Of course," he said, checking a shelf on the right. He pulled down a leather bound book that was more of a folder for the loose pages within and handed it to Paetus. "This version was copied by Sallustius's own apprentice."

Paetus placed it on the desk and began leafing through the pages.

"What are you looking for?" I asked him.

"The black marble temple and the flat mountain tops you described reminded me of something I read in an index of one of Sallustius's lesser known works. He mostly wrote about the Catiline conspiracy sixty years ago and other war histories. But he also dabbled in the religious and spiritual practices of North Africa. I've never read *this* book, but I remember seeing a reference to it in one of my books about—*ah!*"

Paetus pulled out a loose sheet of tanned paper. There was little light in Danel's windowless library, so without asking, Cana siphoned a spark globe and directed it over the paper in Paetus's hand. A sharp gasp came from Danel, but Vitulus's officers didn't even flinch. I didn't recognize them, so I wasn't sure if they'd seen me do it or not. Regardless, they seemed more interested in the paper rather than the spark globe.

"'The Punics,'" Paetus read, "'have many uncouth rituals and beliefs, but the most intriguing is the belief by a small sect regarding a realm of spirit where the underworld and the earth meet. It is a world of purification for souls whose sins and deeds balance, but are not yet worthy of the Punic realm reserved for their honored dead. The Punics believe this world *can be a bridge between the earth and the underworld,* where denizens of each may freely roam *through a doorway of black pillars and flat mountains,* if Ba'al and the gods so allow it.'"

"Obviously," Silanus said. "How else how did my sister and I come back here?"

"The basket," I breathed. "It's an artifact that opens the doorway to that bridge. I was destroying the basket in my third vision! If we can destroy that basket—"

"Then we close the bridge," Paetus said excitedly. "Terentius's army will disappear because they cannot survive on earth without that open bridge!"

"What about that dome you saw?" Helva asked. "That sounds like a powerful spell. I am not sure my brother and I could do such a thing."

"Of course we can do it, sister," he said smoothly. "I will show you. It is not all that different from my column thingy."

I so badly wanted to throw a heavy book at Silanus. Instead I said, "Plus you get a hit of cell magic from Cana and the evergreen glove. Is that what your body did in your visions, Cana? Cana?"

She was deep in thought and flinched when I said her name. "Yes," she said. "I sensed myself pouring all my cell magic into the glove when I raised it. I may have drained myself, too."

I nodded, giving her a long look. Perhaps that was also why she looked so troubled. She was dealing with things no *leerling* should ever have to deal with. As if daemons and battles and a gruesome death weren't enough, now she had to contemplate draining all her magic and its potentially catastrophic implications.

"And I," Silanus said, "am not overly fond of what happened to us when Terentius broke through our dome."

"I'm not overly fond of draining my magic and getting attacked by Himilco and his men," I said, "but I'm willing to do it if that means stopping Terentius."

Silanus stared at me. "Are we expected to drain our magic as well, Natta Magus?"

"I expect you to fulfill your Oath."

"I will fulfill my Oath," he said coldly. "It is my sister that I wish to spare such trifles as madness and death."

"It is my choice, brother," Helva growled. "Do not presume my love for you includes obedience."

"I would never presume such a thing," he said. Then he glanced at me with a raised eyebrow. "I just want to ensure that *Natta Magus* understands what he's asking of us."

"I understand the consequences if we *don't* act," I said. "Our deaths, the deaths of these refugees, the end of the world, that sort of thing. I know exactly what I'm asking. From all of you." I spoke to Silanus, but looked at Helva. "Your sister is a warrior. Without her strength, Invidia would've taken your mind moments after she took you to the underworld. Without her honor, you'd still be there. I wouldn't risk madness and death without her."

I meant every word of what I said. Helva kept a straight face as she returned my stare, but damnation, her deep brown eyes smoldered with a promise that I prayed I'd survive to...

Soul magic. Dangerous. Remember?

I tore my gaze away from Helva's promising eyes and looked at Vitulus. He and his two officers had remained silent the whole time.

"Buddy, I know these visions are...grim for you and your men."

He gave me a dark smile. "Since when are visions from the gods cheerful?"

I couldn't help but return his smile.

"My men and I have taken oaths as well," he said, his face turning stone serious. "If this army of daemons should appear, it is our sworn duty to do all we can to protect the Republic and her citizens. We will fight." His grin returned. "Although I am pleased you prefer the third vision. That one seems to hold the best chances for our survival."

I nodded to him slowly, all the while picturing his wife, Claudia, and their infant son, Lucius, back in Rome. I'd held Lucius in my arms many times and was welcomed by Claudia into their home like an honored member of their gens. Now I was asking my best friend, Claudia's beloved husband and Lucius's proud father, to stand before a wall of daemons that I'd just reported would rip him limb from limb.

And the bastard was perfectly willing to do it. I didn't know if that made this easier or harder.

My gaze swept across them all as they stared at me expectantly. Even Silanus regarded me with questioning eyes as if waiting to hear what I said next. I got that feeling of crushing responsibility again that every decision I made from here on out would decide whether they lived or died.

Leadership is stressful. Some people thrive on it. It mostly turns my guts to water.

"Well then," I said, faking courage. "We have a world to save."

49

Right after our meeting, Vitulus deployed scouts throughout the hills surrounding the valley to warn us of Terentius's approaching horde. The scouts remained out there all day, but returned once the sun set. They reported no enemy movement or activity. Carthage continued to burn and pockets of refugees moved about the countryside, but there was no sign of the daemons Cana and I described.

They didn't even see signs of Seius's legion, which Vitulus was keen on finding. I was pretty conflicted on that, as you can imagine. On one hand, I figured having an angry Seius around might complicate things when we should all be united and focused on one threat. On the other hand, I was still horrified over what I'd done to them and wanted to make sure the remaining legionaries didn't get torn apart in the countryside by Terentius's horde. Nobody deserved that kind of fate. At least they'd have a chance here.

Well as much of a chance as any place else in North Africa.

The lack of daemons made me nervous in the way you get when you're waiting for the monsters to jump out at the heroes in a mirror drama. But the absence of a threat gave us plenty of time to move all of the refugees within Danel's walls. While there was some grumbling over the cramped conditions, I think they'd seen enough of the monsters that had destroyed Carthage to know that they'd be safer crammed into a walled space than outside with breathing room.

Once I'd seen to the refugees, I was free to walk the complex to see how my friends and allies were faring in their preparations.

Vitulus's Praetorians had time to dig trenches that they hoped would at least slow down the daemon attackers. I think Vitulus was mostly giving the men something to do rather than holding any illusions that the trenches would stop leaping and flying daemons. I'm sure his men felt the same, but they attacked their work with typical Roman efficiency and discipline.

Helva and Silanus talked quietly in Danel's library, the one place in all the complex that we'd made off limits to all but the magi and Vitulus. Silanus explained how he'd cast the column in Carthage, and they debated ways they could combine their earth magicks to expand it. Helva spared me a lingering glance whenever I walked by the open library, which I did my best not to return. Not only did I remember my own fears over getting too close to her, I also felt Silanus's warning glare bore into me like arrows.

Which is why I let Danel draw my blood and not Silanus. In addition to being a farmer and a priest, Danel was apparently an accomplished physician. Or at least as accomplished as a physician could be in the ancient world.

"I've done many a bloodletting," he assured me as I nervously placed my left forearm on the desk in his library. He opened a leather pouch filled with knives, tongs, and hooks upon the table. *Instruments of torture*, I thought. When he took out a large metal bowl, I could feel my eyes boggle.

"We only need a few ounces!" I said.

"Yes," he replied with the same confident voice of a twenty-first century doctor, "but we do not want to waste a drop. The bowl is large enough to catch it all. We will put the blood in this." He placed a clay vial on the desk. "Is this sufficient?"

I stared at it. It was the exact same vial that I'd seen in my vision. "That'll do," I said quietly.

About ten minutes later, I left Danel's library with a cloth wrapped tightly around my upper forearm, a light head, and a vial of hot blood in my components vest. I'd never wanted orange juice and donuts more in my life.

Vitulus lent Paetus some spare armor, which he began trying on with martial gusto. He'd never served in the legions, a rarity for male Roman patricians at the time, so he had little experience with how to buckle everything correctly. Vitulus assigned one of his patrician officers to help Paetus, who surprisingly seemed to have the same passion for daemonology as Paetus. I think it took them far longer to get Paetus into his armor than it should have since they were so animated by their opinionated discussions on various daemonology texts.

I made sure to be with Cana when she tried on the evergreen glove for the first time. We stood atop one of the ramparts on Danel's walls, the place where we had stood in our visions. It offered the best view of the now empty valley. The other artifacts were in the leather pack at our feet.

Cana winced when she pulled the glove on. The evergreen needles dug into her skin, but she didn't complain.

I handed her a gladius that Vitulus lent to us. "When I used the glove on Himilco," I said, "I didn't need to siphon any magic into it. It just worked."

I drew my enchanted gladius and adopted a battle stance. There wasn't room atop the wooden ramparts for a full on sparring match, but I just wanted to give her an idea of how the glove worked.

She adopted a battle stance, too, though with a slightly differing placement of her feet and sword angle. She had told me that her father had shown her a few moves when she was a child, just before she was sold into slavery. While she could never practice with a real sword, she had practiced the positions many times in her rare private moments in anticipation of the day she might fight for her freedom.

I stabbed forward, and she easily parried my attack. Her eyes widened, and she looked down at the glove. "I saw what you were going to do before you did it. I even had time to ponder how to defend it."

"Weird, eh?"

"Wonderful," she said. "An army equipped with these would be unstoppable."

"Yeah. Unless the other army had them, too. That would be an interesting battle."

She continued staring at the glove. "I wonder how it—?"

Without warning I swung toward her head. It was a killing attack that I never would've attempted in a normal sparring session, even when I knew she was ready for it.

But she batted my swing away with barely any effort or a shift in her stance.

She smiled at me. I smiled back. "I think you've got it, *leerling*."

She shifted her eyes to the glove, her smile fading. "What will happen after I drain my magic?"

I sheathed my gladius. "Well in both of our visions, you didn't drop dead, so that's a plus. Afterward?" I shrugged. "Other than being drained of magic, did your body do anything different after I disappeared?"

She shook her head thoughtfully. "It makes me wonder if..."

Cana looked uncomfortable as I waited for her to finish.

"If I really *did* drain myself all the way," she said, looking away. "Maybe I held back out of cowardice. Maybe that is why the dome collapses. I did not give it all the magic I could have."

"Hey," I said, "I'm the one who's supposed to carry all the guilt in this party, remember?" The corners of her lips upturned in a slight grin that didn't grow.

"Look, I'm not asking you to drain yourself of magic. I'd never do that. That would be like me ordering you to jump on a hand grenade." Her brow furrowed in confusion, but I went on. "Put as much into it as you can. If you get to a point where you feel like you're about to hurt yourself, then stop. I don't need your death or maiming on my conscience either."

She licked her lips. "What would happen if...Terentius wins?"

"He isn't going to win," I said. "Whatever it is he wants from me, I won't give it to him." *He might just kill everyone I care about, which I've conveniently assembled in one spot for him...*

She nodded slowly. "You rarely speak of your home. What would this world be like if everyone had magic?"

"I've told you how dangerous that would—"

"I know," she said, "we are not ready. You have said this many times. I am not convinced, but I understand that Terentius's way would be terrible. I just want to know what *your* world was like."

That was a deep question that I could've spent a lifetime answering. How could I describe all the billions of little things in my world that I took for granted, but would make her jaw drop through the ramparts? How could I explain the beauty of Detroit's magically reinforced skyscrapers and the floating aero-planes that docked at them? Spark globes on every street corner lighting the way at night? Instantaneous communication with loved ones on the other side of the world? Watching a baseball game on a warm summer day—a hot dog in one hand and a cold beer in the other—knowing the loser wouldn't die a bloody death at the end of the contest if the president gave them a thumb's down?

Simple joys that I could go on listing until the twenty-first century arrived.

There were problems, to be sure. The world was still a dangerous place. Yeah, everyone had magic and could defend themselves, so crimes like murder and robbery were virtually non-existent. But nobody was immortal. While the Aether surrounding the world kept soul magic from being used, people still used mundane weapons and cell magic in terrible ways.

But even though everyone had magic, there were still rich and poor, the brilliant and the not-so-brilliant, the talented and the mediocre, people with ambition and people content with what they had. Predators and victims.

We did the best we could and always hoped for the best.

I gave Cana a rueful grin. "We were human."

She stared at me, waiting for more. "I know that's not what you want to hear," I said, "but it's true. Things were different, yes, but we still had the same human desires as everyone here. We wanted to be free, wanted to be loved, wanted to be respected."

I glanced at Paetus near the main house, still working on his armor and having an animated discussion with the centurion that Vitulus had assigned to help him. My gaze moved to Vitulus and Danel studying the villa's walls and pointing out strengths and weaknesses. Helva and Silanus stood in the center of the courtyard practicing their dome spell, the refugees giving them a wide circle so as to avoid the earth magic they were casting. I saw Elissa handing a water skin to a young Roman officer, both of them smiling shyly at each other as they spoke.

"What gives me hope," I said, "is how even in this world that can be so brutal, people can still get along to achieve a worthy goal. Academics and soldiers. Romans and Carthaginians. Earth magi and cell magi." I tried to keep the cynic in me from snorting at that last one. "My home was different from this one, yes. But not where it counts."

A gleam of metal in the valley caught my eye. I looked up in time to hear one of the Roman sentries on the ramparts call down to Vitulus.

"General, scouts returning!" the sentry yelled.

Vitulus frowned, for I knew that the scout's return was ahead of schedule. Something was up.

As Vitulus ordered Danel to open the gates to allow the scout inside, I turned to watch the scout approach. He was riding fast, forcing his horse to gallop over open terrain. Even I knew that was a dangerous thing to do given the rocks and gravel on the hill he was racing down.

Then I saw an inky black streamer rise into the sky behind the scout. It was like a plume of smoke, but far blacker and denser.

"*Leraar*," Cana whispered beside me.

I followed her pointing finger toward the west. Another streamer was rising there, too. I turned all the way around and saw streamers in every direction, all of them growing thicker by the moment. The tips of the streamers met high above the farm. The blackness expanded outward from where the streamers met in the center eventually creating a black dome that stretched to the horizons around us. The blackness roiled, and red lightning flashed within.

"More scouts returning!" cried the sentries on the walls.

More riders raced toward the farm from the other three cardinal directions. When I looked closer at the riders coming from the east and south, however, I noticed it was just the horses galloping toward us. The men were gone.

Vitulus didn't even wait for the scouts to reach the complex and report. He immediately yelled orders to his officers as he jogged toward the open gate. The officers all ran off to their respective cohorts.

Before Vitulus passed through the gate, he looked up at me as I looked down at him. We'd been through some dire situations during our two-year partnership tracking down daemons and supernatural threats in Rome. There wasn't much else we could say to each other that we hadn't already said each of those times.

So we just nodded. One of his men brought his horse up to him. He mounted and trotted out through the gate toward his mustering legion on the field in front of the walls. The surviving scouts skidded their horses to a stop in front of him and breathlessly made their reports.

I turned to Helva and Silanus, who still stood in the center of the courtyard. But now they both studied the inky blackness covering the sky. Helva wore a grim, worried expression, while Silanus seemed like the only person in the entire complex who looked bored by all the commotion.

"Helva," I cried. When she turned to me, I said, "Now would be a good time."

She nodded curtly, all business. She aimed her open palms toward the ground and then said something to Silanus. The man's posture exuded all the confidence in the world as he also aimed his palms toward the ground. Clear, undulating waves of magical energy rose toward their open palms. After a few moments of pulling in all the magic they could from the earth, they shouted something in Coptic. The energy burst upward from them in a solid column of shimmering white magic, like the way the air looks above a blacksmith's forge. The magic stopped just beneath the point where the black streamers were spreading and ballooned out like an umbrella. It fell back to the earth in the shape of a dome that encompassed the entire walled complex and several hundred paces beyond. We were all cast in a soft white glow.

"Damnation," I breathed, watching the dome form. This was industrial strength magic that would've taken entire teams of magi in my time to perform. I turned to Helva and Silanus. Both of them stared directly at each other with intense concentration, sweat glistening on Helva's brow and even Silanus too. I'd never seen that level of effort from either of them before. Not even on the Capitoline two months ago. This dome was taxing them to the draining point, and they hadn't even begun moving it yet.

Danel and his household, along with several dozen refugees, joined us upon the ramparts. All were armed with bows, arrows, and short swords. The other refugees crammed into the courtyard below, cried and prayed, and hugged their loved ones.

Paetus, his armor creaking and clinking, leaped up the stairs to stand beside Cana and me on the rampart walls. They both looked as terrified as I felt.

"You guys okay?" I asked. I couldn't disguise the tremor in my voice.

Flashes of red lightning from the black sky above the dome added more shadows to their faces than illumination.

"Sure," Paetus said, glancing at the sky.

Cana swallowed. "I will do what is necessary."

"I wish I had some inspiring words for you," I said. "Damnation. I just wish I had some spit in my mouth."

Paetus and Cana both looked at me. Then Paetus barked a laugh and Cana grinned, shaking her head.

With a wide smile, Paetus said, "I wish my bowels were not about to release."

I barked my own laugh at this.

Then Cana said, "Beware the piss puddle at my feet."

This brought laughter from all three of us. I noticed the men on the ramparts nearby eying us as if we were insane. At that moment, perhaps we were.

A wave of vicious, unnatural shrieks rolled over the farm, turning off our laughter like an extinguished spark globe. The red lightning illuminated a dark wave of daemons pouring over the tops of the valley all around us as if a million spider nests had suddenly burst. The daemons, just like in my visions, were all slimy tentacles, rigid carapaces, skittering bug legs, and bladed limbs. They leaped and ran and flew and crawled. There was no symmetry at all to their bodies or their cries.

It was one big wave of chaotic horror, and we were at the center of it.

We all stared a while, our minds numb from the impossible revulsion of it all. After a few moments, Cana turned to me and said, "Should you not turn your cap around, *leraar*?"

"Right," I murmured.

I reached up to my trusty ball cap with shaking hands and turned it around. Play ball.

50

Not even the three visions from Trivia prepared me for actually being here in this battle. I'd felt everything with my mundane five senses, but they'd all been muted and dreamlike. Now every one of my senses blasted me with reality.

I could see every wart, glistening carapace, and hairy spider leg on the daemons rushing down the valley. There were even undead men, women, and—most disturbingly—children among the horde, screaming and running right along with the rest. I wished I could send a spark globe streaking throughout the masses of daemons. But even if I sent it as fast as I could, it would only kill a couple dozen before the rest of the horde plowed into us.

I turned away from that horror to Vitulus's Praetorian legion efficiently forming into maniples. They looked laughably meager, like a colony of ants trying to stop a flood of raw sewage rushing down the Cloaca Maxima. But by Jupiter, they were going to do their duty and try.

The stench of sulfur mixed with burning offal wafted across the valley. I assumed the dome was blocking the worst of it, but the odor coming off the horde was enough to make many of the defenders on the wall cough and gag.

The air grew cold and stale as the inky darkness blocked out the sun. I shivered despite my thundering heartbeat and ramped up adrenaline. If it got any colder, I'd see my breath.

The sounds were the worst. The entire valley was filled with the shrieking of a hundred thousand hellish voices. I've heard some pretty frightening cries from animals when I used to camp with my parents in northern Michigan, but I'd always known that they were just animals. The cacophony from the things outside the dome, however, had no place in nature. Their screams were madness turned into sound.

And beneath all that madness were the cries of terror coming from the refugees behind me. My heart broke for the parents clutching their children, trying to keep their sanity themselves so that they could give their terrified children hope that this was *not* the end.

I saw Alishat sitting on the porch of Danel's main house holding a sobbing boy who was no more than three. Her eyes were terrified, but she spoke to him with a smile and what I could only assume was her best attempt at a soothing song. Somehow, over all the madness, I caught a hint of her voice and the tune.

I turned back to the gibbering horde. I clenched my teeth, my eyes misting with resolute tears. *No, this was not the end. I will make sure of that.*

I looked toward the position where I'd seen Terentius in the visions. It was a solid wall of black and gray and red daemons, but neither Terentius nor his men were among them.

I scanned the entire line of monsters from left to right, and murmured, "Where are you, you son of a..."

Terentius's voice boomed from my left, just outside the dome to the north. "You took some items from me, Natta Magus. I want them back."

I swung my gaze in that direction. I couldn't see anything with all the defenders on the walls, so I weaved around them toward the north end of Danel's complex. I stopped at the wall and stared out at the monstrous horde. Terentius and his blue-turbaned men stood over a hundred paces away just outside the dome.

I felt Cana arrive just behind me, and I gave her glance over my shoulder. Our worried expressions said it all: *This is different from the visions.*

And if this was different, then what else would be different? Optimist that I am, I chose to believe that the visions were more of a basic outline of what would happen as opposed to a word-for-word script.

I *had* to believe that.

"Bring me the artifacts, Natta Magus," Terentius boomed again, his voice fading in and out as if amplified by a faulty speaker system. "We can remake the world in our image." He paused. "Not to mention save the lives of your friends inside that little molehill."

I ignored Terentius and turned to Helva and Silanus in the courtyard below. Both were looking up at me, waiting for my signal: Helva with resolute, confident eyes and Silanus with the same expression, which looked more like arrogance on him. At least he no longer looked bored.

"Shut him up," I yelled to them, pouring as much conviction into the order as I'd heard in my vision voices.

Then I looked at Cana and went off script. "Do what you can, *leerling*. But don't kill yourself."

She nodded, her lips thin. She raised her gloved hand and gladius toward the dome directly above. I felt the cell magic build in her; my skin itched and the hairs on my body stood on end. Her teeth clenched from all the power she held, and the muscles on her face tightened with the effort. But she kept building and building it, layer after layer of magic, siphoning more from her cells than I'd ever seen her draw before. Every instinct in me wanted to tell her to stop, to tell her it was enough.

But my visions had not shown me trying to stop her. They hadn't shown me an inkling of what I thought. I figured that was a good thing. I don't know if I would've let Cana do this if I'd known how helpless and terrified I felt for her.

She screamed and then released all that cell magic in a solid green beam of light that shot up into the dome. It collided at the apex where the shimmering earth magic from Helva and Silanus was forming the dome. The entire dome flared green for an instant and then took on a green iridescence. The display of power from that artifact proceeded just like my visions. At least that part was following the script.

Helva and Silanus screamed their Coptic words. I couldn't understand them, of course, but I understood the tone: It was a battle cry, as if they were charging into the line of daemons with nothing more than a gladius and the desire for a glorious death.

My ears popped from the force of their magic. The dome flared again. It seemed to contract a couple of paces, as if taking a deep breath, and then it exploded outward at the same velocity as my visions. The first lines of daemons surrounding us disintegrated into sizzling, purulent spray. The dome pushed through the hordes almost fifty paces before it began to slow.

Terentius and his men were surrounded by that damned multi-colored shell. The expanding dome flowed toward and then around them, forming a divot in the dome's uniformity. Terentius pushed forward. I was too far to see his face, but I imagined it was straining with the effort of walking into a gale. His bent posture and slow pace indicated as much.

Cana continued pouring cell magic from the glove into the dome. Her eyes were glazed and had a green iridescence similar to that flitting across the entire dome now.

I turned back to Helva and Silanus, saw them straining with equal measure. Both were sweating and their normally olive complexions were turning red from the effort. Veins popped out on Silanus's neck and Helva's teeth were bared.

I clenched my jaw to keep from yelling out to both Cana and Helva to stop draining themselves. There was no way to know what would happen to them, and odds were that it would be something bad. I wanted to rip the glove off my *leerling's* hand and run down to Helva and...I guess shake her to break her concentration. I wasn't thinking clearly. My worry clouded my reason.

If my reason *had* been functioning, it would've told me that both of them had chosen to do this. And that if I wanted to stop them, they'd be just as angry with me as I would if they tried stopping me from doing my part.

As predicted in Trivia's visions, the dome flickered and faltered the more Terentius and his men pushed into it. Its expansion slowed and then stopped when it could not recover from Terentius's penetration.

With a last desperate cry, Helva and Silanus collapsed to the ground, their eyes closed. My focus was on Helva, though. I tried to run down there, but Paetus grabbed my arm.

"Natta, the dome is gone," he yelled over the shrieking horde. "Put on the cloak!"

I'd been so worried about Helva and Cana that I didn't even notice when the dome burst into shimmering green sparks. That was the moment upon which everything had hinged, the one commonality between all the visions where I had made a decision that dictated what happened next.

And I'd missed it. *I hope that's not bad.*

I fumbled with the leather pack of artifacts, opened the straps, and pulled out the cloak. Now I understood why in my visions I had not been wearing it the whole time: I'd been sparring with Cana when the horde arrived and had been so overwhelmed by it all that I'd forgotten. Damnation, this was not starting out well.

Once I had the cloak on, Cana thrust the evergreen glove into the open pack in my hands. Pinpricks of blood oozed upon her hand and arm, but she seemed to be fine otherwise.

"Did you drain yourself?" I asked quickly.

She gave me a haunted look and then nodded. I wanted to assess her, ask her how she felt or if she could still siphon her magic. She was still conscious, so that was good—

But she flung her arms around me in a tight hug. "May the gods favor you, *leraar*," she said into my shoulder.

She let go before I had a chance to return the hug.

"Go!" she said.

I spared a glance at Paetus, his eyes saying basically the same thing as Cana.

Helva still lay motionless on the ground—*not dead, please not dead*—next to an equally still Silanus.

Then I shut my eyes, tried to ignore the victorious daemon shrieks around me, and focused on the basket.

The sudden quiet was just as startling as the daemon shrieks. I opened my eyes and found myself on the mesa.

5I

The quiet, I thought. By the gods, the quiet is so "earie."

Seriously, that was my first thought when I opened my eyes on an otherworldly mesa surrounded by a roiling black fog that could contain a host of daemons and magical terrors.

My first thought was a terrible pun.

That shows you how loopy I was from everything.

After I managed to keep myself from laughing insanely, I drew my enchanted gladius and scanned my surroundings for anything immediately life threatening. Darkness, infinitely tall black columns, and eerie quiet—sorry, I'll stop—surrounded me like prison bars. The same braziers that I'd seen in my vision stood next to each red-veined column, creating a flickering orange light around each one.

I turned around and saw the dais with the wicker basket artifact at the top.

I ran the ten paces to the dais, leaped up the wide steps, and stopped in front of the basket. I dumped the teddy bear, the glove, and the two torches into the empty basket and then took off the cloak and shoved that in as well.

Scraping and scratching came from the edges of the mesa in all directions.

Finally, I took out the vial of blood and unstoppered it in one smooth motion. I held it over the basket...and hesitated. It was only a second or two, but it seemed like the world had slowed and a lifetime of thoughts and internal arguments rolled through my mind in those seconds.

I still didn't know exactly what this would do. My vision said it would defeat Terentius, but what did that mean? I realized this was the worst possible moment to begin having doubts and second thoughts, but my hand just wouldn't move until I thought these things through.

What did Terentius mean in Cana's vision when he said "not him"? What was that flash of light and then his disappearance that she described? Did that mean he died or had pulled an earth-magic style "gating" to a different location?

But the vision and Trivia assured me this was the only way to defeat Terentius without using my soul magic. It was a bit too late to come up with a different plan, even if I had another artifact to...

Wait. The basket was an artifact. It was a bridge to the spirit world. The spirit world was the source of human magic. What if the basket didn't just create a bridge to the spirit world where the two worlds could coexist in the same space at the same time?

What if it was the bridge that brought magic to earth?

I looked at the vial in my hand.

My blood. My magic.

The basket in my vision had flared into a blue and red light before it burned.

The colors of my aura.

Damnation.

Was I about to do what Terentius wanted? Was I about to give magic to humanity? Was that the only way to defeat Terentius?

He could use whatever "aspect" magic he'd obtained to bring underworld daemons to earth, but to give magic to humanity, he needed the magic of a cell magus. If I added my blood, it would also add a bit of me into the mix. Which, if what I suddenly suspected was true, would give all humanity magic and a little bit of my essence. My soul.

Gears and wheels turned in my mind faster now. Maybe this was the part that Terentius wanted to come from him. He'd supply the blood, and I'd supply the magic. Then he could...what? Remake the world in his image with a magical humanity subservient to him?

My hand holding the vial began to tremble.

I know I'm not a perfect guy. I have my faults and weaknesses and then some, never mind the always dangerous urge to siphon my soul magic. If I did this, would those same faults and weaknesses—and then some—get sent out to every person in the world? Would everyone also have that desire for soul magic?

Or worse: Would everyone in the world suddenly believe I was some kind of god?

Terentius believed that's what would happen, and that's the goal he'd been working toward this whole time. Not some altruistic belief in equality and freedom.

He just wanted to be more equal than everyone else.

My hand shook even more. The scraping from the mesa's edges had turned to footfalls closing in on me.

How could I make this kind of decision? Silanus was right: I was just a mediocre scholar from a future that no longer existed. Who was I to make this kind of decision for the entire caccing world?

Or...was this the destiny for which I'd stayed in the ancient world?

Himilco and his men entered the brazier lights and didn't hesitate. They charged up the dais toward me.

Sometimes impossible decisions get made for you.

I poured my blood into the basket full of artifacts and chased it with more cell magic than I'd ever siphoned in my life.

Releasing so much magic at once was beyond exhilarating. I had that same feeling back in Aventicum—surrendering all control and consequences to my magic, breaking down barriers that I'd spent a lifetime erecting to prevent this specific act. It was liberating and frightening and beautiful all at once. I don't remember much of what I saw, and I think I even blacked out for most of it, yet I did not collapse to the dais.

Toward the end, however, it got harder to keep pouring the magic into the basket. My cells were depleting and that lifetime of discipline that had become instinctual was screaming at me to stop. Fear crept into the ecstasy of release, a fear that told me I was going to kill myself if I didn't stop.

I pushed through it. I sensed that I had to give everything or this wouldn't work. I had no proof that this was true other than the visions given me by an artifact. But it was the same sense I got whenever I'd made big decisions since my arrival in Rome. Was it the Unknowable Will, Destiny, the gods, or something else that I couldn't imagine? I didn't know. But it was there, and it was urging me on with gentle firmness.

I can't give any more.

[Yes you can.]

It's too much.

[Just a little more.]

I have no more!

[You do.]

I...I'm afraid. I don't want to die here, all alone.

[You are not alone. And you never will be.]

Wherever that assurance came from, it gave me the courage to drain the last of my cell magic into the basket.

The basket exploded into the red and blue lights of my aura, flinging me backward off the dais and sending me skidding along the rocky mesa. It was indeed as painful as it had looked in my vision. The wind was knocked out of me, I could barely pull in a gasping breath, and I re-dislocated my right shoulder. I don't remember feeling any of that in the vision, but damnation, I sure felt it now.

Two things were the same, however.

One, the basket and its contents were now a smoldering pile of ash. A blue and red shimmer hovered over the ashes and then dissipated.

And two, Himilco looked just as pissed at me. As soon as he recovered from the magical explosion, he lunged toward me with his curved sword upraised. I was completely defenseless. I had no magic left to defend myself. My right shoulder, my sword arm, was dislocated so I couldn't draw my gladius and have a reasonable chance of countering Himilco's blow. Plus I was laying on my stomach still trying to breathe again.

This was the point where the artifact vision had ended. I was entering unknown territory here. The vision said I'd defeat Terentius, but never mentioned whether or not I survived to savor my victory. Is this where Himilco chopped off my head?

Well I suppose I'm not giving anything away when I say I survived.

I watched Himilco come at me. The only thing I could do was sit up and face his attack with as much bravery as I'd seen others demonstrate today.

Bravery, hah! To be honest, there simply wasn't a damned thing I could do besides sit there.

It was the basket artifact that saved me.

It took a few moments, but once the basket's final cinder burned away with a blue-red spark, the bridge between the earth and the spirit world collapsed. This mesa was located within that "in between world."

Himilco stood above me, his curved sword swinging down toward my neck. But then he slowed as if he were at the bottom of the sea pushing his sword through the water. Cracks appeared in the air around us. They widened to reveal bright white light. Even Himilco and his men started to crack, like a drought-ravaged riverbed. Himilco's eyes widened, and his mouth opened in a silent scream.

Pieces of burning ash seemed to fly off him, his men, and the entire reality of the mesa. It looked as if everyone and everything around me were made of slow burning paper with white flames on the edges. The pieces dissolved in the purifying flames and floated away like the killed daemons.

It revealed another reality.

I squinted my eyes in that new reality's brightness. Compared to the darkness of the mesa, this new world was like staring at the sun. Once my eyes adjusted, I was finally able to figure out where I was.

I lay on dusty, gravelly soil. The sky above me was blue and cloudless. Directly in front of me, about twenty paces away, was a line of Roman legionaries. Their shields were raised and their short swords bristled from between the shields. I could even see their eyes behind their helms. Every one of the men I looked at stared at me with disbelief. Beyond them I could see the tips of the walls of Danel's villa.

I heard a choking sound behind me. I turned. Terentius stood just two paces away. Anger cannot begin to describe the look on his face. It was red, his eyes were bulging, and his teeth were bared beneath tight lips. While the darkness above the valley had disappeared, the daemon army had not. They remained, undulating and frothing, but just as shocked to see me as I was to see them.

I had somehow landed in the worst possible spot on the battlefield...in between two armies.

And Terentius made me pay for it by leaping those two paces and kicking me in the face.

52

His foot connected beneath my jaw, and he followed through as if he were kicking a soccer ball. My head sprang backward, and my ball cap actually flew off. My muddled brain was more stunned by my cap flying off than the kick. But then I remembered it was magic that kept my cap on my head.

I no longer had magic.

The back of my head struck the stony soil. I lay there unable to move or see beyond the stars filling my vision. Every nerve ending in my body had gone numb for an instant and then exploded in so much pain that I couldn't draw a breath to scream.

"It was not supposed to be you," Terentius snarled insanely, and then kicked me in the ribs. I doubled over on my side, despite the fact I lay on my dislocated shoulder. At that point I no longer had control. My body was acting on instinct.

"I was to rule them, not you!" he screamed. Some of his insane spittle landed on my cheek, and then he gave me another kick in the stomach. I couldn't make my body move fast enough, and he caught me prone. Gasping for air, I couldn't speak or think. My whole world was pain.

"I was promised this, not *you*! Not a barbarian!"

He stooped down next to me. I felt his hot breath on my face. His mad eyes suddenly flashed with multi-colored light. He was about to use his aspect magic.

"No matter," he snarled. "I will burn you alive with your own gift and scatter your ashes before your worshipers."

I had done everything the third artifact vision had shown me. How exactly was this defeating Terentius?

But at least he stopped kicking me long enough to catch my breath and think for a second about something besides the pain. I couldn't move; I couldn't siphon magic. I didn't know what else to do. So I did the only thing I could:

I would defy him with my last breath. I put as much conviction in my voice as I could and whispered one word.

"Stop."

The multi-colored flame in his eyes immediately died. This time it was Terentius's turn to look shocked. And frightened.

His face twisted in concentration, but whatever he was trying to do wasn't working. "What did you do to me?"

My pain addled mind tried to interpret what the hell he was talking about, but couldn't get beyond figuring out how to avoid another kick. So I stared at him. For one, I barely had the energy to breath. Second, I didn't do anything to him. I just told him to "stop."

Wait. Could I do that now?

"How did you know?" he muttered, almost childlike in his utter disappointment over this turn of events. Then his lips curled into a snarl. "It obeys you."

While no magic lit his eyes, the rage did return to his face. He screamed something incompressible and raised his foot to kick me again, aiming for my face. The only thing I could do to defend myself was close my eyes.

I heard a *thunk* and then several more. I opened my eyes. Two arrows had sprouted from Terentius's chest. More arrows *thunked* into him as if he were an archery range target. His eyes widened, he wavered a second, and then he fell flat on his back.

I made the supreme effort to turn my head back to the Romans and saw a cohort of archers retreat behind the protection of the front line shields.

Romans. They reminded me of the lions I once saw in a circus in Detroit. The lions acted all tame and obedient around their handler...but the handler never turned his back on them.

Right now I was happy to see the tame and obedient versions. At least from my perspective.

Of course the fact that Terentius lay on the ground with a dozen arrows in his chest did nothing about the hundred thousand daemons surrounding us all. The monsters were only a hundred paces away from me, the dome having thinned out their first few ranks by *maybe* ten thousand. That still left ninety thousand insane monsters that wanted nothing more than to rip apart any human, animal, and building they could find.

The daemons finally seemed to realize that Terentius no longer had any control over them. They saw no dome and no obstacles between them and fresh prey. They surged forward as one black ghoulish wave.

Ninety thousand daemons versus a thousand Praetorians and about three hundred refugees.

It looked hopeless.

But hope is a funny thing. I've learned that when my hope flees me, it's usually for relatively minor things, like when the Wolverines were on the verge of clinching the pennant (i.e., "They're gonna blow it just like they do every year!"). And yet it's in the most hopeless situations, like now, when hope seems to burst out of me. When it fuels my muscles for one last push.

Gives me one last idea on how to snatch victory from the jaws of a daemon's feed hole, wrap it up nice and special, and shove it back down its throat.

If I could stop Terentius's magic, could I also *give* magic? Is that how this all worked now?

I turned away from the oncoming horde. Still sitting with my good arm propping up my torso, I transferred my weight and got to my knees. I swayed a bit from the pain in my shoulder, face, and chest, but I maintained my balance. I needed to see as many of the legionaries as I could, and I didn't think I'd be able to get to my feet in time. I could see at least the first three or four ranks.

It would have to do. I took them all in, as many as I could see, trying to ignore the shrieking and skittering and thumping behind me that was getting closer by the second.

"*Vonk globe*," I grunted in my bastardized Dutch. *Best to start with something simple.*

The faces of the men in front of me contorted in surprise, but only for a few seconds. Almost as one, they dropped their shields and swords. Angry shouts came from the centurions behind the men, from the ones I could not see, but the men in the front lines ignored their officers. Each man held up his right hand.

I still couldn't siphon my cell magic, but I could certainly feel all the men in front of me siphon theirs. One by one, a spark globe of varying intensity and size formed above each outstretched hand. Up and down the lines, four men deep, the ethereal spark globes made the daylight all the more brighter.

A globe shot past me, barely missing my head by a foot. I wasn't too concerned since spark globes can't harm humans.

Daemons, on the other hand...

The daemons had come within twenty paces or so of my back when spark globes began shooting past me from the Roman lines like lit rocks. I didn't have to turn around to know the globes were obliterating the daemon lines. Their shrieks of violent pleasure had turned to shrieks of horror. Or at least that's how it sounded to me; they both sounded pretty similar.

I slowly stood, swayed a bit, and then stumbled toward the Roman lines. More spark globes flew past me, hundreds from just the first few ranks alone. It was a lot, but wasn't going to be enough to stop a ninety thousand daemons. We needed more.

So I walked as fast as I could, which wasn't fast at all. I almost tripped over several rocks, but I kept my balance and continued forward. The Roman lines in front of me began to part, which gave me a view of the angry officers who'd been yelling at their men a moment earlier. They now stood in stunned silence watching their men siphon magic.

"*Vonk globe*," I cried through my swollen jaw. It wasn't very loud, but it was enough for the officers to hear. They stared at me a second and then held up their right hands. White spark globes formed in swirling spheres above each hand. They thrust their hands forward like the front line legionaries had. The globes shot toward the daemons behind me, resulting in more horrified shrieks from the daemons.

I kept walking. It felt like I had a knife stuck in my side where Terentius had kicked me. There must've been another knife in my jaw. My steps dragged in the rocky soil. I think my toes were bleeding from me ramming them into sharp rocks on the ground. But damnation, I kept walking.

The legion was tearing apart the daemons directly in front of it with the spark globes, but what about the hordes on the other side of Danel's walls where I couldn't see? If everyone was to survive this, if we were to completely annihilate the horde, I needed to expand my sight.

I didn't know how I'd do that short of flying. I hadn't even known a cell magic spell for flying.

It was time to see how loud my teacher's bullhorn was.

I knew I couldn't scream the spell aloud because I didn't think I could muster more than a mumble through my jaw. So I closed my eyes, dug deep into whatever new power I had, and imagined myself screaming as loud as I could to everyone:

VONK GLOBE!

A wave of vertigo from the agony in my ribs, shoulder, and jaw made the world tilt to the side. My legs couldn't hold me up anymore, and my balance fled.

I fell to the ground, landing mostly on my good arm. I remember choking out a hysterical laugh that I probably just dislocated my other shoulder. Somebody rolled me over on my back, and I looked up to see a group of legionaries surrounding me. Vitulus was suddenly there too. His lips were moving, but I couldn't understand a word.

I was too focused on the thousands of spark globes zipping across the blue sky above the Romans like the spray from a waterfall.

I think I smiled. And then I know I passed out.

53

I floated on a rubber mattress on Lake Michigan in the northeast part of the Lower Peninsula. It was the middle of summer. The lake was calm, almost like glass, which was pretty rare for a Great Lake. The sun shone down on my bare chest, warm and pleasant, and the sky was a deep blue. My fingers caressed the water on either side of me. I glanced up and down the beach, noting the bright sandy dunes covered in beach grass and shrubs. This was Esch Beach, where my family and I would come every summer. It was probably the most peaceful place I'd ever been to.

I smelled meat cooking on a charcoal grill on the shore, just ten or twenty paces away. I turned my head slightly. My dad stood over his red grill flipping burgers and sausages. He wore his plaid swim trunks and a faded Wolverines t-shirt proclaiming them the 2006 American League champs. He refused to get the magically powered grills that didn't require an open flame because he claimed "meat and magic don't mix." I could never tell the difference, but hey, he was the cook.

Mom sat in a beach chair beneath an umbrella wearing a wide-brimmed hat, sun spectacles, and a flowery one-piece bathing suit. She was reading a Steven Saylor paperback novel about ancient Rome. She seemed to sense that I was looking at her, because she looked up at me and smiled.

Then she frowned and called out, "Remi, you're looking a little pink. Did you shield yourself?"

"Twice," I murmured. If I spoke too loudly, my voice would break the peacefulness around me. For some reason I felt like that was the last thing I wanted. "It's just the red in the mattress, mom."

"I don't think so. Come in, I want to work a sun shield on you."

"Mom..."

Dad continued flipping the meat on the grill and said, "It's almost lunch time anyway, champ. Come on in."

I issued a suffering teenager groan and then sat up in my mattress and placed my feet in the soft sand just two feet beneath the smooth warm water. I stood and carried my mattress onto shore, held my arms out as if I were about to be frisked, and said, "Fine, Mom, show me how it's done."

She gave me The Look over the tops of her spectacles as she stood. "A little less attitude, young man. You don't want to die of skin cancer like Grandma Sheila."

I decided it was best *not* to point out that Grandma Sheila died of skin cancer despite a lifetime of sun shielding herself.

Mom siphoned her cell magic. My skin tightened as the shielding spell seemed to close my every pore. It felt like warm rubber was poured over my body where it solidified into a tacky layer.

"Damnation, Mom, astronauts aren't this shielded."

"Language," she said, and then sat back down.

"Lunch is served," Dad said from the grill.

My stomach grumbled, and I felt like I could eat all the burgers and sausages on the grill. I grabbed a tin plate, added buns, and loaded them up.

Dad raised an eyebrow. "Must've worked up an appetite with all that floating, eh?"

"I'm a growing boy," I said, taking a bite of sausage before sitting down beneath the umbrella.

We all sat in our beach chairs beneath the large umbrella, eating and taking in the peaceful scenery in amiable silence. To my right were large, cliff-like dunes about three miles distant that jutted out into the lake. To my left, the shoreline curved for several miles into a small point covered in dunes with trees and shrubs. There was nobody else around us. It was peaceful and relaxing and...

Too peaceful.

I glanced from my mom to my dad. I set my plate down and asked, "Am I dead?"

"What kind of a question is that?" Mom said. Although she didn't say it with the appalled tone of voice that I knew she would've used had I asked that in real life. It was more of a mildly curious tone.

"What do you think?" Dad said, in between bites of sausage.

"I think," I said, "that you guys are answering my question with more questions. I've had enough encounters with spirits and artifacts lately to know when I'm speaking with them."

I blinked. *Now where did those words come from?* I was just a fifteen-year-old on vacation with his parents. Wasn't I?

No. I wasn't. Memories flooded back, memories of daemons and fear and the ancient world. Of giving everything I had to save my friends from madmen and monsters.

"I'm dreaming," I said. "I passed out on the battlefield in front of Danel's villa."

Mom put her plate down, reached over to me, and took me in her arms. Her arms were warm and soft, and she smelled like mom. I wrapped my arms around her and began to cry.

"My brave boy," she whispered. "Don't you think you've earned a little break?"

"Maybe," I said. "Maybe not. I think I did a really bad thing."

Dad tossed his plate into an open garbage sack nearby. "You saved your friends and hundreds of people. Not to mention all of North Africa. What's bad about that?"

"I released magic into the world before it's time."

Mom pulled back from her hug and held my shoulders. "Magic was going to enter the world with or without you, honey."

"But this wasn't the time. It was supposed to come later."

Dad chuckled. "A lot of things were supposed to come later. You weren't supposed to be here at all. But you are. Maybe magic should be, too."

"What if people use it for evil? What if they use soul magic? What if the Dark Wars start two thousand years early?"

"There will always be bad people," Dad said. "Just like there will always be good people who rise up to fight them."

I shook my head. "I don't know if they're ready."

Mom smiled. "Then you will teach them."

"How am I supposed to teach *everyone in the world* how to use their magic without killing themselves or someone else?"

"You'll figure it out," Dad said. "You always do."

"That's helpful," I grumbled.

"When magic first came to our world," Mom said, "do you think there weren't mistakes or conflicts or danger? There always are with new things. But people figured it out. Just like people in this time will. Starting with you and your friends."

I shook my head. I looked out at the peaceful lake and wished I could stay forever. "I can't help but feel like I've traded one big problem for an even bigger problem."

"Perhaps," Dad said, shrugging. "Or perhaps it's one big opportunity."

I glanced at him. "For what?"

He winked. "You'll figure it out."

My dream mind was doing a great job recreating my parents. They were always like this: forcing me to come up with my own answers rather than just giving them to me. It was frustrating as hell at the time—like now—but I knew it had made me a far more creative thinker.

I guess I just had to have faith they were right.

"Well," Mom said, standing up, "the sun is setting, so we should get going. The mosquitos will be out soon, and I don't think you want me to cast another shield on you."

My skin was still tight as a drum from her sun shield. But I would've let her cast a thousand shields if I could spend one more day with them on this beach.

I blinked furiously and then stood up with them. They looked at me with proud smiles. I wrapped my arms around them and drew them into a three-way hug. We all stood that way for a while.

I gave them one big squeeze and then pulled away. "This was a good dream," I said.

"You can always find us here," Dad said solemnly.

"Always," Mom said.

I woke up.

54

I 'd never been in Danel's bedroom, but I immediately knew I was lying on his bed when I awoke. The bed had a soft mattress and finely woven insect netting hanging over it from a central point on the ceiling like a silky chandelier. The room was windowless like most Roman-style bedrooms, but lamplight arranged throughout the room, and sunlight streaming from the atrium just outside the open door, gave it a cozy feel. Frescoes of desert landscapes and exotic African animals—lions, giraffes, alligators—filled the walls.

The netting was open to my left. Cana sat slumped in an armchair next to me; her head leaned back in what looked like a really uncomfortable position. Her mouth was wide open, and she was snoring.

I did an inventory of my body. First I moved my jaw around. *Okay, good, feels normal.* I took a slow deep breath, expanding my rib cage as far as it could go. *Ribs are healed too.* I tentatively rolled my dislocated shoulder. *Back in place.*

I sat up and was pleased that I felt no wearier then I would've waking up any other morning. I looked at Cana and smiled at her sleeping form. "You heal like a champ, *leerling*," I said aloud.

She jerked at the sound of my voice and raised her head, blinking rapidly. When she finally focused on me, she exhaled sharply. She jumped out of her chair and wrapped her arms around my neck.

"I am sorry," she said, her voice breaking. And then she did something I'd never seen her do before: She began to cry.

"Hey," I said, returning her hug. "I'm fine thanks to you. This healing *was* from you, right?"

She nodded against my shoulder.

"So that means you're fine after draining your magic?"

"I believe so," she said, her voice muffled. "It came back an hour afterwards."

"That's great. You might be one of the lucky—"

"I knew," she mumbled.

"What?"

She pulled back from me and sat down in her chair again. However, she stared at her hands in her lap through red, tear-filled eyes.

"I saw it in my vision," she said. "It was the third path that Trivia showed me." She looked up at me. "For us to defeat Terentius...I had to lie to you about what I saw after you destroyed the basket. I *knew* you were going to give magic to the world."

I leaned back against the wall and licked my lips. Then I reached over and put my hand on hers. She still didn't look at me, but she had stopped crying.

"In my first vision," she said, "I told you everything that would happen. You decided not to do it and went with a cell magic strategy. We all died." Her words came out faster and in a heavier Gallic accent. "In my second vision, again you refused the spell on the basket and decided on soul magic. My task was to sleep you after you defeated Terentius's army...and then kill you. Because you would have used up far too much of your soul to be trusted to wake up. So the third path, lying to you, was far better. But it was difficult...you are my teacher and friend. And I knew how much you did not want to—"

"Cana," I said quietly, "you did the right thing."

"You almost died because of my lie."

"I would've died if you hadn't lied."

She looked at me. "*Would* you have performed the spell if I had told you my vision?"

I didn't have to think about it long. "At the time, probably not. I still think the risk is too great...but I just had a good dream. It makes me think that we'll figure it out."

And then my limbs went cold. I looked at Cana and asked, "Where's Helva?"

"She is fine," Cana said quickly. "She did not drain herself during the battle. We think the breaking of the dome sent a jolt of magic back into her." Then she got a sour look and said, "Silanus is fine, too."

I nodded. The only reason I cared whether Silanus lived or died was that it would break Helva's heart if something happened to him. In that respect, I was glad he made it through, too. But I still didn't trust him.

"Where are they?"

I swung my legs over the side of the bed and stood, much to Cana's alarm.

"Danel's library. Should you be walking now? I almost drained myself healing you. I do not want it to be for nothing if you fall down and break your neck."

I rotated my shoulder and twisted my torso. I even opened and closed my mouth. I didn't swoon, and none of my injuries were on fire, so that made me 100% in my book.

"Damnation, *leerling*. After this healing maybe it's *you* who should be in bed resting."

She gave me a weak smile and then glanced at the bed. "Well if you are not going to use it..."

She crawled onto the bed, and I was almost out the door when she called, "*Leraar.*"

I turned in time to see her toss my Wolverine ball cap to me. I caught it.

"We found it on the field next to Terentius's body," she said, lying down on the bed. "I thought you might miss it."

I stared at my trusty, dirty, magical focus, ball cap. Even now I couldn't sense any cell magic in me. Would I still need my cap? It had been a part of me for over a decade. If what I suspected were true—if my cell magic was gone for good—then my cap would be nothing but a style choice.

Worse, a reminder of what I'd lost.

I tossed it back to Cana, who caught it with one hand.

"*Leerling*, you've done more magic in two months than most people in my time do in four years of academy. So I pronounce you 'magus'. You may now have a magical focus. Use it well."

She stared at the cap a moment and then slowly put it on. Her eyes began brimming with tears again, and she looked at me.

"It smells so bad."

I grinned. "Then wash it."

She returned my grin, and then her chin rose with that familiar Cana pride. "Thank you, *leraar*."

"You've graduated," I said. "Call me Natta." And then I left the room through the open door.

And almost ran into a spark globe hovering a foot in front of my face. Beyond the globe came Paetus down the hallway. I didn't know if he was chasing it or directing it.

"*Vonk globe*," he said, and the globe dissipated into ethereal white sparks that floated away. He grinned at me the way he always did when he made some new discovery.

"Magic. This feeling, the power in my own skin, the release," he said breathlessly. "Is that how it is when you use it?"

I swallowed hard and tried to match his enthusiastic grin. "Yeah. It was."

It took him a few seconds to catch the past tense. When he did, his grin wavered. He looked me up and down, and said, "Cana did well with her healing. But I take it she could not heal all things."

"No," I said.

"Did she explain...well, I mean, did she—"

I nodded. "She told me about her visions. Her real visions. I hate that she had to lie to me to get me to do the right thing. At least I pray it was the right thing..."

"She hated it, too," Paetus said. Then his eyes brightened. "Does this mean you are *leraar* to the world now?"

I barked a weary laugh. "We'll see."

"Can you teach me something else right now?" he asked eagerly. "You know, to test your new power."

"Paetus, I really want to go see—"

"Just one quick spell. An easy one."

I glanced past Paetus toward the stairs that led down to the library. "How about later after I've—"

"Oh, teach me the sleep spell! I've always wanted to know how—"

"*Slapen!*" I said, with a quite a bit more irritation than I'd intended.

I didn't feel anything like I had on the battlefield when I had "sent" the spark globe spell to everyone. All I'd done was say the word, which alone had brought up the feelings I had when I actually cast the spell.

Apparently that was all it took. Paetus's eyes grew distant for a second, and then he blinked several times as if coming out of a particularly intense daydream.

He smiled like a kid with a new toy. "I wonder if Cana will let me practice on her."

Then he rushed past me into the bedroom. I hurried down the hallway toward the stairs, but not before I heard Cana's angry voice and Paetus's pleading.

I normally would've smiled at their bickering, but I feared this sort of thing was happening all over North Africa and maybe the world: people using their spark globes like a toy or a game. Had I saved the world for a different sort of chaotic destruction? How were they going to learn—?

They'll figure it out, came Dad's voice.

It was my dream, so obviously there was a part of me that believed humanity would "figure it out." But it warred with a lifetime of lessons regarding caution and magical discipline. Without it laid the path to the Dark Wars and human extinction.

Learning how to reconcile those two sides was just one of the things that *I'd* have to "figure out."

Danel's house was surprisingly quiet, given how chaotic it had been before the battle. I wondered where everyone was, but found that I didn't care too much. With the danger gone, everyone must've left the cramped and crowded complex walls for the elbowroom outside.

I found Helva in Danel's library. She stood with her back to the door, both hands leaning on a table as she read over a scroll she had unfurled, her hips cocked to the right.

When I entered the library, she turned and did a double take when she saw it was me. Her deep brown eyes sparkled.

"Natta, you are awake—"

Before she could finish that sentence, I took two strides toward her, pulled her close to me, and kissed her. A quick, growly noise came from her throat, and then she flung her arms around my neck. She pressed her body into mine and returned the kiss. She had just bathed, for she smelled of fresh jasmine that always seemed to accompany her. I ran my hands down her firm back. Her hips swayed slowly against me. She ran her fingers through my hair. I kissed her even deeper.

Then she pulled away, looking up at me from beneath dark lashes. Her eyes smoldered, and I wasn't sure if it was a reflection of the candle nearby or the fire in my own eyes.

"When the sun sets," she said in a low, husky voice, "we will meet in Danel's bathhouse." She stood on her tip toes and kissed me gently on the lips. "It has locks."

I grinned. "Sounds naughty."

"I do not know 'naughty'," she said, kissing me again softly. Then she gave me a coy smile. "But it will be glorious."

Glorious. Damnation, I thought I was going to explode right then and there.

"What will be glorious?" Silanus said from behind me.

I whirled around, jumped away from Helva, and knocked over half the scrolls on the reading table. Silanus stood in the doorway, shadows covering most of his face. His arms were folded across his chest. At least his hands weren't pointed toward the earth.

"Our victory, brother," Helva said smoothly, and then calmly bent down to pick up the scrolls that I'd knocked over.

Silanus continued to point his shadowed face in my direction. "Is it true, Natta Magus?" he asked quietly. "Did you give up your magic to save all mankind?"

Silanus wasn't stupid, so it was no good trying to make him think that I still had magic. I had...something. But it wasn't the cell magic I once had.

"Yes, my magic is gone. For now."

Silanus stared at me, unmoving. I crossed my forearms to match his posture and returned the stare.

"Then my Oath is fulfilled," he said. He turned around and walked out of the room.

I glanced at Helva. "Should I be worried?"

She paused, looking after Silanus a moment, and then shook her head. "He knows what you mean to me. Though he does not approve, he knows I would never forgive him if he hurt you."

I reached over, took her hands in mine, and gave her a piercing gaze. "Are you sure about...later?"

"I have never been surer about anything. Are you?"

I'd thought about that question ever since I started thinking about "Helva and me." I had loved Brianna with all my heart. Losing her was the most painful thing I'd ever had to deal with in my life. I had worked through some of it during all that time in the Ring of Saturn over a year ago, but I still ached for her. A part of me always would.

But she was gone. I would never see her again.

Helva was fierce, talented, and had her own sense of humor and honor. She was royalty, the granddaughter of Cleopatra, descended from a long line of kings and queens that went all the way back to one of Alexander the Great's trusted generals. She exhibited all the best qualities of royalty: self-sacrifice, wisdom, strength.

Over the last two months, I'd often thought that she was what Brianna would've been had she grown up in the same circumstances. But it wasn't fair to compare Brianna and Helva. They were different women from different times.

I was different, too. I had done things here that I couldn't imagine having the courage to do back in the twenty-first century. I didn't know what kind of relationship Helva and I would have, but I figured if I was going to "move on," then I'd be a fool not to try it with her.

"I am sure. Your highness."

She lifted her chin and crossed her arms over her breasts as if she were holding the royal Egyptian rod and staff. Then she gave me another coy, sideways smile.

"Natta Magus!" cried a voice from behind me in the atrium. I ground my teeth at the interruption and turned. Even though I was happy to see my best friend Vitulus striding toward me with a wide grin, I found that I wanted nothing more at that moment than for the *caccing* sun to set.

I glanced back quickly at Helva. With blazing eyes, she whispered, "Sunset. The bathhouse."

Vitulus still wore his armor from the battle, which creaked and clinked as he walked. He wrapped me in a big bear hug and laughed. "You have more lives than Jupiter has children, my friend."

I slapped him on the back as I returned his hug and said, "Glad you made it, too, buddy."

He pulled away and studied me. "You're well, then? I'd heard your magic was gone, like after Aventicum."

I nodded slowly with a small sigh. "Yeah. My magic is gone. But not like Aventicum. Seems I can...teach people, I guess."

Vitulus held his hand out, palm up. "*Vonk globe*," he murmured. A spark globe swirled into existence above his hand, and he stared at it with the same ecstatic wonder as Paetus had done. "Yes," he breathed. "And I have learned. This is going to change the world."

I winced at that, but said nothing.

He let the spark globe dissipate with a sigh. "Which is why I wanted to find you. I want you to teach my men more spells. With Carthage in ruins and refugees scattered throughout countryside, we are getting reports of banditry. I'd like to send my riders out to eliminate these bandits, but I fear they, too, will have magic at their disposal. So any help you can give my men..."

I exhaled sharply. This felt like my point of no return. I was going to train Roman soldiers how to use their new magic. Damnation, they were going to use it whether or not I trained them. But how much stronger would they be with my experienced instruction? Was I saving the world or dooming it? Memories of those circus lions from years ago flitted across my mind's eye.

Faith in people. I have faith in people.

No, I thought firmly, looking at Vitulus's earnest face. *I have faith in my friend.*

"So a legion of *leerlings*, eh?"

He grinned. "Shall I have new banners made? 'Legio Leerling'?"

I snorted. "Augustus would have a fit. Let's do it."

I spent the next several hours teaching Vitulus's Praetorian legion how to cast a sleep spell without components. A spark globe was one of the first cantrips that every child learned in my century, so they were already pretty adept with those (including the refugees, whose children chased each other about their camp with the white globes of harmless light).

But the spark globes were useless against bandits. The sleep spell was about the only useful offensive spell I knew that would work against other humans. The Romans practiced it on each other with entertaining gusto along with the "wake up" spell that I had developed during my Finder days on the Aventine Hill. Cries of *slapen* and *ontwaken* echoed across the field outside Danel's walls along with plenty of laughter and good-natured cursing. Cell magic was all about positive feelings and emotions, so it didn't surprise me that their practice was playful and humorous.

I tried not to think about what they'd do to the bandits that lay helplessly snoring on the ground.

My jealousy and wistful longing to use cell magic again was partially alleviated by my curiosity over my own new powers. I found that teaching the legionaries was just as easy as thinking through a spell and just "projecting" it out to them with my mind.

And that projecting part was amazingly precise. All I had to do was think about *whom* I wanted to have the spell and then send it. So *only* the legion got the sleep and awaken spells when I projected them, even when Danel's household or refugees were walking nearby.

I thought back to the battle with Terentius and how I'd sent the spark globe to "everyone," thinking at the time that it would only go to the people in the valley. Had it gone, literally, to everyone in the world?

And soul magic...well that was certainly *not* something I was going to teach them. I had no doubt someone somewhere in the world would figure it out on their own. That was inevitable. But, damnation, they weren't going to learn it from me.

While the teaching power seemed limitless, the "stopping" power that I had used on Terentius was far more restricted. Meaning that I could only cut off one person from their magic within my range of vision. After testing the ability on several Roman volunteers, I found that I could certainly do it to any person on which I focused. But all I could do to the men around him was make it much harder for them to siphon their cell magic. With a little more practice, I figured I could soon stop everyone within my field of vision.

Despite all that I learned—and the surprisingly fun time I had with the Romans learning it—the best part of all that training was that it made the hours fly by. The sun was setting and my heart began to thunder as I remembered what that meant.

I approached Vitulus near his personal tent in the orderly Roman camp. "Hey, buddy, I have to go."

"Where?" he asked as he unbuckled his hardened leather breast armor.

"Just something I have to do."

"What is it? Is something wrong?"

"No," I said. "It's just...I have to meet someone, is all."

"Who? Do you need me to go with you?"

I stared at him, my mouth opening and closing as I tried to figure out what to tell him. He looked at me seriously for several moments, and then his serious face broke into a wide grin.

"You heard Helva and me, didn't you?" I said. "You bastard."

He laughed. "Be sure not to produce any of your own."

I shook my head. "That was...all sorts of wrong."

"Seriously, my friend," he said slipping out of his chain mail shirt, "you deserve some happiness. I will *discreetly* ensure that no one approaches the bathhouse tonight."

I could feel my face heating up. I didn't know whether to be grateful for the guards or weirded out that a bunch of legionaries would be standing just outside the door while Helva and I were, um, together.

"Thanks. I guess."

Vitulus made a shooing motion. "Go, go! Before she changes her mind."

"Right, okay," I said, and then almost tripped over my feet hurrying away.

The sun was already set beyond the horizon, so darkness was quickly descending over the land. The walk from the Roman camps to the bathhouse was only a couple hundred paces, but those couple hundred paces gave me plenty of time for my mind to try and sabotage myself.

Helva would be the first woman I'd been with since Brianna. And it had been a long time since I was last with Brianna. What if, I don't know, I *forgot* things? What if I wasn't "glorious" like Helva promised? Damnation, she was royalty! The *caccing* granddaughter of *Cleopatra*!

By the time I got within ten paces of the bathhouse, I was trembling. It was dark, but I noticed flickering candlelight inside beyond the slightly open doorway. I saw movement within and heard the gentle lapping of water. I imagined Helva inside, her naked olive skin glistening in the candlelight as she lounged in the bath.

Waiting for *me*. My heart thundered even louder in my ears and chest, but the shaking suddenly stopped. That's right, she's waiting for me. Confidence and a ton of desire replaced my fear and doubts. I strode forward.

Damnation, this is really going to—

"*Slapen*," came a voice from behind me.

55

Sleep spells technically do not put a victim to sleep. They essentially target the hypothalamus in the victim's brain to shut down their body except for basic life support functions. It's not a sleep where one dreams while under the spell.

So when I "awoke," I was quite disoriented to say the least. One moment I was working up the courage to make love to a beautiful woman, the next, I was sitting on a high-backed chair with a hood over my head, my hands bound to the chair's arms, and my feet to the legs. I jerked with my arms and legs, but they were tied way too tight.

Someone pulled the hood off my head. I blinked in the sudden light, everything blurry like I'd just awoken from a true night's sleep. My head felt squeezed, and my mouth seemed filled with cotton balls and salt. My stomach was painfully empty.

I was sitting in a room that looked out upon a balcony. Outside, I saw an ancient city covering several hills beneath a bright blue sky. The ever-present miasma cinched it for me.

I was back in Rome.

The man who'd taken my hood off stood in front of me with shrewd eyes. *Seius. Oh, cac.*

"Good morning, Natta Magus," he rumbled. "I hope you had a pleasant journey."

The tone of his voice and the look in his eyes suggested the exact opposite.

"Now, now, General," came another voice from behind me. There were soft footsteps on the marble floor, and then Octavian Augustus came into view. He held his palm out and a large spark globe swirled above it. The globe's white light flashed in Augustus's blue eyes.

"Natta Magus is a friend of Rome," he said, staring at his spark globe. Then he slowly shifted his glinting eyes to me. "Aren't you, Natta Magus?"

Read NATTA MAGUS, book four in the Journals of Natta Magus series.

Afterword

Thanks for giving *Wounded Magus* a read. If you enjoyed it and have the time, please leave a review, I'd appreciate it.

If you're ready for more adventures in the Journals of Natta Magus, continue with the next novel *Natta Magus*.

Check my website (https://robsteinerauthor.com) for a full list of my novels.

If you'd like a quick note when I release something new, please sign up for my newsletter on my website. For social media fans, you can find me on Twitter, Facebook, Goodreads, and BookBub.

ACKNOWLEDGMENTS

Many thanks to Edmund R. Schubert at *Orson Scott Card's Intergalactic Medicine Show*. He got this book rolling when he bought two Natta Magus short stories, which convinced me this character might just carry a novel.

Thanks to my publishing team: David Drazul and Jack Baker. David for his nit-pickin' editing (and I mean that in the best possible way) and Jack for an outstanding cover.

And as always, thank you Sarah and Amelia for your support, encouragement, and big hugs on the rough days.